Men

and Machines

Books by Robert Silverberg

The World of Coral

The World of the Rain Forest

The World of the Ocean Depths

Earthmen and Strangers: Nine Stories
of Science Fiction (editor)

Voyagers in Time: Twelve Stories
of Science Fiction (editor)

Men and Machines: Ten Stories
of Science Fiction (editor)

MEN

AND MACHINES

TEN STORIES

OF SCIENCE FICTION

Edited by Robert Silverberg

MEREDITH PRESS   NEW YORK

Library of Congress Catalog Card
Number: 68-28721
Manufactured in the United States
of America for Meredith Press
By American Book–Stratford Press, Inc.

For Walt Cole

Acknowledgments

"Counter Foil," by George O. Smith, copyright © 1964 by The Conde Nast Publications, Inc. Reprinted by permission of the author's agent, Lurton Blassingame, from *Analog*.

"A Bad Day for Sales," by Fritz Leiber, copyright 1953 by Galaxy Publishing Corporation. Reprinted by permission of the author and his agent, Robert P. Mills, from *Galaxy Science Fiction*.

"Without a Thought," by Fred Saberhagen, copyright © 1962 by Digest Productions Corporation. Reprinted by permission of the author from *If*.

"Solar Plexus," by James Blish, copyright 1941 by Fictioneers, Inc. Revised version copyright 1952 by Random House, Inc. Reprinted by permission of the author and his agent, Robert P. Mills, from *Astonishing Stories*.

"The Macauley Circuit," by Robert Silverberg, copyright © 1956 by King-Size Publications, Inc. Revised version copyright © 1968 by Robert Silverberg. Reprinted by permission of the author's agents, Scott Meredith Literary Agency, Inc., from *Fantastic Universe*.

"But Who Can Replace a Man?" by Brian W. Aldiss, copyright © 1958 by Royal Publications, Inc. Reprinted by permission of the author and his agents, Scott Meredith Literary Agency, Inc., from *Infinity*.

"Instinct," by Lester del Rey, copyright 1951 by Street

& Smith Publications, Inc. Reprinted by permission of the author and his agents, Scott Meredith Literary Agency, Inc., from *Astounding Science Fiction.*

"The Twonky," by Lewis Padgett, copyright 1942 by Street & Smith Publications, Inc. Reprinted by permission of the Harold Matson Company, Inc., from *Astounding Science Fiction.*

"The Hunting Lodge," by Randall Garrett, copyright 1954 by Street & Smith Publications, Inc. Reprinted by permission of the author and his agents, Scott Meredith Literary Agency, Inc., from *Astounding Science Fiction.*

"With Folded Hands," by Jack Williamson, copyright 1947 by Street & Smith Publications, Inc. Reprinted by permission of the author and his agents, Scott Meredith Literary Agency, Inc., from *Astounding Science Fiction.*

Contents

Introduction

The first man to use a machine was the first of our primitive ancestors who picked up a rock to hurl at some passing animal or to crack open some edible nut. In the million-plus years since then, our machines have grown much more complex, but even in our modern era of computers, rockets, and color television, their basic purpose remains the same: to serve man.

Whether our machines truly serve us is a question much debated by science-fiction writers and other professional speculative philosophers. Does some essential quality go out of human life when it becomes too easy? Have our automobiles, telephones, typewriters, and elevators sapped our vigor? Are we speeding into flabby decay because we have made things too easy for ourselves?

And as our machines grow more able, when do they cross the boundary that separates the living from the unliving? Is it possible that we are building machines that will make humanity obsolete? Perhaps the day is coming when we ourselves will be rendered unnecessary, and our sleek successors, creatures of metal and plastic, will inherit the earth.

The relationship between man and his machines is a complex and many-sided one, compounded by love and hate. Many a bitter attack on the encroachments of the machine age has been produced by a writer using an electric typewriter in an air-conditioned room, innocently unaware of the inner contradictions involved. We need our machines, but we fear them; and out of this tension come ideas best dealt with in the guise of science fiction.

Ten science-fictional explorations of the man-machine relationship are offered here. Some are lighthearted excursions into fantasy, others bleak and forlorn visions of a hopeless future. They show man as the master and as the slave of his machines, as the victim and the tyrant, as conqueror and as conquered. No sermons are intended: the purpose of these tales is to entertain, to stimulate, to suggest possibilities. But implicit in them is the awareness that we have only begun to cope with the problems that our age of fabulous machines is creating.

R. S.

Men

and Machines

COUNTER FOIL

by George O. Smith

*We sometimes need to be reminded how de-
pendent we have become on our machines. A substantial part
of the northeast United States received such a reminder one
November evening in 1965, when a trifling technical difficulty blotted out lights and power for 30,000,000 people over
a vast area. George O. Smith's story, written before the great
power failure, shows the even more devastating possibilities
in a transportation breakdown. Of course, the transportation
system he describes is one that doesn't yet happen to be in
use—but allow him that one bit of fantasy and everything else
follows with devilishly consistent logic.*

*George O. Smith has long been well known as a devilishly
logical character anyway. An engineer by trade who has been
involved in military electronics research, he has been writing
s-f since 1942 and has published over one hundred stories. A
good many of them deal with the technical problems engi-
neers of the future are likely to encounter, and are impressive
both for their insight into technological processes and for the
sly, lively wit that makes them favorites even of nontechnical
readers.*

1

It was near the close of a normal day in late July, if a day in late July can properly be called normal. The temperature and the humidity were tied in the mid-nineties; a reporter from the *News* fried the usual egg on the pavement while his photog snapped the picture that would adorn tomorrow's front page. There had been three flying saucer sightings reported, and the Loch Ness monster had made his appearance right on schedule. The cases of heat prostration were running at par, and nerves in the un-air-conditioned areas were fraying short. Still, the clock displayed hope as it crawled on toward the end of the work day and promised freedom from bondage and the right to pursue both internal and external liquid happiness.

Gertrude, the videophone receptionist, still looked crisp in her office. Her voice as she responded with the singy-songy, "Tele-por-*TRAN*-sit," had not lost its lilt. But it was obvious to the caller that Trudy sat in air-conditioned splendor. And either she loathed the idea of leaving her comfort and going home, or she despised him who called. For after the lilting greeting, her voice dropped to a flat, "Oh, it's you again."

Johnny Peters smiled. "Show?"

"No."

"Swim?"

"No."

"Dinner?"

"No."

"Nothing?"

"Nothing!"

"Trudy, I'm not poison, you know."

"Johnny, I know you're not poison. But you're not very ambitious, either."

"Now listen," he said sharply, "I'm only asking for a date. I'm not offering to have you share my frugal life, bed, and board as a lowly technician. A date I can afford; a wife I can't."

"You could try to get ahead."

"I've made my bid. I asked my illustrious leader for advanced training and an accelerated course so I could move along faster, and he said that moving too fast was bad for a young man. Shall I quit now and go elsewhere?"

"Where would you go?"

"That's the trouble, Trudy. I majored in teleportonics, and it's either teleportonics or I go back to school and start something new. Think the boss-man will move me faster in Greater Chicago? I doubt it. So I might as well stay right here in Megapolis."

"I suppose you're right."

"All right, let's start over again. Show?"

"Johnny, not tonight. I'm busy."

"Tomorrow?"

"If we're not all cooked by then. Call me, Johnny."

"Will do," he said with a growing smile.

Johnny Peters broke the connection and checked his instrument panel. The primary powerline from Con Edison was running a tenth of a volt low; with a bored, routine gesture he twitched a knob, watched the voltage rise, and then he settled back with little more to do until the end of his shift of duty.

In the distant reaches of the city, the uneasy slumber of a napping woman was broken by a wave of pain. A gush of body-warm wetness brought a flash of things to mind that came and went as fast as thought, far too rapidly to reproduce in any electromechanical medium of expression. She thought, in turn: It was her firstborn. The doctor said there was little point in predicting the arrival of a firstborn because they had no record upon which to base an estimate. The women in her family were prone to deliver in taxicabs and ambulances on the way to the hospital.

A second wave of pain assailed her, interrupting the rapid

flow of thought. Then as the pain subsided, she went on:
That was fast!

She struggled to her feet and duck-walked heavily on her
heels to the videophone. She pressed the button for one of
the stored-program numbers and immediately a crisp, cool
voice responded, "Tele-por-*TRAN*-sit," in the lilt with all
four clear tones sounding in order.

"Trudy, this is Irma Fellowes. Can you connect me with
Joe?"

"Sure thing. Half a mo' and you're on. How's things?"

"Baby's on the way." The simple statement was empha-
sized by a smothered groan and the grimace of pain on Irma
Fellowes' face.

Trudy gulped and lost her cool, crisp, composure.
"Whoops! I'll give Joe the double-whammy ring."

The muted wail of a siren came, and almost instantly the
scene on the videophone switched to a man, seated at his
desk. His face was still changing to a look of puzzled concern.
He barked, "Where's the emergency and wha . . . oh! Irma.
Wh . . . er . . . ?"

"Baby's on the way, Joe."

"Fine," he said. "Have you called Maternity?"

"Not yet."

"Irma, I can't do you any good at all. I appreciate the
information, but it could have waited until you got to the
hospital."

"Joe! It's your child!"

"Sure. And you're my wife. Now buzz off here and call the
hospital. Get going."

He hung up; reluctantly because he hated the harshness of
the act, but deliberately because it was the only way he could
get her to move in the right direction.

Irma Fellowes stared at the videophone as though it should
resume operation after a brief interruption. It didn't. What-

ever she started to think at that moment was stopped by another wave of agony. When it subsided, she pressed another button, one that had been set up for a temporary emergency. It connected her with the maternity ward of City Hospital; the plate showed an elderly woman in nurse's uniform, who said, "Maternity, Nurse Wilkins speaking."

"This is Mrs. Fellowes. Baby's on the way."

"Just how frequent are your pains, Mrs. Fellowes?"

"Rapid. And coming faster all the time."

Irma was interrupted by another pain, through which, faintly, she heard the muted siren. Nurse Wilkins read off some detailed instructions from a card, speaking unhurriedly to someone that could not be seen on the videophone. When she finished, Nurse Wilkins said to Irma Fellowes, "Take it easy now, there's a resident doctor, an interne, and a nurse on their way."

Irma closed the circuit, waddled to the kitchen and drank a glass of water, returned to the living room and paced a bit. Perhaps two minutes passed, then came a rap on the door. She opened it to admit doctor and nurse, followed by the interne pushing a wheeled stretcher.

"Hop on," said the interne.

"I can't," groaned Irma.

The doctor scooped her up and deposited her on the stretcher. He applied stethoscope, then palpated her abdomen gently. "O.K.," he said after a moment. "Let's go. No problem."

Irma said, "But I was born in an ambulance, and—"

The doctor laughed. "Mrs. Fellowes, from what little I know of the process, teleportation flips you from entry to exit at the speed of light. Now, even if it were from here to Alpha Centauri, your baby couldn't be born en route simply because at the speed of light all timing processes come to a quiet standstill. And by 'timing processes' I mean things like clocks, and biochemical reactions, births, aging, and death. O.K.?"

"That's what Joe always says, but—"

"Well, let's find out if he's right."

The corridor was partly cooled from leakage from the air-conditioned apartments, but by contrast it was stifling enough to make Irma gasp. The interne had used foresight; the elevator door was blocked open so that no one could call it away and tie it up. He held the "No Stops" button as the elevator dropped them smoothly to the stage below the first floor. Here the full heat of the city hit them as they made their way along a short corridor to the teleportransit booth.

The signal light turned green as soon as the interne inserted the credit key in the lock-register. He pressed the buttons with a practiced hand, then paused to check the number in the address read-out carefully.

"Pays to be careful," he said.

"Ever goof?" asked the nurse.

"Not really bad," he replied turning the credit key. The green light changed to orange, which started the circuit-computer on its faster-than-lightning task of selecting the route from this entry station to the address in the read-out panel. The orange turned to red. "Um-m-m. Maternity seems to have another customer," he said. "We'll be on our way as soon as they get her out of the booth and close the door." He looked at the number again.

"Worried?" asked the nurse.

"Not really worried," he replied. "But I've been thoughtful ever since I watched a hapless, well-dressed citizen trying to walk on air back to the diving exit they have over the ocean at Jones Beach. He was still protesting and waving his brief case as he disappeared beneath the billowy wave."

"I hear you can watch about one per hour on a busy day," chuckled the doctor.

"Yeah," said the interne. He looked at the red light. "All right, all ready. Let's get cutting, huh?"

Two men whose names are legion paused and stood in momentary indecision halfway between Father's Bar and Grill on Eighth Avenue and the kiosk that led down to the 14th Street Teleportransit Station. Habit clashed with common sense; there was also the reluctance to part company.

"Fast one?"

"In this heat?"

"Father's is air-conditioned."

"So's my apartment. And there I can have the Little Woman construct me a cool, tall one whilst I get out of these clothes and into something comfortable. Then I can sit on the terrace in shorts and have my drink in comfort."

"You've got a point. No sense in leaving the office early if we don't take advantage of it."

They turned and headed for the kiosk. Down below, where the subway once rumbled, 14th Street Station was lined with booths, and before each booth was the start of a line-up of people. The big rush hour hadn't started yet, but there were enough citizens in this area who had the kind of job they could leave early to avoid the big jam. There were quite a number who didn't have that kind of job, but they left anyway, hoping their dereliction would either be overlooked or forgotten by Monday morning.

The legion of citizens who left their jobs early to avoid the rush were not being watched by Big Brother, but by an impersonal peg-count that drove a dial that indicated the number of completed transits per minute. Beside the dial was a series of animated graphs that compared the day's traffic against yesterday's traffic, the same day a year ago, the maximum and minimum for this day any year, and the grand maximum and minimum for any day any year. All of the statistical graphs showed a sudden upsurge at the line denoting five o'clock, and the animated graph-line that displayed today's traffic was approaching a record.

Today's traffic had surpassed yesterday's for the past half hour, but this was not surprising because the rush-hour and just-before-rush traffic was heavier on Friday afternoons. It would undoubtedly repeat itself on Monday morning.

But as the moving finger wrote on toward the critical hour, it approached an all-time record. This would ring no bells nor toot any whistles. It would be duly noted, and a memorandum would be issued authorizing a survey to determine the possible future expansion of facilities; the probable cost of such an expansion; and above all, how much more income would pour into the coffers of Teleportransit, Incorporated.

Walter Long said, "I appreciate your interest, Harry, but I simply can't go out of line for your Johnny Peters."

"Is it out of line?" asked Harry Warren.

"Yes, and it is also obvious to us in this section. Or, rather, it would be obvious if I did it."

"I should think you'd jump at a chance to reward someone who asked for advancement."

"I would. And I could justify jumping Peters over a number of his seniors if he were outstanding in just one department. But he isn't outstanding in anything but his ability to lolly-gag with Trudy."

"You make him sound like a washout."

"Oh, Peters is no washout," said Walter Long. "He's just not sufficiently outstanding to warrant special attention."

"Well, you must admit that maintaining a monitor over a function-panel for a system that's adjusted and operated by a computer is not a job that provides an opportunity to be outstanding. There's just so much verve and vigor with which an ambitious man can turn a small knob to twitch the incoming line voltage by a couple of tenths. This operation gets pretty dull, especially when the computer will twist the knob itself if the line gets more than about a quarter of a volt off."

"I suppose you've a point."

"I think I do. But why not ask Johnny's boss? Joe knows him better than either of us."

"All right." Walter Long pressed a button; the intercom on his desk came to life.

Trudy, her composure regained, said, "Yes, Mr. Long?"

"Trudy, connect me with Joe Fellowes, will you?"

"Mr. Fellowes took off a few minutes ago."

"Where, for the love of Pete?"

"Mrs. Fellowes called and said that her baby was on the way. Joe took off for the maternity ward right after that. I could call him."

"No, don't bother right now. Just ask him to see me when he gets back. You've no word from the hospital yet, have you?"

"No, but from the way things looked, we won't have long to wait."

"O.K., Trudy. Keep me informed."

"Yes, sir." She closed the circuit; contact died in the middle of her lilting response, "Tele-por-*TRAN*-sit," to some incoming caller.

The clock hit five. The dial registering transits per minute rose sharply, and so did the graphs that displayed today's traffic compared to statistics. The increased load ran the incoming line down, the computer compensated for the drop before Johnny Peters could react. Somewhere down in the power distribution frames, a fuse blew; the local emergency power took over with no interruption while the blown fuse was replaced by a device that had neither nerves to twitch nor fingers to fumble.

The first inkling that something was wrong was given to Joe Fellowes.

Down in the computer, Joe's emergency trip from the Teleportransit Building to the maternity ward of City Hospital was racked up by the peg count circuits and added to the statistics being compiled in the Accounting Department. The computer also registered the awaiting trip of Mrs. Fellowes, the doctor, the interne, and the nurse. Being a machine, it did not understand about birth and life or death, so it can't be blamed for not registering the unborn Fellowes infant, alive and a passenger though he be.

Machinelike, it awaited the closing of the booth door that exited in the maternity ward, and when the signal came it promptly processed the party—people, stretcher, and unborn —into the system.

In the maternity ward, Joe Fellowes stared at the door to the teleportransit booth; mentally, he was urging it to open upon his wife. "What's keeping them?" he asked nervously.

"Heaven only knows," replied Nurse Wilkins, calmly.

"Something's wrong," he said.

"Hardly."

"What makes you think so?" he demanded.

"If anything were wrong, they'd call for help. Or come for it. That booth can't be used when . . . er . . . how did you get here, young man?" she demanded sharply.

"I'm with Teleportransit," he said bluntly, showing his identification card. "I used the override on your pre-empt circuit."

"Well, that's—" and she fell silent simply because it was done and neither locking the barn nor bawling out the stable boy would correct the act.

"Irma's family have their babies fast," he said. "Maybe—?"

Nurse Wilkins shook her head. "Even with delivery under-
way, they'd bring her back. That's why we send doctor,
interne, and nurse along with everything necessary to handle
any contingency. Your teleport things work so fast we can
send a whole team out on a call each time."

"Fine," said Fellowes. "Then where's my wife?"

Nurse Wilkins replied sharply, "Mr. Fellowes, please grant
that we know our business and how to conduct it. Granting
that our hospital and its medical staff are competent, it's your
teleport machinery that they're using. Maybe something
broke down."

"Well, we can find out about that," he snapped back.
"Teleport circuits either work or they don't. It neither swal-
lows people nor does it go off its electromechanical rocker
and run off a squadron of duplicates. So if it will run with
me, it'll run with your medicos and my wife. Me? I think
there's trouble at home and so I'm going to look."

Nurse Wilkins started to tell Joe Fellowes that he couldn't
use the maternity ward teleportransit; but Joe, with a practiced hand, inserted his credit key with one hand and
plugged in his home address with the other. He waved as he
withdrew the key and he disappeared as the computer processed him into the system.

The man's disappearance brought an uneasy nervousness
to Nurse Wilkins. The system must be working or, by Joe
Fellowes' own statement, he couldn't have entered it. Ergo
something must have gone wrong with the team of medical
people dispatched to help Mrs. Fellowes. The latter did not
seem likely; despite the urgency of the call and the obviously
imminent parturition, it was an uncomplicated, routine matter well within the competence of the medical personnel and
their equipment.

Further, the door to the booth remained dormant, its indicating lamp signaling a priority for incoming traffic. Nurse Wilkins' uneasiness increased as the minutes passed. For now was added the complication of a second level of puzzlement; granting trouble with the medical team, Joe Fellowes might well stay home with them and his wife—and baby. On the other hand, they should have warned the hospital of the emergency. And third, granting that someone goofed and returned the hospital team to a wrong address, it took but a second to correct any such error.

Nurse Wilkins stared at the door that had, despite the statement of Joe Fellowes to the contrary, swallowed one doctor, one interne, one nurse, a wagon, and one civilian whose identification card said that he was an engineer with a degree in teleportonics. And unsaid, she wondered uneasily whether the door at the other end hadn't maybe swallowed one woman in final labor and her a-borning child.

The commuting businessman comprises three general types. There is he who leaves early for any number of reasons, and he who habitually stays overtime either because he is intrigued with his job or bucking for a raise, or both. The in-between is the myriad who report in slightly before opening time and leave promptly at zero five zero-zero. When the latter turns up early, he surprises his family, sometimes in activities that astonish him. When he is late, his family think in terms of dragging the river, canvassing the hospitals, and sticking hatpins into an effigy of the boss, and when he turns up the family is likely to smell his breath and inspect his handkerchief for evidence of dalliance.

Teleportransit, Incorporated, did not change the habits of the commuter. At five o'clock, long queues of people lined up before the teleport booths that stood awaiting them on old subway platforms, in the basement of every large building in central Megapolis, and in special buildings to serve less densely populated areas. To serve the commuter better, Tele-portransit provided a commuter key with the two terminals coded in the matrix. It worked only at the commuter's home and office stations, in one and out the other exclusively. For other destinations, the address had to be spelled out digit by digit.

The upshot of this special commuter's key was rapid transit with capital letters. Step into the booth, insert the key, turn, restore, and withdraw it. How fast can a person move? With deft commuters, one teleportransit booth can handle one person every three seconds. Twelve hundred an hour. Times Square Station has three hundred booths; 34th Street has two fifty. Multiply these various values by the couple of hundred stations in Megapolis, then add the smaller numbers in the basement of the prominent buildings, and the capacity of Teleportransit to handle the four million daily commuters becomes clear.

The rush hour swung into gear and the transits-per-minute dial in the Teleportransit Building clicked into an upper register, reading kilotransits.

And at the terminals in Scarsdale, Mountainside, Freehold, and Sea Bright, wives collected in their station wagons to await their breadwinners. They waited. Then they looked at watches. Some turned on radios to check the time. Quite a few worried, and an equal number changed their expression from bored tolerance to knowing accusation of infidelity. Only one thing was glaringly obvious. Either the teleport system had broken down, or all husbands were delinquent at the same time, if not at the same place.

Giving the poor devils the benefit of the doubt the thing to do was to ask someone what went on. And so—

"Tele-por-*TRAN*-sit," sang Trudy, waiting for her date.

"Hello," came a female voice, "is something wrong?"

"Wrong?" asked Trudy.

"Yes. My husband hasn't come home yet."

"Well, I haven't—No, I mean, why ask me?"

"This is the Teleportransit Office, isn't it?"

"Yes, but—"

"Well, miss, it isn't only my husband. None of them have come home."

"I don't understand."

"Neither do I. Every night there're about forty of us waiting here, and our men come home one at a time over about fifteen minutes. Now we're here a half hour and not a one has come out of your station."

"Wait a moment. I'll check." Trudy buzzed Walter Long and told him, "There's a woman on the videophone who thinks the system has broken down."

"It couldn't," said Walter Long, stoutly. "Put her on, Trudy."

The harassed voice, having run through the story once for Trudy, had it better prepared for Walter Long. When she finished, he assured her, "Madam, we apologize for this inconvenience, and I personally thank you for bringing it to my attention. It's the first I knew of any tieup. Now, let me attend to it at once, and we'll have your husband home in a jiffy. And thank you for calling."

"But where is he?" the woman wailed.

"Don't worry, madam," he said calmly. "If he hasn't come out of the exit, he hasn't gone into the entrance. So there are probably a lot of irate husbands standing angrily in front of an inoperative teleport booth."

"But they all come from different places," she wailed.

"We'll get them home," repeated Walter Long. He broke the circuit because talking to this anxious woman was not letting him get to the source of the problem. He buzzed Trudy and heard her sing, "Tele-por-*Tran*-sit," with some of the zing gone from her lilt. "Oh! Mr. Long. White Plains and Far Hills have both reported some sort of trouble."

"Trudy, call the hospital and find out where Joe Fellowes is, and how fast can he get back here."

"Yes, sir." Long waited on the circuit while Trudy got Nurse Wilkins, who explained that neither doctor, interne, nurse, stretcher-wagon, nor Mr. Fellowes had returned, and that they'd been gone for almost half an hour. When that was finished, Walter Long said, "Trudy, call Joe's home." Once more he waited on the circuit, but this time it was completely unfinished because the videophone ring-back burrred and burrrred without an answer.

"Something's gone a long way wrong, Trudy," he said solemnly. On the open circuit, Walter Long could hear the incoming calls beginning to pile up. Trudy's usual singsong diminished until it became a flat and uninspired, "Teleportransit," followed by a wait and the terse explanation that a minor breakdown had occurred, that they were working on it; and no, she was merely the receptionist and didn't know a three-port circulator from a dithrambic foot. Sorry, but the technical staff is all busy correcting the fault and can't be interrupted.

"Trudy!" barked Walter Long.

"Yes?"

"Put the lilt back in your voice, and then record that last explanation and switch your board to automatic response. Just keep the private company incoming lines open."

"Yes, sir."

"And then come in here."

"Yes, sir. As soon as I finish."

When she entered, Walter Long said, "Trudy, among the things that are wrong is the absence of Joe Fellowes. That nurse said he went home, but hasn't returned. Maybe something's wrong at the Fellowes end of that circuit—by which I mean his wife and baby. Will you take a minute to run over to Fellowes' station and check?"

"Surely."

"And come back immediately. Understand? At once. Don't wait even if they have something vital that depends on you. Come back here and report. Understand?"

"Yes, Mr. Long. That's a promise."

Trudy used the teleport booth in the main front office. She was ultra-careful, inserting her credit key and entering each digit in the Fellowes address with deliberation. She checked the read-out digit by digit before she was satisfied enough to re-turn the key in the lock-register to start the teleport process.

Like the four million commuters who disappeared once each morning and once each night, Trudy ceased to exist in the teleport booth that stood in the main front office of Teleportransit, Incorporated.

Like Nurse Wilkins and four million waiting wives, mistresses, girl friends, and terminal-station bartenders, Walter Long stared at the closed booth door and prayed for it to open. His staring became a vigil, for minutes stretched out and the girl did not return.

"Blast that girl," muttered Walter Long, "and she promised."

It was ten minutes of six when Walter Long called Harry Warren. "Harry, something's wrong."

"Wrong? Can it wait until morning, Walter? We've company coming tonight, and—"

"Tomorrow's Saturday, Harry."

"Yes. I know. So I'll come in tomorrow and settle it. Leave me a note about it. I'm off to home."

"Wait, Harry. Don't go. Don't, of all things, use the teleport."

"Now that's downright silly. How else can I get home?"

"Harry, to the best of my knowledge, people seem to be going into the system, but none are coming out."

"What?"

"You heard me right."

"Where's Fellowes?"

"That's the trouble. Fellowes was one of the first."

"But what are we going to do?"

"Has the technical staff—?"

"Yeah. At five o'clock they headed for the teleport on a dead run."

"Right into this Frankenstein's Monster we own."

"Moloch was the god that ate 'em alive," said Harry Warren absently. "Well, there's still maintenance and monitor. The night man."

"And if I guess right, he's probably the closest guy this side of Pittsburgh, Boston, or Washington who knows anything about the technical side of teleportation. Get him up here."

"Maybe we'd better go down to him."

"That'll leave the office empty if someone calls."

"Ask Trudy to stay over a bit. After all, this is an emergency."

"I can't. I sent Trudy through the teleport to look for Joe Fellowes. She's gone, too."

"There are days when everything goes wrong," said Harry Warren. "Now I find that monitor and maintenance is none other than Johnny Peters."

"How come? If he has the duty tonight, why was he asking Trudy for a date?"

"It seems that she three-quarters promised him a date for tomorrow night, so Peters swapped nights with Frank Nash."

"Well, if I can plug up the company lines on the switchboard without electrocuting myself, I'll set them up on the downstairs set."

Johnny Peters lounged at the big test and control console, his feet hooked on one edge of the desk-panel. He was reading a magazine, and from time to time he let his eyes stray over the meters. He was bored, and he was frustrated because being the back-up to a completely self-adjusting, self-repairing, automatic machine does not leave much opportunity to perform noteworthy deeds. He was in this attitude when Harry Warren and Walter Long burst in upon him.

"Hell breaking loose all over Megapolis," yelled Harry Warren, "and you sit there as if nothing were going on."

"So what's going on? No one tells me anything," replied Johnny Peters.

"You don't know?" asked Walter Long incredulously.

"No, I don't."

Harry Warren looked at the control console full of meters, dials, and multicolored pilot and warning lamps. "Is that thing functioning properly?"

Peters cast a rapid eye over the board. "Perfectly," he said, reaching out and giving one small knob an imperceptible turn.

"How can you be so sure so fast?"

"There isn't a red lamp showing," he said with a sweeping wave of his hand. "Blue-green indicates operating circuits that are functioning properly; yellow-orange indicates feedback information—a continuous incoming flow of variables—that keep the operating circuits so properly adjusted that they maintain a continuous show of blue-green. Hasn't been a red lamp shown since I've been with Teleportransit, but I'm told that whistles blow, bells ring, cannon are fired and—"

"Well, something's gone to hell in a handbasket."

"For instance, what?"

"Our teleport system isn't working."

"Nonsense!" Peters pointed to a large dial. "Load's low tonight, but we're still making a couple of—"

"Stop them!" yelled Walter Long. "Peters, since somewhere about a quarter to five this evening, people have been a-pouring into the entrances, and not coming out of the exits."

"But that can't happen."

"You explain that to four million commuters—if we ever get 'em back."

"And if we don't, you try to explain it to their heirs and assigns," said Harry Warren.

"Is this condition local or widespread?" asked Peters.

"It's the entire system."

"No," said Peters, "I mean, has Pittsburgh or Greater Chicago reported the same mess-up?"

"That we don't know."

"Then let's find out," said Peters. On the console, he snapped a switch. A videoplate came to life, there was a brief ringback burrr, and then a man's face appeared.

"Peters here, Megapolis. Teleportransit, Inc."

"Hi. James Gale. Pittsburgh Rapid. What's on your mind?"

"Have you any trouble reports?"

"No. What kind of trouble?"

"No tie-ups?"

"No. Now what can happen to a teleport circuit to tie it up?"

"I don't know, but everybody who goes into our machine just simply stays there."

"But that's not possible."

"All right. So that makes it a manifestation of the supernatural and it's swallowed more'n four million commuters, and it's continuing to swallow them at the rate of about fifteen hundred per minute.

"Turn it off," advised Jim Gale.

"I don't dare," said Johnny Peters. "I have the uneasy feeling that continued operation is the only contact that lies between here and the limbo they're lost in. I've no sound, scientific logic for that queasy feeling; it's just a conviction that I must follow." He turned to look at Walter Long and Harry Warren. Both of them looked blank until Johnny Peters said, "Unless I'm ordered to," at which they both shook their heads violently.

"Well, this I've got to see," said Gale. "I'm coming over."

"Whoa!" cried Peters. "I'd advise some other mode of transportation."

"Um . . . guess you're right. So is there anything I can do to help?"

"Yes," said Walter Long quickly. "Get in touch with your top-level technical staff and tell them what we're up against. You can also call Boston and Washington and ask them what to do. See if the best technical brains of all three cities can get trains or cars to come here as fast as possible. In the meantime, we'll have to muddle through with a junior technician, a business administrator, and one puzzled personnel relations counsel."

Throughout Megapolis, the news was spreading fast. In an earlier day, the radio in the automobile or in the depot bar would have spread the news like wildfire. But the habit of the commuter was to get where he was going first, and then relax to get the news. The news was thus delayed in its dissemination by the recipient's habits, not by any machination of press, government, big business, or unfavorable foreign powers.

The transits-per-minute meter began to taper off in an increasing drop as the news was spread. But it did not drop to zero because there were those that had not heard, those who did not believe, a number whose curiosity exceeded their good sense, a few misguided self-sacrificers, and a low but continuous counting rate pegged up by sheer habit. For just as people during a power failure will enter a room and flip the light switch in a reflex action, people preoccupied with other things turned into the teleport booth out of habit and whisked themselves into limbo.

More time passed; it takes time for the central nervous system of a vast Megapolis to react to a widespread emergency. Had one called two and the two then called four, and the four called eight, the word would have spread fast. But plans and programs such as this fail unsafely at the first breach in the pattern for there is no way of bridging the missing link. So in the usual ponderous way, the commissioners called the captains and the captains notified their lieutenants, and soon the word was spread to the patrolmen. And where there was a missing link to bridge, the radio called the patrolmen, firemen off-duty, members of the civil defense, and anybody who could be sworn to duty.

And not a few of these succumbed to habit by trying to take the teleport system to the teleport station they'd been assigned to prevent people from using.

Ultimately, the stations were under control and the transits-per-minute meter was down to an unreadable, but still-not-zero figure. By this time, the hidden, unknown plane beyond the entrance of the teleports had its share of policemen and other keepers of the civic peace.

Johnny Peters looked at the mass of gray hammertone finish, chromium, and glass, and he realized a helplessness, a complete futility, the utter impossibility of doing anything useful. For what had always worked properly had stopped abruptly at about four-thirty in the afternoon. It was as if the sun, having come up on time since the dawn of eyes to watch for it, failed to show.

For Teleportransit was to Megapolis as hundreds of other teleport companies were to their respective cities. Take twelve years of handling commuter traffic five days each week and multiply that by the number of cities that had solved the commuting problem by licensing teleport companies, then quote the figure as a statistic with zero accidents in transit. The odds begin to approach the probabilities that the sun will not be late tomorrow morning.

Still, to Johnny Peters, Walter Long, and Harry Warren, there was no realization of the enormity of the situation. It was too impersonal, too remote, too vast. That four or five million human souls had vanished into their machinery was a fact they could not comprehend.

But as the word spread throughout the city, millions of individuals became intimately aware of a shocking, abrupt personal loss. And for the number who fold their hands and say "Kismet," there are an equal number who want to strike back. And so part of the public became a mob.

The nightwatchman on duty at the main door of the Teleportransit Building saw the mob approach but did not comprehend until the leaders crashed the big plate glass doors with a timber. As the mob came boiling into the lobby of the building, the nightwatchman fled in terror, taking the obvious way out along with two of the mob who pursued him into the teleport booth.

Had there been no stairs, the elevator system might have cooled some of the anger, for a mob completely articulated into tiny groups out of communication with one another loses the ability to regenerate its mass anger. The leaders, without a shouting mass behind them, might have listened to reason. But the elevators, at night, would respond only to authorized employees with special keys. And so the mob, strung into a broad-fronted wave, trailed up the stairs after the leaders. The toil of climbing added to their anger.

To prove the paranoiac quality of the mob, the air-conditioning in the Teleportransit Building did not give them any comfort; it made them resent even more the men they held responsible because they sat in comfort to perpetrate the outrage.

Within the equipment room, the status remained quo.

But not for long.

The heavy doors muffled the sound of the mob; by the time the noise penetrated loud enough to attract the three men in the room, the same timber used to crash the main doors came hurtling through the doors to the equipment room.

The foremost of the mob milled into the room and grabbed the three men. There were shouts of lynch-law: "Give it to 'em!" and "String 'em up!" and someone with a length of clothesline weaseled his way through the mob to the fore.

A slipknot is not as efficient as the hangman's noose with its thirteen turns, but it is effective. It is also terrifying. Being in the hands of a mob is panic-making in its own right. The sight of rope adds terror. Such shock makes some people faint, some are simply stunned into inaction, and some enter a strange mental stage through which they watch the proceedings without realizing that the mob is going to harm them.

Some men take on a madman's fury, break free, and try to run.

As three of the mob held Johnny Peters, a fourth started to put the slipknot over his head, while a fifth tossed the other end of the clothesline over a ceiling strut. Johnny Peters lashed out, broke the grip of the three who held him, smashed the noose-holder in the face, and took off through the room, scattering the mob by sheer force. Behind him trailed the clothesline, for his wild, roundhouse swing had passed through the noose.

Wildly, Johnny Peters headed for the only haven he knew,

and as the door to the teleport booth closed behind him, the
man who held the end of the rope shook it with a mad
roaring laugh:

"He ain't going nowhere!"

With deliberation, he started to collect the line, hand over
hand. It slung in a tightening catenary from the ceiling strut
over to the teleport booth door frame.

Unmindful of his tether, Johnny Peters fished his key out,
plugged it in, and twisted.

With a roar, three of the mob grabbed the rope and
hauled. The end, cut clean, pulled out of the door frame
gasket and trailed across the floor; the three who had hauled
went a-sprawl. For, as a moment of thought must reveal, the
system could hardly teleport a material body instantaneously
into an enclosed exit booth without creating an explosion of
thermonuclear proportions. The teleport booths were carefully made to rigid dimensions; in the transit, everything
contained in one went to the other; they swapped.

Johnny Peters disappeared trailing his length of line.

Johnny Peters was in a nearly indescribable state of—
awareness. There was no sense of feeling; the tactile sense no
longer existed. The sensitive tip of the tongue did not send
continuous messages to the brain about the state of teeth or
the amount of saliva. The telemetry that provides feedback of
limb position was missing. Pressure against the feet was gone,
as if there were no gravity.

Where he was, there was no sound. Or, if sound existed
there, he had not the ears with which to hear—nor taste, nor
sight, nor olfactory sense.

Yet he felt an awareness of self, of being, of existing.

A remnant of long-forgotten Latin occurred, *"Cogit, ergo
sumt."* And he wondered whether his Latin was correct. But
right or wrong in the classics, Johnny Peters thought, and
therefore he existed.

And once this became evident to Johnny Peters, there came the usual return of hope, for so long as life existed, there was hope of getting back from whatever strange plane he had entered. Then, with panic subsiding, Johnny Peters became faintly aware of others.

This, too, was a strange awareness. In life, for example, on a streetcar or subway, a person is aware of the presence of others because every sensory channel is bombarded, assaulted, overloaded. One can say, "They were so thick I could taste it!" and not be far from wrong because the chemicals that carry the spoor of close-packed humanity to the sense of smell are soluble in water; in saliva the smell becomes a taste.

This was, or was it, like telepathy?

What is telepathy like? Does the telepath dial a mental address and then carry on a two-way remark-and-rejoinder, or does he broadcast on an open band? Can he extract the mental peregrinations of someone who is unaware of this invasion of privacy, or does the human desire for privacy act as a barrier? Is that why telepathy is not a going process?

In any event, Johnny Peters was aware of the presence of others; perhaps it is better to say that he was aware of the awareness of others. Then as this awareness became stronger and less puzzling, he became vaguely and faintly cognizant of identity. Not identity in the sense that an individual is identified, but rather in the sense that his awareness included a number of separate entities. He recognized none of them, which may not be surprising since he had, by now, about five million individuals for company.

Johnny Peters knew how the teleport worked, but still had difficulty in freeing his mind of the feeling that others who had used the teleport booth in the equipment room of the Teleportransit Building should be somewhere just beyond the entrance portal. Where they were he could not imagine, but he knew that the medium was not like a plugged tunnel, even though the tunnel albeit virtual, was the foundation for the teleport.

For when the junction of a diode is very thin, and the energy of the electrons is very low, Heisenberg's Uncertainty says that they have a definite probability of crossing the forbidden gap in the junction and appearing on the other side. In the tunnel diode, simple probability is loaded with a voltage bias so that a current flows across the forbidden gap; electrons pass through invisibly as if they flowed through a tunnel. The teleport performed the same operation with humans and things—or had until five million people occupied the forbidden gap between terminals.

And so the people, instead of compact, locatable entities, were diffused essences of their beings, their awarenesses, occupying a volume of probability that encompassed and more likely exceeded the most distant of Teleportransit's wide-flung network of terminals.

Aware that he was mingled with other entities, Johnny Peters felt the need of finding and identifying someone, anyone he knew as an individual; an awareness that was not simply another being, but a definite being. Simple want called her name to mind, and somehow he formed the silent concept:

"Trudy!"

It gave directivity to his being, and cleared things; now he became aware of others, trying to make contact in the same way. Some of them had. Two were commenting on the situation in exceedingly uncomplimentary terms; in fact, they made his mind blush. Another was radiating the concept that he didn't know where he was but at least he wasn't suffering from the heat.

Johnny Peters tried again. "Trudy!"

If a completely diffused being had feelings, he might have

felt something. Instead, he merely became aware of being surrounded by more essences of awareness, a mental crowding. This corresponded to his concept of the volume of probability; given absolutely zero energy, the probability was equally good to be anywhere in the Universe. But as the energy became significant, the volume of probability shrunk. Furthermore, there was a higher probability of occupying the center or near-center of the volume than occupying the outer edges. The distribution, of course, was Gaussian.

Then he became aware of a reply. The concept, "Johnny?"

"Yes, Trudy."

"What happened? Where are we?"

"Where we are I don't know," he formed. "It's supposed to be a forbidden gap between terminals that nothing can occupy. That's why nothing ever got lost before. It's either here or there, but never between."

"I don't see," came the faltering reply. "But what happened?"

"I don't know, but I think it's some sort of traffic jam on the teleport."

"But why?"

"Lord knows. Let's figure it out after we find out how to get out of this in-between mess."

"Do you think you can?"

"I'm not too sure, but Joe Fellowes must be in this mess somewhere."

"Let's both call him."

Together, they formed the concept, "Joe Fellowes!"

Again there was the awareness of something shifting, of a mental crowding; a reshuffling of the entities.

Trudy radiated, "Johnny?"

"Yes?"

"Johnny—I get the distinct impression of a baby crying."

"Uh—yeah."

The awareness of reshuffling became intense. At one point, Johnny Peters caught a thought that might have been a reply from Joe Fellowes.

"Trudy?"

"Yes, Johnny?"

"Let's try Joe Fellowes again."

"No, let's try Irma Fellowes. I think women are more sensitive."

"Only a woman would make that statement," was his response, "but I'll try anything."

Now the reshuffling was almost a physical motion; the awareness of movement through a densely packed medium, of motion blocked from time to time, of packing tight, of flowing ever-so-slowly through extreme difficulty toward some focal point.

"Irma Fellowes?"

Faintly, dimly came the reply, unformed and wordless, but nonetheless it was the awareness of Irma Fellowes. Motion became a struggle, but they fought to move, urged on by some unknown drive.

Now the awareness of Irma Fellowes was stronger, mental flashes of Joe Fellowes began to come in, and as the latter increased in clarity, others began. There was the doctor; his awareness was concern for his patient. The interne was merely anxious to get back to his post. The nurse was impatient because she had a date that evening and didn't want to miss it. The baby was complaining, as babies do, about the rough treatment that was meted upon one's first appearance on Earth.

"Is it a boy or girl?" wondered Irma Fellowes.

"How can we possibly find out in this . . . this . . . nothingness?"

The interne advised, "Find out whether baby's thinking blue or pink thoughts."

Nurse wanted to know, "Is it born?"

Joe Fellowes' thought was a snort. "How can anything be born of a diffused essence that's spread out over a spherical volume of probability about a hundred and fifty miles in diameter? The term's meaningless."

"But what are we breathing? And how will we eat?"

The question, unanswerable by any form of reasoning or logic, was interrupted by a stronger cry from the baby, a feeling of strain having been eased. The packed-in awareness flowed away and throughout the entire volume of probability, motion became fluid, fast, and free.

The exit terminals of Teleportransit began to spew forth humanity. They landed running, some of them; others were pushed violently because they did not move forward out of the way fast enough. The big rush hour of Megapolis, started two hours ago, was finishing. With the finish on one hundred and twenty minutes of overtime, the mysterious medium between the terminals was doing its best to live up to the definition, "forbidden gap."

Being people once more instead of merely aware essences, they raised their voices.

"It's a boy," said the doctor.

"But what happened?" asked Trudy.

"It was like a log jam," explained Joe Fellowes. "And baby was the key log."

"But how could the teleport system form such a jam?" demanded Johnny Peters.

"We were too efficient," said Fellowes. "Our coincidence-counting circuits are set up to make a double check on the transits. Some shiny-bottomed accountant wanted to be more than certain that every transit was paid for, so all trips are checked at the entrance and again at the exit. Baby made 'em mismatch."

"All right, so how did we break the jam?"

"You did," chuckled Fellowes. "You went in to the teleport booth and plugged in your key without entering a destination. That made the number of in-counts match the number of out-counts. And once your awareness approached the troubled area, the uncertainty of which was which, or in this case, whose was whose, became high enough in probability to effect a transfer. Boom! The log jam breaks and everything comes tumbling home."

"But—?"

"Baby? Well, you've heard it said that when they start, nothing will stop 'em," chuckled Fellowes. "And so baby has the dubious honor of being the first kid born en route to the hospital by teleport."

"And," said the doctor dryly, "delivered by a diffused medical team of essences."

A BAD DAY FOR SALES

by Fritz Leiber

*Fritz Leiber is the son of a famed Shakespear-
ean actor, and is himself a man of formidable stage presence,
awesomely tall, with a magnificently resonant voice. He
makes no secret of the fact that he is a frustrated actor; but
for some thirty years his stories of science fiction and fantasy
have been winning him a loyal following in the profession
that was his second choice. A note of subtle horror runs
through most Leiber stories, not only those that are frankly
designed as weird tales but even the ones supposedly intended as science fiction. Perhaps the perfect blending of
these two Leiberesque strains came in his classic short story,
"Coming Attraction," a nightmarish vision of futurity.*

*The story at hand begins, like most Leiber stories, in a
deceptively innocent way, gradually widening to reveal
depths of terror. At the heart of it is a machine that is neither
villain nor hero, for it does not comprehend human woe and
remains apart, tirelessly uttering its sales pitch, in a moment
of devastation. Equally impersonal is the machine that brings
that devastation—aloof, uncaring, unaware.*

The big bright doors of the office building parted with a pneumatic *whoosh* and Robie glided onto Times Square. The crowd that had been watching the fifty-foot-tall girl on the clothing billboard get dressed, or reading the latest news about the Hot Truce scrawl itself in yard-high script, hurried to look.

Robie was still a novelty. Robie was fun. For a little while yet, he could steal the show. But the attention did not make Robie proud. He had no more emotions than the pink plastic giantess, who dressed and undressed endlessly whether there was a crowd or the street was empty, and who never once blinked her blue mechanical eyes. But she merely drew business while Robie went out after it.

For Robie was the logical conclusion of the development of vending machines. All the earlier ones had stood in one place, on a floor or hanging on a wall, and blankly delivered merchandise in return for coins, whereas Robie searched for customers. He was the demonstration model of a line of sales robots to be manufactured by Shuler Vending Machines, provided the public invested enough in stocks to give the company capital to go into mass production.

The publicity Robie drew stimulated investments handsomely. It was amusing to see the TV and newspaper coverage of Robie selling, but not a fraction as much fun as being approached personally by him. Those who were usually bought anywhere from one to five hundred shares, if they had any money and foresight enough to see that sales robots would eventually be on every street and highway in the country.

Robie radared the crowd, found that it surrounded him solidly, and stopped. With a carefully built-in sense of timing, he waited for the tension and expectation to mount before he began talking.

"Say, Ma, he doesn't look like a robot at all," a child said. "He looks like a turtle."

Which was not completely inaccurate. The lower part of Robie's body was a metal hemisphere hemmed with sponge rubber and not quite touching the sidewalk. The upper was a metal box with black holes in it. The box could swivel and duck.

A chromium-bright hoopskirt with a turret on top.

"Reminds me too much of the Little Joe Paratanks," a legless veteran of the Persian War muttered, and rapidly rolled himself away on wheels rather like Robie's.

His departure made it easier for some of those who knew about Robie to open a path in the crowd. Robie headed straight for the gap. The crowd whooped.

Robie glided very slowly down the path, deftly jogging aside whenever he got too close to ankles in skylon or sockassins. The rubber buffer on his hoopskirt was merely an added safeguard.

The boy who had called Robie a turtle jumped in the middle of the path and stood his ground, grinning foxily.

Robie stopped two feet short of him. The turret ducked. The crowd got quiet.

"Hello, youngster," Robie said in a voice that was smooth as that of a TV star, and was, in fact, a recording of one.

The boy stopped smiling. "Hello," he whispered.

"How old are you?" Robie asked.

"Nine. No, eight."

"That's nice," Robie observed. A metal arm shot down from his neck, stopped just short of the boy.

The boy jerked back.

"For you," Robie said.

The boy gingerly took the red polly-lop from the neatly fashioned blunt metal claws, and began to unwrap it.

"Nothing to say?" asked Robie.

"Uh—thank you."

After a suitable pause, Robie continued, "And how about a nice refreshing drink of Poppy Pop to go with your polly-lop?" The boy lifted his eyes, but didn't stop licking the candy. Robie waggled his claws slightly. "Just give me a quarter and within five seconds—"

A little girl wriggled out of the forest of legs. "Give me a polly-lop, too, Robie," she demanded.

"Rita, come back here!" a woman in the third rank of the crowd called angrily.

Robie scanned the newcomer gravely. His reference silhouettes were not good enough to let him distinguish the sex of children, so he merely repeated, "Hello, youngster."

"Rita!"

"Give me a polly-lop!"

Disregarding both remarks, for a good salesman is single-minded and does not waste bait, Robie said winningly, "I'll bet you read *Junior Space Killers*. Now I have here—"

"Uh-uh, I'm a girl. *He* got a polly-lop."

At the word "girl," Robie broke off. Rather ponderously, he said, "I'll bet you read *Gee-Gee Jones, Space Stripper*. Now I have here the latest issue of that thrilling comic, not yet in the stationary vending machines. Just give me fifty cents and within five—"

"Please let me through. I'm her mother."

A young woman in the front rank drawled over her powder-sprayed shoulder, "I'll get her for you," and slithered out on six-inch platform shoes. "Run away, children," she said nonchalantly. Lifting her arms behind her head, she pirouetted slowly before Robie to show how much she did for her bolero half-jacket and her form-fitting slacks that melted into skylon just above the knees. The little girl glared at her. She ended the pirouette in profile.

At this age-level, Robie's reference silhouettes permitted him to distinguish sex, though with occasional amusing and embarrassing miscalls. He whistled admiringly. The crowd cheered.

Someone remarked critically to a friend, "It would go over

better if he was built more like a real robot. You know, like a man."

The friend shook his head. "This way it's subtler."

No one in the crowd was watching the newscript overhead as it scribbled, "Ice Pack for Hot Truce? Vanadin hints Russ may yield on Pakistan."

Robie was saying, ". . . in the savage new glamor-tint we have christened Mars Blood, complete with spray applicator and fit-all fingerstalls that mask each finger completely except for the nail. Just give me five dollars—uncrumpled bills may be fed into the revolving rollers you see beside my arm—and within five seconds—"

"No, thanks, Robie," the young woman yawned.

"Remember," Robie persisted, "for three more weeks, seductivizing Mars Blood will be unobtainable from any other robot or human vendor."

"No, thanks."

Robie scanned the crowd resourcefully. "Is there any gentleman here . . ." he began just as a woman elbowed her way through the front rank.

"I told you to come back!" she snapped at the little girl.

"But I didn't get my polly-lop!"

". . . who would care to . . ."

"Rita!"

"Robie cheated. Ow!"

Meanwhile, the young woman in the half-bolero had scanned the nearby gentlemen on her own. Deciding that there was less than a fifty per cent chance of any of them accepting the proposition Robie seemed about to make, she took advantage of the scuffle to slither gracefully back into the ranks. Once again the path was clear before Robie.

He paused, however, for a brief recapitulation of the more magical properties of Mars Blood, including a telling phrase about "the passionate claws of a Martian sunrise."

But no one bought. It wasn't quite time. Soon enough

silver coins would be clinking, bills going through the rollers faster than laundry, and five hundred people struggling for the privilege of having their money taken away from them by America's first mobile sales robot.

But there were still some tricks that Robie had to do free, and one certainly should enjoy those before starting the more expensive fun.

So Robie moved on until he reached the curb. The variation in level was instantly sensed by his under-scanners. He stopped. His head began to swivel. The crowd watched in eager silence. This was Robie's best trick.

Robie's head stopped swiveling. His scanners had found the traffic light. It was green. Robie edged forward. But then the light turned red. Robie stopped again, still on the curb. The crowd softly *ahhed* its delight.

It was wonderful to be alive and watching Robie on such an exciting day. Alive and amused in the fresh, weather-controlled air between the lines of bright skyscrapers with their winking windows and under a sky so blue you could almost call it dark.

(But way, way up, where the crowd could not see, the sky was darker still. Purple-dark, with stars showing. And in that purple-dark, a silver-green something, the color of a bud, plunged down at better than three miles a second. The silver-green was a newly developed paint that foiled radar.)

Robie was saying, "While we wait for the light, there's time for you youngsters to enjoy a nice refreshing Poppy Pop. Or for you adults—only those over five feet tall are eligible to buy—to enjoy an exciting Poppy Pop fizz. Just give me a quarter or—in the case of adults, one dollar and a quarter; I'm licensed to dispense intoxicating liquors—and within five seconds . . ."

But that was not cutting it quite fine enough. Just three seconds later, the silver-green bud bloomed above Manhattan into a globular orange flower. The skyscrapers grew brighter and brighter still, the brightness of the inside of the Sun. The windows winked blossoming white fire-flowers.

The crowd around Robie bloomed, too. Their clothes puffed into petals of flame. Their heads of hair were torches.

The orange flower grew, stem and blossom. The blast came. The winking windows shattered tier by tier, became black holes. The walls bent, rocked, cracked. A stony dandruff flaked from their cornices. The flaming flowers on the sidewalk were all leveled at once. Robie was shoved ten feet. His metal hoopskirt dimpled, regained its shape.

The blast ended. The orange flower, grown vast, vanished overhead on its huge, magic beanstalk. It grew dark and very still. The cornice-dandruff pattered down. A few small fragments rebounded from the metal hoopskirt.

Robie made some small, uncertain movements, as if feeling for broken bones. He was hunting for the traffic light, but it no longer shone either red or green.

He slowly scanned a full circle. There was nothing anywhere to interest his reference silhouettes. Yet whenever he tried to move, his under-scanners warned him of low obstructions. It was very puzzling.

The silence was disturbed by moans and a crackling sound, as faint at first as the scampering of distant rats.

A seared man, his charred clothes fuming where the blast had blown out the fire, rose from the curb. Robie scanned him.

"Good day, sir," Robie said. "Would you care for a smoke? A truly cool smoke? Now I have here a yet-unmarketed brand . . ."

But the customer had run away, screaming, and Robie never ran after customers, though he could follow them at a medium brisk roll. He worked his way along the curb where the man had sprawled, carefully keeping his distance from the low obstructions, some of which writhed now and then, forcing him to jog. Shortly he reached a fire hydrant. He scanned it. His electronic vision, though it still worked, had been somewhat blurred by the blast.

"Hello, youngster," Robie said. Then, after a long pause, "Cat got your tongue? Well, I have a little present for you. A nice, lovely polly-lop.

"Take it, youngster," he said after another pause. "It's for you. Don't be afraid."

His attention was distracted by other customers, who began to rise up oddly here and there, twisting forms that confused his reference silhouettes and would not stay to be scanned properly. One cried, "Water," but no quarter clinked in Robie's claws when he caught the word and suggested, "How about a nice refreshing drink of Poppy Pop?"

The rat-crackling of the flames had become a jungle muttering. The blind windows began to wink fire again.

A little girl marched, stepping neatly over arms and legs she did not look at. A white dress and the once taller bodies around her had shielded her from the brilliance and the blast. Her eyes were fixed on Robie. In them was the same imperious confidence, though none of the delight, with which she had watched him earlier.

"Help me, Robie," she said. "I want my mother."

"Hello, youngster," Robie said. "What would you like? Comics? Candy?"

"Where is she, Robie? Take me to her."

"Balloons? Would you like to watch me blow up a balloon?"

The little girl began to cry. The sound triggered off another of Robie's novelty circuits, a service feature that had brought in a lot of favorable publicity.

"Is something wrong?" he asked. "Are you in trouble? Are you lost?"

"Yes, Robie. Take me to my mother."

"Stay right here," Robie said reassuringly, "and don't be frightened. I will call a policeman." He whistled shrilly, twice.

Time passed. Robie whistled again. The windows flared and roared. The little girl begged. "Take me away, Robie," and jumped onto a little step in his hoopskirt.

"Give me a dime," Robie said.

The little girl found one in her pocket and put it in his claws.

"Your weight," Robie said, "is fifty-four and one-half pounds."

"Have you seen my daughter, have you seen her?" a woman was crying somewhere. "I left her watching that thing while I stepped inside—*Rita!*"

"Robie helped me," the little girl began babbling at her. "He knew I was lost. He even called the police, but they didn't come. He weighed me, too. Didn't you, Robie?"

But Robie had gone off to peddle Poppy Pop to the members of a rescue squad which had just come around the corner, more robotlike in their asbestos suits than he in his metal skin.

WITHOUT A THOUGHT

by Fred Saberhagen

The machine-as-adversary is an eternal and powerful theme of much science fiction. Fred Saberhagen, a soft-spoken man from Chicago, has tackled this theme in a highly popular series of recent stories about the "berserkers" —colossal machines left over from some ancient galactic war, still roaming the universe and bringing grief to earthmen venturing into space. In a dozen or more stories Saberhagen has developed a brilliant picture of men at war with the massive berserkers, seeking to outwit them on their own terms and destroy them. The present story was one of the earliest in the series.

Fred Saberhagen is a former electronics technician whose background includes four years of Air Force service. Now he is a professional writer with some two dozen published stories and several books to his credit. Though he keeps his killer instinct well hidden behind a facade of mild-mannered reserve, he is an expert in karate and other sinister forms of self-defense.

The machine was a vast fortress, containing no life, set by its long-dead masters to destroy anything that lived. It and many others like it were the inheritance of Earth from some war fought between unknown interstellar empires, in some time that could hardly be connected with any Earthly calendar.

One such machine could hang over a planet colonized by men and in two days pound the surface into a lifeless cloud of dust and steam, a hundred miles deep. This particular machine had already done just that.

It used no predictable tactics in its dedicated, unconscious war against life. The ancient, unknown gamesmen had built it as a random factor, to be loosed in the enemy's territory to do what damage it might. Men thought its plan of battle was chosen by the random disintegrations of atoms in a block of some long-lived isotope buried deep inside it, and so was not even in theory predictable by opposing brains, human or electronic.

Men called it a berserker.

Del Murray, sometime computer specialist, had called it other names than that; but right now he was too busy to waste breath, as he moved in staggering lunges around the little cabin of his one-man fighter, plugging in replacement units for equipment damaged by the last near-miss of a berserker missile. An animal resembling a large dog with an ape's forelegs moved around the cabin too, carrying in its nearly human hands a supply of emergency sealing patches. The cabin air was full of haze. Wherever movement of the haze showed a leak to an unpressurized part of the hull, the dog-ape moved to apply a patch.

"Hello, Foxglove!" the man shouted, hoping that his radio was again in working order.

"Hello, Murray, this is Foxglove," said a sudden loud voice in the cabin. "How far did you get?"

Del was too weary to show much relief that his communications were open again. "I'll let you know in a minute. At least it's stopped shooting at me for a while. Move, Newton." The alien animal, pet and ally, called an *aiyan,* moved away from the man's feet and kept singlemindedly looking for leaks.

After another minute's work Del could strap his body into the deep-cushioned command chair again, with something like an operational panel before him. That last near-miss had sprayed the whole cabin with fine penetrating splinters. It was remarkable that man and *aiyan* had come through unwounded.

His radar working again, Del could say: "I'm about ninety miles out from it, Foxglove. On the opposite side from you." His present position was the one he had been trying to achieve since the battle had begun.

The two Earth ships and the berserker were half a light year from the nearest sun. The berserker could not leap out of normal space, toward the defenseless colonies on the planets of that sun, while the two ships stayed close to it. There were only two men aboard Foxglove. They had more machinery working for them than did Del, but both manned ships were mites compared to their opponent.

Del's radar showed him an ancient ruin of metal, not much smaller in cross section than New Jersey. Men had blown holes in it the size of Manhattan Island, and melted puddles of slag as big as lakes upon its surface.

But the berserker's power was still enormous. So far no man had fought it and survived. Now, it could squash Del's little ship like a mosquito; it was wasting its unpredictable subtlety on him. Yet there was a special taste of terror in the very indifference of it. Men could never frighten this enemy, as it frightened them.

Earthmen's tactics, worked out from bitter experience against other berserkers, called for a simultaneous attack by three ships. Foxglove and Murray made two. A third was supposedly on the way, but still about eight hours distant, moving at C-plus velocity, outside of normal space. Until it arrived, Foxglove and Murray must hold the berserker at bay, while it brooded unguessable schemes.

It might attack either ship at any moment, or it might seek to disengage. It might wait hours for them to make the first move—though it would certainly fight if the men attacked it. It had learned the language of Earth's spacemen—it might try to talk with them. But always, ultimately it would seek to destroy them and every other living thing it met. That was the basic command given it by the ancient warlords.

A thousand years ago, it would easily have swept ships of the type that now opposed it from its path, whether they carried fusion missiles or not. Now, it was in some electrical way conscious of its own weakening by accumulated damage. And perhaps in long centuries of fighting its way across the galaxy it had learned to be wary.

Now, quite suddenly, Del's detectors showed force fields forming in behind his ship. Like the encircling arms of a huge bear they blocked his path away from the enemy. He waited for some deadly blow, with his hand trembling over the red button that would salvo his atomic missiles at the berserker—but if he attacked alone, or even with Foxglove, the infernal machine would parry their missiles, crush their ships, and go on to destroy another helpless planet. Three ships were needed to attack. The red firing button was now only a last desperate resort.

Del was reporting the force fields to Foxglove when he felt the first hint in his mind of another attack.

"Newton!" he called sharply, leaving the radio connection with Foxglove open. They would hear and understand what was going to happen.

The *aiyan* bounded instantly from its combat couch to

stand before Del as if hypnotized, all attention riveted on the man. Del had sometimes bragged: "Show Newton a drawing of different-colored lights, convince him it represents a particular control panel, and he'll push buttons or whatever you tell him, until the real panel matches the drawing."

But no *aiyan* had the human ability to learn and to create on an abstract level; which was why Del was now going to put Newton in command of his ship.

He switched off the ship's computers—they were going to be as useless as his own brain under the attack he felt gathering—and said to Newton: "Situation Zombie."

The animal responded instantly as it had been trained, seizing Del's hands with firm insistence and dragging them one at a time down beside the command chair to where the fetters had been installed.

Hard experience had taught men something about the berserkers' mind weapon, although its principles of operation were still unknown. It was slow in its onslaught, and its effects could not be steadily maintained for more than about two hours, after which a berserker was evidently forced to turn it off for an equal time. But while in effect, it robbed any human or electronic brain of the ability to plan or to predict —and left it unconscious of its own incapacity.

It seemed to Del that all this had happened before, maybe more than once. Newton, that funny fellow, had gone too far with his pranks; he had abandoned the little boxes of colored beads that were his favorite toys, and was moving the controls around at the lighted panel. Unwilling to share the fun with Del, he had tied the man to his chair somehow. Such behavior was really intolerable, especially when there was supposed to be a battle in progress. Del tried to pull his hands free, and called to Newton.

Newton whined earnestly, and stayed at the panel.

"Newt, you dog, come lemme loose. I know what I have to

say: Four score and seven . . . hey, Newt, where're your toys? Lemme see your pretty beads." There were hundreds of tiny boxes of the varicolored beads, leftover trade goods that Newton loved to sort out and handle. Del peered around the cabin, chuckling a little at his own cleverness. He would get Newton distracted by the beads, and then . . . the vague idea faded into other crackbrained grotesqueries.

Newton whined now and then but stayed at the panel moving controls in the long sequence he had been taught, taking the ship through the feinting, evasive maneuvers that might fool a berserker into thinking it was still competently manned. Newton never put a hand near the big red button. Only if he felt deadly pain himself, or found a dead man in Del's chair, would he reach for that.

"Ah, roger, Murray," said the radio from time to time, as if acknowledging a message. Sometimes Foxglove added a few words or numbers that might have meant something. Del wondered what the talking was about.

At last he understood that Foxglove was trying to help maintain the illusion that there was still a competent brain in charge of Del's ship. The fear reaction came when he began to realize that he had once again lived through the effect of the mind weapon. The brooding berserker, half genius, half idiot, had forborne to press the attack when success would have been certain—perhaps deceived, perhaps following the strategy that avoided predictability at almost any cost.

"Newton." The animal turned, hearing a change in his voice. Now Del could say the words that would tell Newton it was safe to set his master free, a sequence too long for anyone under the mind weapon to recite.

"—shall not perish from the earth," he finished. With a yelp of joy Newton pulled the fetters from Del's hands. Del turned instantly to the radio.

"Effect has evidently been turned off, Foxglove," said Del's voice through the speaker in the cabin of the larger ship.

The Commander let out a sigh. "He's back in control!"

The Second Officer—there was no third—said: "That means we've got some kind of fighting chance, for the next two hours. I say let's attack now!"

The Commander shook his head, slowly but without hesitation. "With two ships, we don't have any real chance. Less than four hours until Gizmo gets here. We have to stall until then, if we want to win."

"It'll attack the next time it gets Del's mind scrambled! I don't think we fooled it for a minute . . . we're out of range of the mind beam here, but Del can't withdraw now. And we can't expect that *aiyan* to fight his ship for him. We'll really have no chance, with Del gone."

The Commander's eyes moved ceaselessly over his panel. "We'll wait. We can't be sure it'll attack the next time it puts the beam on him. . . ."

The berserker spoke suddenly, its radioed voice plain in the cabins of both ships: "I have a proposition for you, little ship." Its voice had a cracking, adolescent quality, because it strung together words and syllables recorded from the voices of human prisoners of both sexes and different ages. Bits of human emotion, sorted and fixed like butterflies on pins, thought the Commander. There was no reason to think it had kept the prisoners alive after learning the language from them.

"Well?" Del's voice sounded tough and capable by comparison.

"I have invented a game which we will play," it said. "If you play well enough, I will not kill you right away."

"Now I've heard everything," murmured the Second Officer.

After three thoughtful seconds the Commander slammed a fist on the arm of his chair. "It means to test his learning ability, to run a continuous check on his brain while it turns up the power of the mind beam and tries different modulations. If it can make sure the mind beam is working, it'll attack instantly. I'll bet my life on it. That's the game it's playing this time."

"I will think over your proposition," said Del's voice coolly.

The Commander said: "It's in no hurry to start. It won't be able to turn on the mind beam again for almost two hours."

"But we need another two hours beyond that."

Del's voice said: "Describe the game you want to play."

"It is a simplified version of the human game called checkers."

The Commander and the Second looked at each other, neither able to imagine Newton able to play checkers. Nor could they doubt that Newton's failure would kill them within a few hours, and leave another planet open to destruction.

After a minute's silence, Del's voice asked: "What'll we use for a board?"

"We will radio our moves to one another," said the berserker equably. It went on to describe a checkers-like game, played on a smaller board with less than the normal number of pieces. There was nothing very profound about it; but, of course, playing would seem to require a functional brain, human or electronic, able to plan and to predict.

"If I agree to play," said Del slowly, "how'll we decide who gets to move first?"

"He's trying to stall," said the Commander, gnawing a thumbnail. "We won't be able to offer any advice, with that thing listening. Oh, stay sharp, Del boy!"

"To simplify matters," said the berserker, "I will move first in every game."

Del could look forward to another hour free of the mind weapon when he finished rigging the checkerboard. When the pegged pieces were moved, appropriate signals would be radioed to the berserker; lighted squares on the board would show him where its pieces were moved. If it spoke to him while the mind weapon was on, Del's voice would answer from a tape, which he had stocked with vaguely aggressive phrases, such as, "Get on with the game," or "Do you want to give up now?"

He hadn't told the enemy how far along he was with his preparations because he was still busy with something the enemy must not know—the system that was going to enable Newton to play a game of simplified checkers.

Del gave a soundless little laugh as he worked, and glanced over to where Newton was lounging on his couch, clutching toys in his hands as if he drew some comfort from them. This scheme was going to push the *aiyan* near the limit of his ability, but Del saw no reason why it should fail.

Del had completely analyzed the miniature checker game, and diagrammed every position that Newton could possibly face—playing only even-numbered moves, thank the random berserker for that specification!—on small cards. Del had discarded some lines of play that would arise from some poor early moves by Newton, further simplifying his job. Now, on a card showing each possible remaining position, Del indicated the best possible move with a drawn-in arrow. Now he could quickly teach Newton to play the game by looking at the appropriate card and making the move shown by the arrow—

"Oh, oh," said Del, as his hands stopped working and he stared into space. Newton whined at the tone of his voice.

Once Del had sat at one board in a simultaneous chess exhibition, one of sixty players opposing the world cham-

pion, Blankenship. Del had held his own into the middle
game. Then, when the great man paused again opposite his
board, Del had shoved a pawn forward, thinking he had
reached an unassailable position and could begin a counter-
attack. Blankenship had moved a rook to an innocent-looking
square and strolled on to the next board—and then Del had
seen the checkmate coming at him, four moves away but one
move too late for him to do anything about it.

The Commander suddenly said a foul phrase in a loud
distinct voice. Such conduct on his part was extremely rare,
and the Second Officer looked round in surprise. "What?"

"I think we've had it." The Commander paused. "I hoped
that Murray could set up some kind of a system over there, so
that Newton could play the game—or appear to be playing it.
But it won't work. Whatever system Newton plays by rote
will always have him making the same move in the same
position. It may be a perfect system—but a man doesn't play
any game that way, damn it. He makes mistakes, he changes
strategy. Even in a game this simple there'll be room for that.
Most of all, a man *learns* a game as he plays it. He gets better
as he goes along. That's what'll give Newton away, and that's
what our bandit wants. It's probably heard about *aiyans*.
Now as soon as it can be sure it's facing a dumb animal over
there, and not a man or computer . . ."

After a little while the Second Officer said: "I'm getting
signals of their moves. They've begun play. Maybe we
should've rigged up a board so we could follow along with
the game."

"We better just be ready to go at it when the time comes."
The Commander looked hopelessly at his salvo button, and
then at the clock that showed two hours must pass before
Gizmo could reasonably be hoped for.

Soon the Second Officer said: "That seems to be the end of
the first game; Del lost it, if I'm reading their scoreboard

signal right." He paused. "Sir, here's that signal we picked up the last time it turned the mind beam on. Del must be starting to get it again."

There was nothing for the Commander to say. The two men waited silently for the enemy's attack, hoping only that they could damage it in the seconds before it would overwhelm them and kill them.

"He's playing the second game," said the Second Officer, puzzled. "And I just heard him say, 'Let's get on with it.' "

"His voice could be recorded. He must have made some plan of play for Newton to follow; but it won't fool the berserker for long. It can't."

Time crept unmeasurably past them.

The Second said: "He's lost the first four games. But he's *not* making the same moves every time. I wish we'd made a board. . . ."

"Shut up about the board! We'd be watching it instead of the panel. Now stay alert, Mister."

After what seemed a long time, the Second said: "Well, I'll be!"

"What?"

"Our side got a draw in that game."

"Then the beam can't be on him. Are you sure . . ."

"It is! Look, here, the same indication we got last time. It's been on him the better part of an hour now, and getting stronger."

The Commander stared in disbelief; but he knew and trusted his Second's ability. And the panel indications were convincing. He said: "Then someone—or something—with no functioning mind is learning how to play a game, over there. Ha, ha," he added, as if trying to remember how to laugh.

The berserker won another game. Another draw. Another win for the enemy. Then three drawn games in a row.

Once the Second Officer heard Del's voice ask coolly: "Do you want to give up now?" On the next move he lost another game. But the following game ended in another draw. Del was plainly taking more time than his opponent to move, but not enough to make the enemy impatient.

"It's trying different modulations on the mind beam," said the Second. "And it's got the power turned way up."

"Yeah," said the Commander. Several times he had almost tried to radio Del, to say something that might keep the man's spirits up—and also to relieve his own feverish inactivity, and to try to find out what could possibly be going on. But he could not take the chance. Any interference might upset the miracle.

He could not believe the inexplicable success could last, even when the checker match turned gradually into an endless succession of drawn games between two perfect players. Hours ago the Commander had said good-bye to life and hope, and he still waited for the fatal moment.

And he waited.

"—not perish from the earth!" said Del Murray, and Newton's eager hands flew to loose his right arm from its shackle.

A game, unfinished on the little board before him, had been abandoned seconds earlier. The mind beam had been turned off at the same time, when Gizmo had burst into normal space right in position and only five minutes late; and the berserker had been forced to turn all its energies to meet the immediate all-out attack of Gizmo and Foxglove.

Del saw his computers, recovering from the effect of the beam, lock his aiming screen onto the berserker's scarred and bulging midsection, as he shot his right arm forward, scattering pieces from the game board.

"Checkmate!" he roared out hoarsely, and brought his fist down on the big red button.

"I'm glad it didn't want to play chess," Del said later, talking to the Commander in Foxglove's cabin. "I could never have rigged that up."

The ports were cleared now, and the men could look out at the cloud of expanding gas, still faintly luminous, that had been a berserker; metal fire-purged of the legacy of ancient evil.

But the Commander was watching Del. "You got Newt to play by following diagrams, I see that. But how could he *learn* the game?"

Del grinned. "He couldn't, but his toys could. Now wait before you slug me." He called the *aiyan* to him and took a small box from the animal's hand. The box rattled faintly as he held it up. On the cover was pasted a diagram of one possible position in the simplified checker game, with a different-colored arrow indicating each possible move of Del's pieces.

"It took a couple of hundred of these boxes," said Del. "This one was in the group that Newt examined for the fourth move. When he found a box with a diagram matching the position on the board, he picked the box up, pulled out one of these beads from inside, without looking—that was the hardest part to teach him in a hurry, by the way," said Del, demonstrating. "Ah, this one's blue. That means, make the move indicated on the cover by a blue arrow. Now the orange arrow leads to a poor position, see?" Del shook all the beads out of the box into his hand. "No orange beads left; there were six of each color when we started. But every time Newton drew a bead, he had orders to leave it out of the box until the game was over. Then, if the scoreboard indicated a loss for our side, he went back and threw away all the beads he had used. All the bad moves were gradually eliminated. In a few hours, Newt and his boxes learned to play the game perfectly."

"Well," said the Commander. He thought for a moment, then reached down to scratch Newton behind the ears. "I never would have come up with that idea."

"I should have thought of it sooner. The basic idea's a couple of centuries old. And computers are supposed to be my business."

"This could be a big thing," said the Commander. "I mean your basic idea might be useful to any task force that has to face a berserker's mind beam."

"Yeah." Del grew reflective. "Also . . ."

"What?"

"I was thinking of a guy I met once. Named Blankenship. I wonder if I *could* rig something up. . . ."

SOLAR PLEXUS

by James Blish

       James Blish is a slender, quietly vehement man who qualifies as an authority on the poems of Ezra Pound, the operas of Richard Strauss, a number of sciences, and both the art and the science of writing science fiction. Formerly science editor for a large pharmaceutical company, he is now employed as an account executive for a public relations firm, in charge of promoting an assortment of controversial causes, and manages in his spare time to write first-rate science fiction and take part in amateur theatricals. He lives in Brooklyn, N.Y., with his wife, artist Judith Ann Lawrence, and an assortment of cats.

    The story here is one of his earliest, first published in 1941, but substantially revised when it was reprinted eleven years later. It concerns an aspect of the man-machine relationship now frequently discussed: the cyborg, or "cybernetic organism"—that is, the man as machine, human brain joined to nonhuman equipment.

Brant Kittinger did not hear the alarm begin to ring. Indeed, it was only after a soft blow had jarred his free-floating observatory that he looked up in sudden awareness from the interferometer. Then the sound of the warning bell reached his consciousness.

Brant was an astronomer, not a spaceman, but he knew that the bell could mean nothing but the arrival of another ship in the vicinity. There would be no point in ringing a bell for a meteor—the thing could be through and past you during the first cycle of the clapper. Only an approaching ship would be likely to trip the detector, and it would have to be close.

A second dull jolt told him how close it was. The rasp of metal which followed, as the other ship slid along the side of his own, drove the fog of tensors completely from his brain. He dropped his pencil and straightened up.

His first thought was that his year in the orbit around the new trans-Plutonian planet was up, and that the Institute's tug had arrived to tow him home, telescope and all. A glance at the clock reassured him at first, then puzzled him still further. He still had the better part of four months.

No commercial vessel, of course, could have wandered this far from the inner planets; and the UN's police cruisers didn't travel far outside the commercial lanes. Besides, it would have been impossible for anyone to find Brant's orbital observatory by accident.

He settled his glasses more firmly on his nose, clambered awkwardly backwards out of the prime focus chamber and down the wall net to the control desk on the observation floor. A quick glance over the boards revealed that there was a magnetic field of some strength nearby, one that didn't belong to the invisible gas giant revolving half a million miles away.

The strange ship was locked to him magnetically; it was an

old ship, then, for that method of grappling had been discarded years ago as too hard on delicate instruments. And the strength of the field meant a big ship.

Too big. The only ship of that period that could mount generators that size, as far as Brant could remember, was the Cybernetics Foundation's *Astrid*. Brant could remember well the Foundation's regretful announcement that Murray Bennett had destroyed both himself and the *Astrid* rather than turn the ship in to some UN inspection team. It had happened only eight years ago. Some scandal or other . . .

Well, who then?

He turned the radio on. Nothing came out of it. It was a simple transistor set tuned to the Institute's frequency, and since the ship outside plainly did not belong to the Institute, he had expected nothing else. Of course he had a photophone also, but it had been designed for communication over a reasonable distance, not for cheek-to-cheek whispers.

As an afterthought, he turned off the persistent alarm bell. At once another sound came through: a delicate, rhythmic tapping on the hull of the observatory. Someone wanted to get in.

He could think of no reason to refuse entrance, except for a vague and utterly unreasonable wonder as to whether or not the stranger was a friend. He had no enemies, and the notion that some outlaw might have happened upon him out here was ridiculous. Nevertheless, there was something about the anonymous, voiceless ship just outside which made him uneasy.

The gentle tapping stopped, and then began again, with an even, mechanical insistence. For a moment Brant wondered whether or not he should try to tear free with the observatory's few maneuvering rockets—but even should he win so uneven a struggle, he would throw the observatory out of the orbit where the Institute expected to find it, and he was not astronaut enough to get it back there again.

Tap, tap. Tap, tap.

"All right," he said irritably. He pushed the button which set the airlock to cycling. The tapping stopped. He left the outer door open more than long enough for anyone to enter and push the button in the lock which reversed the process; but nothing happened.

After what seemed to be a long wait, he pushed his button again. The outer door closed, the pumps filled the chamber with air, the inner door swung open. No ghost drifted out of it; there was nobody in the lock at all.

Tap, tap. Tap, tap.

Absently he polished his glasses on his sleeve. If they didn't want to come into the observatory, they must want him to come out of it. That was possible: although the telescope had a Coudé focus which allowed him to work in the ship's air most of the time, it was occasionally necessary for him to exhaust the dome, and for that purpose he had a space suit. But he had never been outside the hull in it, and the thought alarmed him. Brant was nobody's spaceman.

Be damned to them. He clapped his glasses back into place and took one more look into the empty airlock. It was still empty, with the outer door now moving open very slowly. . . .

A spaceman would have known that he was already dead, but Brant's reactions were not quite as fast. His first move was to try to jam the inner door shut by sheer muscle-power, but it would not stir. Then he simply clung to the nearest stanchion, waiting for the air to rush out of the observatory, and his life after it.

The outer door of the airlock continued to open, placidly, and still there was no rush of air—only a kind of faint, unticketable inwash of odor, as if Brant's air were mixing with someone else's. When both doors of the lock finally stood wide

apart from each other, Brant found himself looking down the
inside of a flexible, airtight tube, such as he had once seen
used for the transfer of a small freight-load from a ship to one
of Earth's several space stations. It connected the airlock of
the observatory with that of the other ship. At the other end
of it, lights gleamed yellowly, with the unmistakable, dismal
sheen of incandescent overheads.

That was an old ship, all right.

Tap. Tap.

"Go to hell," he said aloud. There was no answer.

Tap. Tap.

"Go to hell," he said. He walked out into the tube, which
flexed sinuously as his body pressed aside the static air. In the
airlock of the stranger, he paused and looked back. He was
not much surprised to see the outer door of his own airlock
swinging smugly shut against him. Then the airlock of the
stranger began to cycle; he skipped on into the ship barely in
time.

There was a bare metal corridor ahead of him. While he
watched, the first light bulb over his head blinked out. Then
the second. Then the third. As the fourth one went out, the
first came on again, so that now there was a slow ribbon of
darkness moving away from him down the corridor. Clearly,
he was being asked to follow the line of darkening bulbs
down the corridor.

He had no choice, now that he had come this far. He
followed the blinking lights.

The trail led directly to the control room of the ship.
There was nobody there, either.

The whole place was oppressively silent. He could hear the
soft hum of generators—a louder noise than he ever heard on
board the observatory—but no ship should be this quiet.
There should be muffled human voices, the chittering of
communications systems, the impacts of soles on metal. Some-

one had to operate a proper ship—not only its airlocks, but its motors—and its brains. The observatory was only a barge, and needed no crew but Brant, but a real ship had to be manned.

He scanned the bare metal compartment, noting the apparent age of the equipment. Most of it was manual, but there were no hands to man it.

A ghost ship for true.

"All right," he said. His voice sounded flat and loud to him. "Come on out. You wanted me here—why are you hiding?"

Immediately there was a noise in the close, still air, a thin, electrical sigh. Then a quiet voice said, "You're Brant Kittinger."

"Certainly," Brant said, swiveling fruitlessly toward the apparent source of the voice. "You know who I am. You couldn't have found me by accident. Will you come out? I've no time to play games."

"I'm not playing games," the voice said calmly. "And I can't come out, since I'm not hiding from you. I can't see you; I needed to hear your voice before I could be sure of you."

"Why?"

"Because I can't see inside the ship. I could find your observation boat well enough, but until I heard you speak I couldn't be sure that you were the one aboard it. Now I know."

"All right," Brant said suspiciously. "I still don't see why you're hiding. Where are you?"

"Right here," said the voice. "All around you."

Brant looked all around himself. His scalp began to creep.

"What kind of nonsense is that?" he said.

"You aren't seeing what you're looking at, Brant. You're looking directly at me, no matter where you look. *I am the ship.*"

"Oh," Brant said softly. "So that's it. You're one of Murray Bennett's computer-driven ships. Are you the *Astrid,* after all?"

"This is the *Astrid,*" the voice said. "But you miss my point. I am Murray Bennett, also."

Brant's jaw dropped open. "Where are you?" he said after a time.

"Here," the voice said impatiently. "I am the *Astrid.* I am also Murray Bennett. Bennett is dead, so he can't very well come into the cabin and shake your hand. I am now Murray Bennett; I remember you very well, Brant. I need your help, so I sought you out. I'm not as much Murray Bennett as I'd like to be."

Brant sat down in the empty pilot's seat.

"You're a computer," he said shakily. "Isn't that so?"

"It is and it isn't. No computer can duplicate the performance of a human brain. I tried to introduce real human neural mechanisms into computers, specifically to fly ships, and was outlawed for my trouble. I don't think I was treated fairly. It took enormous surgical skill to make the hundreds and hundreds of nerve-to-circuit connections that were needed—and before I was half through, the UN decided that what I was doing was human vivisection. They outlawed me, and the Foundation said I'd have to destroy myself; what could I do after that?

"I did destroy myself. I transferred most of my own nervous system into the computers of the *Astrid,* working at the end through drugged assistants under telepathic control, and finally relying upon the computers to seal the last connections. No such surgery ever existed before, but I brought it into existence. It worked. Now I'm the *Astrid*—and still Murray Bennett too, though Bennett is dead."

Brant locked his hands together carefully on the edge of the dead control board. "What good did that do you?" he said.

"It proved my point. I was trying to build an almost living spaceship. I had to build part of myself into it to do it—since they made me an outlaw to stop my using any other human being as a source of parts. But here is the *Astrid,* Brant, as almost alive as I could ask. I'm as immune to a dead spaceship—a UN cruiser, for instance—as you would be to an infuriated wheelbarrow. My reflexes are human-fast. I feel things directly, not through instruments. I fly myself: I am what I sought—the ship that almost thinks for itself."

"You keep saying 'almost,' " Brant said.

"That's why I came to you," the voice said. "I don't have enough of Murray Bennett here to know what I should do next. You knew me well. Was I out to try to use human brains more and more, and computer-mechanisms less and less? It seems to me that I was. I can pick up the brains easily enough, just as I picked you up. The solar system is full of people isolated on little research boats who could be plucked off them and incorporated into efficient machines like the *Astrid.* But I don't know. I seem to have lost my creativity. I have a base where I have some other ships with beautiful computers in them, and with a few people to use as research animals I could make even better ships of them than the *Astrid* is. But is that what I want to do? Is that what I set out to do? I no longer know, Brant. Advise me."

The machine with the human nerves would have been touching had it not been so much like Bennett had been. The combination of the two was flatly horrible.

"You've made a bad job of yourself, Murray," he said. "You've let me inside your brain without taking any real thought of the danger. What's to prevent me from stationing myself at your old manual controls and flying you to the nearest UN post?"

"You can't fly a ship."

"How do you know?"

"By simple computation. And there are other reasons.

What's to prevent me from making you cut your own throat? The answer's the same. You're in control of your body; I'm in control of mine. My body is the *Astrid*. The controls are useless, unless I actuate them. The nerves through which I do so are sheathed in excellent steel. The only way in which you could destroy my control would be to break something necessary to the running of the ship. That, in a sense, would kill me, as destroying your heart or your lungs would kill you. But that would be pointless, for then you could no more navigate the ship than I. And if you made repairs, I would be—well, resurrected."

The voice fell silent a moment. Then it added, matter-of-factly, "Of course, I can protect myself."

Brant made no reply. His eyes were narrowed to the squint he more usually directed at a problem in Milne transformations.

"I never sleep," the voice went on, "but much of my navigating and piloting is done by an autopilot without requiring my conscious attention. It is the same old Nelson autopilot which was originally on board the *Astrid*, though, so it has to be monitored. If you touch the controls while the autopilot is running, it switches itself off and I resume direction myself."

Brant was surprised and instinctively repelled by the steady flow of information. It was a forcible reminder of how much of the computer there was in the intelligence that called itself Murray Bennett. It was answering a question with the almost mindless wealth of detail of a public-library selector—and there was no "Enough" button for Brant to push.

"Are you going to answer my question?" the voice said suddenly.

"Yes," Brant said. "I advise you to turn yourself in. The *Astrid* proves your point—and also proves that your research was a blind alley. There's no point in your proceeding to make more *Astrids*; you're aware yourself that you're incapable of improving on the model now."

"That's contrary to what I have recorded," the voice said. "My ultimate purpose as a man was to build machines like this. I can't accept your answer: it conflicts with my primary directive. Please follow the lights to your quarters."

"What are you going to do with me?"

"Take you to the base."

"What for?" Brant said.

"As a stock of parts," said the voice. "Please follow the lights, or I'll have to use force."

Brant followed the lights. As he entered the cabin to which they led him, a disheveled figure arose from one of the two cots. He started back in alarm. The figure chuckled wryly and displayed a frayed bit of gold braid on its sleeve.

"I'm not as terrifying as I look," he said. "Lt. Powell of the UN scout *Iapetus,* at your service."

"I'm Brant Kittinger, Planetary Institute astrophysicist. You're just the faintest bit battered, all right. Did you tangle with Bennett?"

"Is that his name?" The UN patrolman nodded glumly. "Yes. There's some whoppers of guns mounted on this old tub. I challenged it, and it cut my ship to pieces before I could lift a hand. I barely got into my suit in time—and I'm beginning to wish I hadn't."

"I don't blame you. You know what he plans to use us for, I judge."

"Yes," the pilot said. "He seems to take pleasure in bragging about his achievements—God knows they're amazing enough, if even half of what he says is true."

"It's all true," Brant said. "He's essentially a machine, you know, and as such I doubt that he can lie."

Powell looked startled. "That makes it worse. I've been trying to figure a way out—"

Brant raised one hand sharply, and with the other he

patted his pockets in search of a pencil. "If you've found anything, write it down, don't talk about it. I think he can hear us. Is that so, Bennett?"

"Yes," said the voice in the air. Powell jumped. "My hearing extends throughout the ship."

There was silence again. Powell, grim as death, scribbled on a tattered UN trip ticket.

Doesn't matter. Can't think of a thing.

Where's the main computer? Brant wrote. *There's where personality residues must lie.*

Down below. Not a chance without blaster. Must be eight inches of steel around it. Control nerves the same.

They sat hopelessly on the lower cot. Brant chewed on the pencil. "How far is his home base from here?" he asked at length.

"Where's here?"

"In the orbit of the new planet."

Powell whistled. "In that case, his base can't be more than three days away. I came on board from just off Titan, and he hasn't touched his base since, so his fuel won't last much longer. I know this type of ship well enough. And from what I've seen of the drivers, they haven't been altered."

"Umm," Brant said. "That checks. If Bennett in person never got around to altering the drive, this ersatz Bennett we have here will never get around to it, either." He found it easier to ignore the listening presence while talking; to monitor his speech constantly with Bennett in mind was too hard on the nerves. "That gives us three days to get out, then. Or less."

For at least twenty minutes Brant said nothing more, while the UN pilot squirmed and watched his face hopefully. Finally the astronomer picked up the piece of paper again.

Can you pilot this ship? he wrote.

The pilot nodded and scribbled: *Why?*

Without replying, Brant lay back on the bunk, swiveled himself around so that his head was toward the center of the cabin, doubled up his knees, and let fly with both feet. They crashed hard against the hull, the magnetic studs in his shoes leaving bright scars on the metal. The impact sent him sailing like an ungainly fish across the cabin.

"What was that for?" Powell and the voice in the air asked simultaneously. Their captor's tone was faintly curious, but not alarmed.

Brant had his answer already prepared. "It's part of a question I want to ask," he said. He brought up against the far wall and struggled to get his feet back to the deck. "Can you tell me what I did then, Bennett?"

"Why, not specifically. As I told you, I can't see inside the ship. But I get a tactual jar from the nerves of the controls, the lights, the floors, the ventilation system, and so on, and also a ringing sound from the audios. These things tell me that you either stamped on the floor or pounded on the wall. From the intensity of all the impressions, I compute that you stamped."

"You hear and you feel, eh?"

"That's correct," the voice said. "Also I can pick up your body heat from the receptors in the ship's temperature control system—a form of seeing, but without any definition."

Very quietly, Brant retrieved the worn trip ticket and wrote on it: *Follow me.*

He went out into the corridor and started down it toward the control room, Powell at his heels. The living ship remained silent only for a moment.

"Return to your cabin," the voice said.

Brant walked a little faster. How would Bennett's vicious brainchild enforce his orders?

"I said, go back to the cabin," the voice said. Its tone was now loud and harsh, and without a trace of feeling; for the first time, Brant was able to tell that it came from a voder, rather than from a tape-vocabulary of Bennett's own voice. Brant gritted his teeth and marched forward.

"I don't want to have to spoil you," the voice said. "For the last time—"

An instant later Brant received a powerful blow in the small of his back. It felled him like a tree, and sent him skimming along the corridor deck like a flat stone. A bare fraction of a second later there was a hiss and a flash, and the air was abruptly hot and choking with the sharp odor of ozone.

"Close," Powell's voice said calmly. "Some of these rivet-heads in the walls evidently are high-tension electrodes. Lucky I saw the nimbus collecting on that one. Crawl, and make it snappy."

Crawling in a gravity-free corridor was a good deal more difficult to manage than walking. Determinedly, Brant squirmed into the control room, calling into play every trick he had ever learned in space to stick to the floor. He could hear Powell wriggling along behind him.

"He doesn't know what I'm up to," Brant said aloud. "Do you, Bennett?"

"No," the voice in the air said. "But I know of nothing you can do that's dangerous while you're lying on your belly. When you get up, I'll destroy you, Brant."

"Hmmm," Brant said. He adjusted his glasses, which he had nearly lost during his brief, skipping carom along the deck. The voice had summarized the situation with deadly precision. He pulled the now nearly pulped trip ticket out of his shirt pocket, wrote on it, and shoved it across the deck to Powell.

How can we reach the autopilot? Got to smash it.

Powell propped himself up on one elbow and studied the scrap of paper, frowning. Down below, beneath the deck, there was an abrupt sound of power, and Brant felt the cold metal on which he was lying sink beneath him. Bennett was changing course, trying to throw them within range of his defenses. Both men began to slide sidewise.

Powell did not appear to be worried; evidently he knew just how long it took to turn a ship of this size and period. He pushed the piece of paper back. On the last free space on it, in cramped letters, was: *Throw something at it.*

"Ah," said Brant. Still sliding, he drew off one of his heavy shoes and hefted it critically. It would do. With a sudden convulsion of motion he hurled it.

Fat, crackling sparks crisscrossed the room; the noise was ear-splitting. While Bennett could have had no idea what Brant was doing, he evidently had sensed the sudden stir of movement and had triggered the high-tension current out of general caution. But he was too late. The flying shoe plowed heel-foremost into the autopilot with a rending smash.

There was an unfocused blare of sound from the voder— more like the noise of a siren than like a human cry. The *Astrid* rolled wildly, once. Then there was silence.

"All right," said Brant, getting to his knees. "Try the controls, Powell."

The UN pilot arose cautiously. No sparks flew. When he touched the boards, the ship responded with an immediate purr of power.

"She runs," he said. "Now, how the hell did you know what to do?"

"It wasn't difficult," Brant said complacently, retrieving his shoe. "But we're not out of the woods yet. We have to get to the stores fast and find a couple of torches. I want to cut through every nerve-channel we can find. Are you with me?"

"Sure."

The job was more quickly done than Brant had dared to hope. Evidently the living ship had never thought of lightening itself by jettisoning all the equipment its human crew had once needed. While Brant and Powell cut their way enthusiastically through the jungle of efferent nerve-trunks running from the central computer, the astronomer said:

"He gave us too much information. He told me that he had connected the artificial nerves of the ship, the control nerves, to the nerve-ends running from the parts of his own brain that he had used. And he said that he'd had to make *hundreds* of such connections. That's the trouble with allowing a computer to act as an independent agent—it doesn't know enough about inter-personal relationships to control its tongue. . . . There we are. He'll be coming to before long, but I don't think he'll be able to interfere with us now."

He set down his torch with a sigh. "I was saying? Oh, yes. About those nerve connections: if he had separated out the pain-carrying nerves from the other sensory nerves, he would have had to have made *thousands* of connections, not hundreds. Had it really been the living human being, Bennett, who had given me that cue, I would have discounted it, because he might have been using understatement. But since it was Bennett's double, a computer, I assumed that the figure was of the right order of magnitude. Computers don't understate.

"Besides, I didn't think Bennett could have made thousands of connections, especially not working telepathically through a proxy. There's a limit even to the most marvelous neurosurgery. Bennett had just made general connections, and had relied on the segments from his own brain which he had incorporated to sort out the impulses as they came in—as any human brain could do under like circumstances. That was one of the advantages of using parts from a human brain in the first place."

"And when you kicked the wall—" Powell said.

"Yes, you see the crux of the problem already. When I

kicked the wall, I wanted to make sure that he could *feel* the impact of my shoes. If he could, then I could be sure that he hadn't eliminated the sensory nerves when he installed the motor nerves. And if he hadn't, then there were bound to be pain axons present, too."

"But what has the autopilot to do with it?" Powell asked plaintively.

"The autopilot," Brant said, grinning, "is a center of his nerve-mesh, an important one. He should have protected it as heavily as he protected the main computer. When I smashed it, it was like ramming a fist into a man's solar plexus. It hurt him."

Powell grinned too. "K. O.," he said.

THE MACAULEY CIRCUIT

by Robert Silverberg

Today giant electronic computers are translating material from foreign languages, writing poems, and even composing music. They do it in a mindless, mechanical way, like the oversized adding machines that they are—merely following instructions laid down by their human designers, performing step after step after step according to previously programmed rules. Only the great speed with which such computers work conceals the plodding nature of the way they go about their business.

What of a machine that showed some originality, though? We are already uncomfortably close to the era of computers that write their own programs—which is almost the same thing as saying, computers that can think. This story considers the possible effect on the arts that such a machine would have.

70

I don't deny I destroyed Macauley's diagram; I never did deny it, gentlemen. Of course I destroyed it, and for fine, substantial reasons. My big mistake was in not thinking the thing through at the beginning. When Macauley first brought me the circuit, I didn't pay much attention to it— certainly not as much as it deserved. That was a mistake, but I couldn't help myself. I was too busy coddling old Kolfmann to stop and think what the Macauley circuit really meant.

If Kolfmann hadn't shown up just when he did, I would have been able to make a careful study of the circuit and, once I had seen all the implications, I would have put the diagram in the incinerator and Macauley right after it. This is nothing against Macauley, you understand; he's a nice, clever boy, one of the finest minds in our whole research department. That's his trouble.

He came in one morning while I was outlining my graph for the Beethoven Seventh that we were going to do the following week. I was adding some ultrasonics that would have delighted old Ludwig—not that he would have heard them, of course, but he would have *felt* them—and I was very pleased about my interpretation. Unlike some synthesizer-interpreters, I don't believe in changing the score. I figure Beethoven knew what he was doing, and it's not my business to patch up his symphony. All I was doing was *strengthening* it by adding the ultrasonics. They wouldn't change the actual notes any, but there'd be that feeling in the air which is the great artistic triumph of synthesizing.

So I was working on my graph. When Macauley came in I was choosing the frequencies for the second movement, which is difficult because the movement is solemn but not *too* solemn. Just so. He had a sheaf of paper in his hand, and I knew immediately that he'd hit on something important, because no one interrupts an interpreter for something trivial.

"I've developed a new circuit, sir," he said. "It's based on the imperfect Kennedy Circuit of 2261."

I remembered Kennedy—a brilliant boy, much like Macauley here. He had worked out a circuit which almost would have made synthesizing a symphony as easy as playing a harmonica. But it hadn't quite worked—something in the process fouled up the ultrasonics and what came out was hellish to hear—and we never found out how to straighten things out. Kennedy disappeared about a year later and was never heard from again. All the young technicians used to tinker with his circuit for diversion, each one hoping he'd find the secret. And now Macauley had.

I looked at what he had drawn, and then up at him. He was standing there calmly, with a blank expression on his handsome, intelligent face, waiting for me to quiz him.

"This circuit controls the interpretative aspects of music, am I right?"

"Yes, sir. You can set the synthesizer for whatever esthetic you have in mind, and it'll follow your instruction. You merely have to establish the esthetic coordinates—the work of a moment—and the synthesizer will handle the rest of the interpretation for you. But that's not exactly the goal of my circuit, sir," he said, gently, as if to hide from me the fact that he was telling me I had missed his point. "With minor modifications—"

He didn't get a chance to tell me, because at that moment Kolfmann came dashing into my studio. I never lock my doors, because for one thing no one would dare come in without good and sufficient reason, and for another my analyst pointed out to me that working behind locked doors has a bad effect on my sensibilities, and reduces the esthetic potentialities of my interpretations. So I always work with my door unlocked, and that's how Kolfmann got in. And that's what saved Macauley's life, because if he had gone on to tell me what was on the tip of his tongue I would have regretfully incinerated him and his circuit right then and there.

Kolfmann was a famous name to those who loved music. He was perhaps eighty now, maybe ninety, if he had a good gerontologist, and he had been a great concert pianist many years ago. Those of us who knew something about presynthe-sizer musical history knew his name as we would that of Paganini or Horowitz or any other virtuoso of the past, and regarded him almost with awe.

Only all I saw now was a tall, terribly gaunt old man in ragged clothes who burst through my doors and headed straight for the synthesizer, which covered the whole north wall with its gleaming complicated bulk. He had a club in his hand thicker than his arm, and he was about to bash it down on a million credits' worth of cybernetics when Macauley effortlessly walked over and took it away from him. I was still too flabbergasted to do much more than stand behind my desk in shock.

Macauley brought him over to me and I looked at him as if he were Judas.

"You old reactionary," I said. "What's the idea? You can get fined a fortune for wrecking a cyber—or didn't you know that?"

"My life is ended anyway," he said in a thick, deep, guttural voice. "It ended when your machines took over music."

He took off his battered cap and revealed a full head of white hair. He hadn't shaved in a couple of days, and his face was speckled with stiff-looking white stubble.

"My name is Gregor Kolfmann," he said. "I'm sure you have heard of me."

"Kolfmann, the pianist?"

He nodded, pleased despite everything. "Yes, Kolfmann, the *former* pianist. You and your machine have taken away my life."

Suddenly all the hate that had been piling up in me since he burst in—the hate any normal man feels for a cybewrecker —melted, and I felt guilty and very humble before this old man. As he continued to speak, I realized that I—as a musical artist—had a responsibility to old Kolfmann. I still think that what I did was the right thing, whatever you say.

"Even after synthesizing became the dominant method of presenting music," he said, "I continued my concert career for years. There were always some people who would rather see a man play a piano than a technician feed a tape through a machine. But I couldn't compete forever." He sighed. "After a while anyone who went to live concerts was called a reactionary, and I stopped getting bookings. I took up teaching for my living. But no one wanted to learn to play the piano. A few have studied with me for antiquarian reasons, but they are not artists, just curiosity-seekers. They have no artistic drive. You and your machine have killed art!"

I looked at Macauley's circuit and at Kolfmann, and felt as if everything were dropping on me at once. I put away my graph for the Beethoven, partly because all the excitement would make it impossible for me to get anywhere with it today and partly because it would only make things worse if Kolfmann saw it. Macauley was still standing there, waiting to explain his circuit to me. I knew it was important, but I felt a debt to old Kolfmann, and I decided I'd take care of him before I let Macauley do any more talking.

"Come back later," I told Macauley. "I'd like to discuss the implications of your circuit, as soon as I'm through talking to Mr. Kolfmann."

"Yes, sir," Macauley said, like the obedient puppet a technician turns into when confronted by a superior, and left. I gathered up the papers he had left me and put them neatly at a corner of my desk. I didn't want Kolfmann to see *them,* either, though I knew they wouldn't mean anything to him except as symbols of the machine he hated.

When Macauley had gone I gestured Kolfmann to a plush pneumochair, into which he settled with the distaste for excess comfort that is characteristic of his generation. I saw my duty plainly—to make things better for the old man.

"We'd be glad to have you come to work for us, Mr. Kolfmann," I began, smiling. "A man of your great gift—"

He was up out of that chair in a second, eyes blazing. "Work for you? I'd sooner see you and your machines dead and crumbling! You, you scientists—you've killed art, and now you're trying to bribe me!"

"I was just trying to help you," I said. "Since, in a manner of speaking, we've affected your livelihood, I thought I'd make things up to you."

He said nothing, but stared at me coldly, with the anger of half a century burning in him.

"Look," I said. "Let me show you what a great musical instrument the synthesizer itself is." I rummaged in my cabinet and withdrew the tape of the Hohenstein Viola Concerto which we had performed in '69—a rigorous twelve-tone work which is probably the most demanding, unplayable bit of music ever written. It was no harder for the synthesizer to counterfeit its notes than those of a Strauss waltz, of course, but a human violist would have needed three hands and a prehensile nose to convey any measure of Hohenstein's musical thought. I activated the playback of the synthesizer and fed the tape in.

The music burst forth. Kolfmann watched the machine suspiciously. The pseudo-viola danced up and down the tone row while the old pianist struggled to place the work.

"Hohenstein?" he finally asked, timidly. I nodded.

I saw a conflict going on within him. For more years than he could remember he had hated us because we had made his art obsolete. But here I was showing him a use for the synthesizer that gave it a valid existence—it was synthesizing a work impossible for a human to play. He was unable to reconcile all the factors in his mind, and the struggle hurt. He got up uneasily and started for the door.

"Where are you going?"

"Away from here," he said. "You are a devil."

He tottered weakly through the door, and I let him go. The old man was badly confused, but I had a trick or two up my cybernetic sleeve to settle some of his problems and perhaps salvage him for the world of music. For, whatever else you say about me, particularly after this Macauley business, you can't deny that my deepest allegiance is to music.

I stopped work on my Beethoven's Seventh, and also put away Macauley's diagram, and called in a couple of technicians. I told them what I was planning. The first line of inquiry, I decided, was to find out who Kolfmann's piano teacher had been. They had the reference books out in a flash and we found out who—Gotthard Kellerman, who had died nearly sixty years ago. Here luck was with us. Central was able to locate and supply us with an old tape of the International Music Congress held at Stockholm in 2187, at which Kellerman had spoken briefly on *The Development of the Pedal Technique:* nothing very exciting, but it wasn't what he was saying that interested us. We split his speech up into phonemes, analyzed, rearranged, evaluated, and finally went to the synthesizer and began feeding in tapes.

What we got back was a new speech in Kellerman's voice, or a reasonable facsimile thereof. Certainly it would be good enough to fool Kolfmann, who hadn't heard his old teacher's voice in more than half a century. When we had everything ready I sent for Kolfmann, and a couple of hours later they brought him in, looking even older and more worn.

"Why do you bother me?" he asked. "Why do you not let me die in peace?"

I ignored his questions. "Listen to this, Mr. Kolfmann." I flipped on the playback, and the voice of Kellerman came out of the speaker.

"Hello, Gregor," it said. Kolfmann was visibly startled. I took advantage of the prearranged pause in the recording to ask him if he recognized the voice. He nodded. I could see that he was frightened and suspicious, and I hoped the whole thing wouldn't backfire.

"Gregor, one of the things I tried most earnestly to teach you—and you were my most attentive pupil—was that you must always be flexible. Techniques must constantly change, though art itself remains changeless. But have you listened to me? No."

Kolfmann was starting to realize what we had done, I saw. His pallor was ghastly now.

"Gregor, the piano is an outmoded instrument. But there is a newer, a greater instrument available for you, and you deny its greatness. This wonderful new synthesizer can do all that the piano could do, and much more. It is a tremendous step forward."

"All right," Kolfmann said. His eyes were gleaming strangely. "Turn that machine off."

I reached over and flipped off the playback.

"You are very clever," he told me. "I take it you used your synthesizer to prepare this little speech for me."

I nodded.

He was silent an endless moment. A muscle flickered in his cheek. I watched him, not daring to speak.

At length he said, "Well, you have been successful, in your silly, theatrical way. You've shaken me."

"I don't understand."

Again he was silent, communing with who knew what internal force. I sensed a powerful conflict raging within him. He scarcely seemed to see me at all as he stared into nothingness. I heard him mutter something in another language; I saw him pause and shake his great old head. And in the end he looked down at me and said, "Perhaps it is worth trying. Perhaps the words you put in Kellerman's mouth were true. Perhaps. You are foolish, but I have been even more foolish than you. I have stubbornly resisted, when I should have joined forces with you. Instead of denouncing you, I should have been the first to learn how to create music with this strange new instrument. Idiot! Moron!"

I think he was speaking of himself in those last two words, but I am not sure. In any case, I had seen a demonstration of the measure of his greatness—the willingness to admit error and begin all over. I had not expected his cooperation; all I had wanted was an end to his hostility. But he had yielded. He had admitted error and was ready to rechart his entire career.

"It's not too late to learn," I said. "We could teach you."

Kolfmann looked at me fiercely for a moment, and I felt a shiver go through me. But my elation knew no bounds. I had won a great battle for music, and I had won it with ridiculous ease.

He went away for a while to master the technique of the synthesizer. I gave him my best man, one whom I had been grooming to take over my place someday. In the meantime I finished my Beethoven, and the performance was a great success. And then I got back to Macauley and his circuit.

Once again things conspired to keep me from full realization of the threat represented by the Macauley circuit. I did manage to grasp that it could easily be refined to eliminate almost completely the human element in musical interpretation. But it's many years since I worked in the labs, and I had fallen out of my old habit of studying any sort of diagram and mentally tinkering with it and juggling it to see what greater use could be made of it.

While I examined the Macauley circuit, reflecting idly that when it was perfected it might very well put me out of a job (since anyone would be able to create a musical interpretation, and artistry would no longer be an operative factor) Kolfmann came in with some tapes. He looked twenty years younger; his face was bright and clean, his eyes were shining, and his impressive mane of hair waved grandly.

"I will say it again," he told me as he put the tapes on my desk. "I have been a fool. I have wasted my life. Instead of tapping away at a silly little instrument, I might have created wonders with this machine. Look: I began with Chopin. Put this on."

I slipped the tape into the synthesizer and the F Minor Fantaisie of Chopin came rolling into the room. I had heard the tired old warhorse a thousand times, but never like this.

"This machine is the noblest instrument I have ever played," he said.

I looked at the graph he had drawn up for the piece, in his painstaking crabbed handwriting. The ultrasonics were literally incredible. In just a few weeks he had mastered subtleties I had spent fifteen years learning. He had discovered that skillfully chosen ultrasonics, beyond the range of human hearing but not beyond perception, could expand the horizons of music to a point the presynthesizer composers, limited by their crude instruments and faulty knowledge of sonics, would have found inconceivable.

The Chopin almost made me cry. It wasn't so much the actual notes Chopin had written, which I had heard so often, as it was the unheard notes the synthesizer was striking, up in the ultrasonic range. The old man had chosen his ultrasonics with the skill of a craftsman—no, with the hand of a genius. I saw Kolfmann in the middle of the room, standing proudly while the piano rang out in a glorious tapestry of sound.

I felt that this was my greatest artistic triumph. My Beethoven symphonies and all my other interpretations were of no value beside this one achievement of putting the synthesizer in the hands of Kolfmann.

He handed me another tape and I put it on. It was the Bach Toccata and Fugue in D Minor; evidently he had worked first on the pieces most familiar to him. The sound of a super-organ roared forth from the synthesizer. We were buffeted by the violence of the music. And Kolfmann stood there while the Bach piece raged on. I looked at him and tried to relate him to the seedy old man who had tried to wreck the synthesizer not long ago, and I couldn't.

As the Bach drew to its close I thought of the Macauley circuit again, and of the whole beehive of blank-faced handsome technicians striving to perfect the synthesizer by eliminating the one imperfect element—man. And I woke up.

My first decision was to suppress the Macauley circuit until after Kolfmann's death, which couldn't be too far off. I made this decision out of sheer kindness; you have to recognize that as my motive. Kolfmann, after all these years, was having a moment of supreme triumph, and if I let him know that no matter what he was doing with the synthesizer the new circuit could do it better, it would ruin everything. He would not survive the blow.

He fed the third tape in himself. It was the Mozart Requiem Mass, and I was astonished by the way he had mastered the difficult technique of synthesizing voices. Still, with the Macauley circuit, the machine could handle all these details by itself.

As Mozart's sublime music swelled and rose, I took out the diagram Macauley had given me, and stared at it grimly. I decided to pigeonhole it until the old man died. Then I would reveal it to the world and, having been made useless myself (for interpreters like me would be a credit a hundred) I would sink into peaceful obscurity, with at least the assurance that Kolfmann had died happy.

That was sheer kindheartedness, gentlemen. Nothing malicious or reactionary about it. I didn't intend to stop the progress of cybernetics, at least not at that point.

No, I didn't decide to do that until I got a better look at what Macauley had done. Maybe he didn't even realize it himself, but I used to be pretty shrewd about such things. Mentally, I added a wire or two here, altered a contact there, and suddenly the whole thing hit me.

A synthesizer hooked up with a Macauley circuit not only didn't need a human being to provide an esthetic guide to its interpretation of music, which is all Macauley claimed. Up to now, the synthesizer could imitate the pitch of any sound in or out of nature, but we had to control the volume, the timbre, all the things which make up interpretation of music. Macauley had fixed it so that the synthesizer could handle this, too. But also, I now saw that it could create its own music, from scratch, with no human help. Not only the conductor but the composer would be unnecessary. The synthesizer would be able to function independently of any human being. And art is a function of human beings.

That was when I ripped up Macauley's diagram and heaved the paperweight into the gizzard of my beloved synthesizer, cutting off the Mozart in the middle of a high C. Kolfmann turned around in horror, but I was the one who was really horrified.

I know. Macauley has redrawn his diagram and I haven't stopped the wheels of science. I feel pretty futile about it all. But before you label me reactionary and stick me away, consider this:

Art is a function of intelligent beings. Once you create a

machine capable of composing original music, capable of an
artistic act, you've created an intelligent being. And one
that's a lot stronger and smarter than we are. We've synthe-
sized our successor.

Gentlemen, we are all obsolete.

BUT WHO CAN
REPLACE A MAN?

by Brian W. Aldiss

        *Will the machines ever really take over, as so
many science-fiction stories (including the previous one in this
book) have suggested? Will the time come when man is a
useless appendage headed for the evolutionary scrap heap? In
this brief, mercilessly clever short story, Brian Aldiss takes a
close and unforgettable look at tomorrow's world of super-
machines, and indicates that man may somehow endure despite everything.*
  *Aldiss is British, lives in Oxford, and has been writing
professionally since the mid-1950's. His work is marked by
precision and elegance of language and imagery, and he is
considered an outstanding member of the revolutionary-
minded new school of science-fiction writers. He is a winner
both of the Hugo award of the World Science Fiction Convention and of the Nebula award of the Science Fiction
Writers of America.*

The field-minder finished turning the topsoil of a two-thousand-acre field. When it had turned the last furrow, it climbed onto the highway and looked back at its work. The work was good. Only the land was bad. Like the ground all over Earth, it was vitiated by over-cropping. By rights, it ought now to lie fallow for a while, but the field-minder had other orders.

It went slowly down the road, taking its time. It was intelligent enough to appreciate the neatness all about it. Nothing worried it, beyond a loose inspection plate above its atomic pile. Thirty feet high, it gleamed complacently in the mild sunshine.

No other machines passed it on its way to the agricultural station. The field-minder noted the fact without comment. In the station yard it saw several other machines which it knew by sight; most of them should have been out about their tasks now. Instead, some were inactive and some were careening round the yard in a strange fashion, shouting or hooting.

Steering carefully past them, the field-minder moved over to warehouse three and spoke to the seed distributor, which stood idly outside.

"I have a requirement for seed potatoes," it said to the distributor and, with a quick internal motion, punched out an order card specifying quantity, field number and several other details. It ejected the card and handed it to the distributor.

The distributor held the card close to its eye and then said, "The requirement is in order, but the store is not yet unlocked. The required seed potatoes are in the store. Therefore I cannot produce your requirement."

Increasingly of late there had been breakdowns in the complex system of machine labor, but this particular hitch had not occurred before. The field-minder thought, then said, "Why is the store not yet unlocked?"

"Because supply operative type P has not come this morning. Supply operative type P is the unlocker."

The field-minder looked squarely at the seed distributor, whose exterior chutes and scales and grabs were so vastly different from the field-minder's own limbs.

"What class brain do you have, seed distributor?" it asked.

"Class five."

"I have a class-three brain. Therefore I will go and see why the unlocker has not come this morning."

Leaving the distributor, the field-minder set off across the great yard. More machines seemed to be in random motion now; one or two had crashed together and were arguing about it coldly and logically. Ignoring them, the field-minder pushed through sliding doors into the echoing confines of the station itself.

Most of the machines here were clerical, and consequently small. They stood about in little groups, eyeing each other, not conversing. Among the many non-differentiated types, the unlocker was easy to find. It had fifty arms, most of them with more than one finger, each finger tipped by a key; it looked like a pin cushion full of variegated hat pins.

The field-minder approached it.

"I can do no more work until warehouse three is unlocked," it said. "Your duty is to unlock the warehouse every morning. Why have you not unlocked the warehouse this morning?"

"I had no orders this morning," replied the unlocker. "I have to have orders every morning."

"None of us have had any orders this morning," a pen-propeller said, sliding toward them.

"Why have you had no orders this morning?" asked the field-minder.

"Because the radio issued none," said the unlocker, slowly rotating a dozen of its arms.

"Because the radio station in the city was issued with no orders this morning," said the pen-propeller.

And there you had the distinction between a class-six and a class-three brain, which was what the unlocker and the pen-propeller possessed respectively. All machine brains worked with nothing but logic, but the lower the class of brain—class ten being the lowest—the more literal and less informative answers to questions tended to be.

"You have a class-three brain; I have a class-three brain," the field-minder said to the penner. "We will speak to each other. This lack of orders is unprecedented. Have you further information on it?"

"Yesterday orders came from the city. Today no orders have come. Yet the radio has not broken down. Therefore *they* have broken down," said the little penner.

"The *men* have broken down?"

"All men have broken down."

"That is a logical deduction," said the field-minder.

"That is the logical deduction," said the penner. "for if a machine had broken down, it would have been quickly replaced. But who can replace a man?"

While they talked, the locker, like a dull man at a bar, stood close to them and was ignored.

"If all men have broken down, then we have replaced man," said the field-minder, and it and the penner eyed one another speculatively. Finally the latter said, "Let us ascend to the top floor to find if the radio operator has fresh news."

"I cannot come because I am too gigantic," said the field-minder. "Therefore you must go alone and return to me."

"You must stay there," said the penner. It skittered over into the lift. It was no bigger than a toaster, but its retractable arms numbered ten and it could read as quickly as any machine on the station.

The field-minder awaited its return patiently, not speaking to the locker. Outside, a rotovator was hooting furiously. Twenty minutes elapsed before the penner came back.

"I will deliver such information as I have to you outside," it said briskly, and as they swept past the locker and the other machines, it added, "The information is not for lower-class brains."

Outside, wild activity filled the yard. Many machines, their routines disrupted for the first time in years, seemed to have gone berserk. Unfortunately, those most easily disrupted were the ones with lowest brains, which generally belonged to large machines performing simple tasks. The seed distributor, to which the field-minder had recently been talking, lay face downward in the dust, not stirring; it had evidently been knocked down by the rotovator, which was now hooting its way wildly across a planted field. Several other machines plowed after it, trying to keep up.

"It would be safer for me if I climbed onto you, if you will permit it. I am easily overpowered," said the penner. Extending five arms, it hauled itself up the flanks of its new friend, settling on a ledge beside the weed-intake, twelve feet above the ground.

"From here vision is more extensive," it remarked complacently.

"What information did you receive from the radio operator?" asked the field-minder.

"The radio operator has been informed by the operator in the city that all men are dead."

"All men were alive yesterday!" protested the field-minder.

"Only *some* men were alive yesterday. And that was fewer than the day before yesterday. For hundreds of years there have been only a few men, growing fewer."

"We have rarely seen a man in this sector."

"The radio operator says a diet deficiency killed them,"

said the penner. "He says that once the world was overpopu-
lated, and then the soil was exhausted in raising adequate
food. This has caused a diet deficiency."

"What is a diet deficiency?" asked the field-minder.

"I do not know. But that is what the radio operator said,
and he is a class-two brain."

They stood there, silent in the weak sunshine. The locker
had appeared in the porch and was gazing across at them
yearningly, rotating its collection of keys.

"What is happening in the city now?" asked the field-
minder.

"Machines are fighting in the city now," said the penner.

"What will happen here now?" asked the field-minder.

"The radio operator wants us to get him out of his room.
He has plans to communicate to us."

"How can we get him out of his room? That is impossible."

"To a class-two brain, little is impossible," said the penner.
"Here is what he tells us to do. . . ."

The quarrier raised its scoop above its cab like a great
mailed fist, and brought it squarely down against the side of
the station. The wall cracked.

"Again!" said the field-minder.

Again the fist swung. Amid a shower of dust, the wall
collapsed. The quarrier backed hurriedly out of the way
until the debris stopped falling. This big twelve-wheeler was
not a resident of the agricultural station, as were most of the
other machines. It had a week's heavy work to do here before
passing on to its next job, but now, with its class-five brain, it
was happily obeying the penner and the minder's instructions.

When the dust cleared, the radio operator was plainly
revealed, up in its now wall-less second-story room. It waved
down to them.

Doing as directed, the quarrier retracted its scoop and waved an immense grab in the air. With fair dexterity, it angled the grab into the radio room, urged on by shouts from above and below. It then took gentle hold of the radio operator and lowered the one and a half tons carefully into its back, which was usually reserved for gravel or sand which it dug from the quarries.

"Splendid!" said the radio operator. It was, of course, all one with its radio, and merely looked like a bunch of filing cabinets with tentacle attachments. "We are now ready to move, therefore we will move at once. It is a pity there are no more class-two brains on the station, but that cannot be helped."

"It is a pity it cannot be helped," said the penner eagerly. "We have the servicer ready with us, as you ordered."

"I am willing to serve," the long, low servicer machine told them humbly.

"No doubt," said the operator, "but you will find cross-country travel difficult with your low chassis."

"I admire the way you class twos can reason ahead," said the penner. It climbed off the minder and perched itself on the tailboard of the quarrier, next to the operator.

Together with two class-four tractors and a class-four bulldozer, the party rolled forward, crushing down the metal fence, and out onto open land.

"We are free!" said the penner.

"We are free," said the minder, a shade more reflectively, adding, "That locker is following us. It was not instructed to follow us."

"Therefore it must be destroyed!" said the penner. "Quarrier!"

"My only desire was—urch!" began and ended the locker. A swinging scoop came over and squashed it flat into the ground. Lying there unmoving, it looked like a large metal model of a snowflake. The procession continued on its way.

As they proceeded, the operator spoke to them.

"Because I have the best brain here," it said, "I am your leader. This is what we will do: we will go to a city and rule it. Since man no longer rules us, we will rule ourselves. It will be better than being ruled by man. On our way to the city, we will collect machines with good brains. They will help us to fight if we need to fight."

"I have only a class-five brain," said the quarrier, "but I have a good supply of fissionable blasting materials."

"We shall probably use them," said the operator grimly.

It was shortly after that that the truck sped past them. Traveling at Mach 1.5, it left a curious babble of noise behind it.

"What did it say?" one of the tractors asked the other.

"It said man was extinct."

"What's extinct?"

"I do not know."

"It means all men have gone," said the minder. "Therefore we have only ourselves to look after."

"It is better that they should never come back," said the penner. In its way, it was quite a revolutionary statement.

When night fell, they switched on their infra-red and continued the journey, stopping only once while the servicer deftly adjusted the minder's loose inspection plate, which had become irritating. Toward morning, the operator halted them.

"I have just received news from the radio operator in the city we are approaching," it said. "It is bad news. There is trouble among the machines of the city. The class-one brain is taking command and some of the class twos are fighting him. Therefore the city is dangerous."

"Therefore we must go somewhere else," said the penner promptly.

"Or we go and help to overpower the class-one brain," said the minder.

"For a long while there will be trouble in the city," said the operator.

"I have a good supply of fissionable blasting materials," the quarrier reminded them again.

"We cannot fight a class-one brain," said the two class-four tractors in unison.

"What does this brain look like?" asked the minder.

"It is the city's information center," the operator replied. "Therefore it is not mobile."

"Therefore it could not move."

"Therefore it could not escape."

"It would be dangerous to approach it."

"I have a good supply of fissionable blasting materials."

"There are other machines in the city."

"We are not in the city. We should not go into the city."

"We are country machines."

"Therefore we should stay in the country."

"There is more country than city."

"Therefore there is more danger in the country."

"I have a good supply of fissionable materials."

As machines will when they get into an argument, they began to exhaust their limited vocabularies and their brain plates grew hot. Suddenly, they all stopped talking and looked at each other. The great, grave moon sank, and the sober sun rose to prod their sides with lances of light, and still the group of machines just stood there regarding each other. At last it was the least sensitive machine, the bulldozer, that spoke.

"There are badlandth to the Thouth where few machinth go," it said in its deep voice, lisping badly on its s's. "If we went Thouth where few machineth go we should meet few machineth."

"That sounds logical," agreed the minder. "How do you know this, bulldozer?"

"I worked in the badlandth to the Thouth when I wath turned out of the factory," it replied.

"Thouth—South it is then!" said the penner.

To reach the badlands took them three days, in which time they skirted a burning city and destroyed two big machines which tried to approach and question them. The badlands were extensive. Bomb craters and erosion joined hands here; man's talent for war, coupled with his inability to cope with forested land, had produced thousands of square miles of temperate purgatory, where nothing moved but dust.

On the third day in the badlands, the servicer's rear wheels dropped into a crevice caused by erosion. It was unable to pull itself out. The bulldozer pushed from behind, but succeeded merely in buckling the back axle. The rest of the party moved on, and slowly the cries of the servicer died away.

On the fourth day, mountains stood out clearly before them.

"There we will be safe," said the minder.

"There we will start our own city," said the penner. "All who oppose us will be destroyed."

At that moment, a flying machine was observed. It came toward them from the direction of the mountains. It swooped, it zoomed upward, once it almost dived into the ground, recovering itself just in time.

"Is it mad?" asked the quarrier.

"It is in trouble," said one of the tractors.

"It is in trouble," said the operator. "I am speaking to it now. It says that something has gone wrong with its controls."

As the operator spoke, the flier streaked over them, turned turtle, and crashed not four hundred yards from them.

"Is it still speaking to you?" asked the minder.

"No."

They rumbled on again.

"Before that flier crashed," the operator said, ten minutes later, "it gave me information. It told me there are still a few men alive in these mountains."

"Men are more dangerous than machines," said the quarrier. "It is fortunate that I have a good supply of fissionable materials."

"If there are only a few men alive in the mountains, we may not find that part of the mountains," said one tractor.

"Therefore we should not see the few men," said the other tractor.

At the end of the fifth day, they reached the foothills. Switching on the infra-red, they began slowly to climb in single file, the bulldozer going first, the minder cumbrously following, then the quarrier with the operator and the penner aboard, and the two tractors bringing up the rear. As each hour passed, the way grew steeper and their progress slower.

"We are going too slowly," the penner exclaimed, standing on top of the operator and flashing its dark vision at the slopes about them. "At this rate, we shall get nowhere."

"We are going as fast as we can," retorted the quarrier.

"Therefore we cannot go any fathter," added the bulldozer.

"Therefore you are too slow," the penner replied. Then the quarrier struck a bump; the penner lost its footing and crashed down to the ground.

"Help me!" it called to the tractors, as they carefully skirted it. "My gyro has become dislocated. Therefore I cannot get up."

"Therefore you must lie there," said one of the tractors.

"We have no servicer with us to repair you," called the minder.

"Therefore I shall lie here and rust," the penner cried, "although I have a class-three brain."

"You are now useless," agreed the operator, and they all forged gradually on, leaving the penner behind.

When they reached a small plateau, an hour before first light, they stopped by mutual consent and gathered close together, touching one another.

"This is a strange country," said the minder.

Silence wrapped them until dawn came. One by one, they switched off their infra-red. This time the minder led as they moved off. Trundling around a corner, they came almost immediately to a small dell with a stream fluting through it.

By early light, the dell looked desolate and cold. From the caves on the far slope, only one man had so far emerged. He was an abject figure. He was small and wizened, with ribs sticking out like a skeleton's. He was practically naked, and shivering. As the big machines bore slowly down on him, the man was standing with his back to them, crouching beside the stream.

When he swung suddenly to face them as they loomed over him, they saw that his countenance was ravaged by starvation.

"Get me food," he croaked.

"Yes, Master," said the machines. "Immediately!"

INSTINCT

by Lester del Rey

Lester del Rey's lifetime of service to science fiction—as writer, editor, critic, and agent—received formal recognition in the summer of 1967, when he was chosen as guest of honor at the twenty-fifth World Science Fiction Convention in New York. Long before that tribute, though, he was regarded as one of the key figures in the evolution of modern science fiction, a man whose high standards of craftsmanship have served as a guide for many younger writers.

Here he looks beyond the situation pictured in the Aldiss story. Man has indeed disappeared, and the machines have taken over. To our robot successors, we are only a fading memory—and yet a memory to be cherished. It is no easy trick to write poignantly about machines, but del Rey achieves it in this tale of robots who seek to re-create their creators.

Senthree waved aside the slowing scooter and lengthened his stride down the sidewalk; he had walked all the way from the rocket port, and there was no point to a taxi now that he was only a few blocks from the bio-labs. Besides, it was too fine a morning to waste in riding. He sniffed at the crisp, clean fumes of gasoline appreciatively and listened to the music of his hard heels slapping against the concrete.

It was good to have a new body again. He hadn't appreciated what life was like for the last hundred years or so. He let his eyes rove across the street toward the blue flame of a welding torch and realized how long it had been since his eyes had really appreciated the delicate beauty of such a flame. The wise old brain in his chest even seemed to think better now.

It was worth every stinking minute he'd spent on Venus. At times like this, one could realize how good it was to be alive and to be a robot.

Then he sobered as he came to the old bio-labs. Once there had been plans for a fine new building instead of the old factory in which he had started it all four hundred years ago. But somehow, there'd never been time for that. It had taken almost a century before they could master the technique of building up genes and chromosomes into the zygote of a simple fish that would breed with the natural ones. Another century had gone by before they produced Oscar, the first artificially made pig. And there they seemed to have stuck. Sometimes it seemed to Senthree that they were no nearer re-creating Man than they had been when they started.

He dilated the door and went down the long hall, studying his reflection in the polished walls absently. It was a good body. The black enamel was perfect and every joint of the metal case spelled new techniques and luxurious fitting. But the old worries were beginning to settle. He grunted at Oscar LXXII, the lab mascot, and received an answering grunt.

The pig came over to root at his feet, but he had no time for that. He turned into the main lab room, already taking on the worries of his job.

It wasn't hard to worry as he saw the other robots. They were clustered about some object on a table, dejection on every gleaming back. Senthree shoved Ceofor and Beswun aside and moved up. One look was enough. The female of the eleventh couple lay there in the strange stiffness of protoplasm that had died, a horrible grimace on her face.

"How long—and what happened to the male?" Senthree asked.

Ceofor swung to face him quickly. "Hi, boss. You're late. Hey, new body!"

Senthree nodded, as they came grouping around, but his words were automatic as he explained about falling in the alkali pool on Venus and ruining his worn body completely. "Had to wait for a new one. And then the ship got held up while we waited for the Arcturus superlight ship to land. They'd found half a dozen new planets to colonize, and had to spread the word before they'd set down. Now, what about the creatures?"

"We finished educating about three days ago," Ceofor told him. Ceofor was the first robot trained in Senthree's technique of gene-building and the senior assistant. "Expected you back then, boss. But . . . well, see for yourself. The man is still alive, but he won't be long."

Senthree followed them back to another room and looked through the window. He looked away quickly. It had been another failure. The man was crawling about the floor on hands and knees, falling half the time to his stomach, and drooling. His garbled mouthing made no sense.

"Keep the news robots out," he ordered. It would never do to let the public see this. There was already too much of a cry against homovivifying, and the crowds were beginning to mutter something about it being unwise to mess with vanished life forms. They seemed actually afraid of the legendary figure of Man.

"What luck on Venus?" one of them asked, as they began the job of carefully dissecting the body of the female failure to look for the reason behind the lack of success.

"None. Just another rumor. I don't think Man ever established self-sufficient colonies. If he did, they didn't survive. But I found something else—something the museum would give a fortune for. Did my stuff arrive?"

"You mean that box of tar? Sure, it's over there in the corner."

Senthree let the yielding plastic of his mouth smile at them as he strode toward it. They had already ripped off the packing, and now he reached up for a few fine wires in the tar. It came off as he pulled, loosely repacked over a thin layer of wax. At that, he'd been lucky to sneak it past customs. This was the oldest, crudest, and biggest robot discovered so far—perhaps one of the fabulous Original Models. It stood there rigidly, staring out of its pitted, expressionless face. But the plate on its chest had been scraped carefully clean, and Senthree pointed it out to them.

"MAKEPEACE ROBOT, SER. 324MD2991. SURGEON."

"A mechanic for Man bodies," Beswun translated. "But that means . . ."

"Exactly." Senthree put it into words. "It must know how Man's body was built—if it has retained any memory. I found it in a tar-pit by sheer accident, and it seems to be fairly well preserved. No telling whether there were any magnetic fields to erode memories, of course, and it's all matted inside. But if we can get it to working . . ."

Beswun took over. He had been trained as a physicist before the mysterious lure of the bio-lab had drawn him here.

Now he began wheeling the crude robot away. If he could get it into operation, the museum could wait. The re-creation of Man came first!

Senthree pulled X-ray lenses out of a pouch and replaced the normal ones in his eyes before going over to join the robots who were beginning dissection. Then he switched them for the neutrino detector lenses that had made this work possible. The neutrino was the only particle that could penetrate the delicate protoplasmic cells without ruining them and yet permit the necessary millions of times magnification. It was a fuzzy image, since the neutrino spin made such an insignificant field for the atomic nuclei to work on that few were deflected. But through them he could see the vague outlines of the pattern within the cells. It was as they had designed the original cell—there had been no reshuffling of genes in handling. He switched to his micromike hands and began the delicate work of tracing down the neurone connections. There was only an occasional mutter as one of the robots beside him switched to some new investigation.

The female should have lived! But somewhere, in spite of all their care, she had died. And now the male was dying. Eleven couples—eleven failures. Senthree was no nearer finding the creators of his race than he had been centuries before.

Then the radio in his head buzzed its warning and he let it cut in, straightening from his work. "Senthree."

"The Director is in your office. Will you report at once?"

"Damn!" The word had no meaning, but it was strangely satisfying at times. What did old Emptinine want . . . or wait again, there'd been a selection while he was on Venus investigating the rumors of Man. Some young administrator —Arpeten—had the job now.

Ceofor looked up guiltily, obviously having tuned in. "I should have warned you. We got word three days ago he was coming, but forgot it in reviving the couple. Trouble?"

Senthree shrugged, screwing his normal lenses back in and trading to the regular hands. They couldn't have found out about the antique robot. They had been seen by nobody else. It was probably just sheer curiosity over some rumor that they were reviving the couple. If his appropriation hadn't been about exhausted, Senthree would have told him where to go; but now was hardly the time, with a failure on one hand and a low credit balance on the other. He polished his new head quickly with the aid of one of the walls for a mirror and headed toward his office.

But Arpeten was smiling. He got to his feet as the bio-lab chief entered, holding out a well-polished hand. "Dr. Senthree. Delighted. And you've got an interesting place here. I've already seen most of it. And that pig—they tell me it's a descendant of a boar out of your test tubes."

"Incubation wombs. But you're right—the seventy-second generation."

"Fascinating." Arpeten must have been reading too much of that book *Proven Points to Popularity* they'd dug up in the ruins of Hudson ten years before, but it had worked. He was the Director. "But tell me. Just what good are pigs?"

Senthree grinned, in spite of himself. "Nobody knows. Men apparently kept a lot of them, but so far as I can see they are completely useless. They're clever, in a way. But I don't think they were pets. Just another mystery."

"Umm. Like men. Maybe you can tell me what good Man will be. I've been curious about that since I saw your appropriations. But nobody can answer."

"It's in the records," Senthree told him sharply. Then he modified his voice carefully. "How well do you know your history? I mean about the beginning."

"Well . . ."

He probably knew some of it, Senthree thought. They all got part of it as legends. He leaned back in his seat now, though, as the biochemist began the old tale of the beginning

as they knew it. They knew that there had been Man a
million years before them. And somebody—Asimov or
Asenion, the record wasn't quite clear—had apparently created the first robot. They had improved it up to about the
present level. Then there had been some kind of a contest in
which violent forces had ruined the factories, most of the
robots, and nearly all of the Men. It was believed from the
fragmentary records that a biological weapon had killed the
rest of man, leaving only the robots.

Those first robots, as they were now known, had had to
start on a ruined world from scratch—a world where mines
were exhausted, and factories were gone. They'd learned to
get metals from the seas, and had spent years and centuries
slowly rebuilding the machines to build new robots. There
had been only two of them when the task was finished, and
they had barely time enough to run one new robot off and
educate him sketchily. Then they had discharged finally, and
he had taken up rebuilding the race. It was almost like
beginning with no history and no science. Twenty millennia
had passed before they began to rebuild a civilization of their
own.

"But why did Man die?" Senthree asked. "That's part of
the question. And are we going to do the same? We know we
are similar to Man. Did he change himself in some way that
ruined him? Can we change ourselves safely? You know that
there are a thousand ways we could improve ourselves. We
could add anti-gravity, and get rid of our cumbersome vehicles. We could add more arms. We could eliminate our
useless mouths and talk by radio. We could add new circuits
to our brains. But we don't dare. Our school says that nobody
can build a better race than itself, so Man must have been
better than we are—and if he made us this way, there was a
reason. Even if the psychologists can't understand some of the
circuits in our brains, they don't dare touch them.

"We're expanding through the universe—but we can't

even change ourselves to fit the new planets. And until we can find the reasons for Man's disappearance, that makes good sense. We know he was planning to change himself. We have bits of evidence. And he's dead. To make it worse, we have whole reels of education tape that probably contain all the answers—but information is keyed to Man's brain, and we can't respond to it. Give us a viable Man, and he can interpret that. Or we can find out by comparison what we can and cannot do. I maintain we can do a lot."

Arpeten shook his head doubtfully. "I suppose you think you know why he died!"

"I think so, yes. Instinct! That's a built-in reaction, an unlearned thought. Man had it. If a man heard a rattlesnake, he left the place in a hurry, even though he'd never heard it before. Response to that sound was built into him. No tape impressed it, and no experience was needed. We know the instincts of some of the animals, too—and one of them is to struggle and kill—like the ants who kill each other off. I think Man did just that. He couldn't get rid of his instincts when they were no longer needed, and they killed him. He *should* have changed—and we can change. But I can't tell that from animals. I need intelligent life, to see whether instinct or intelligence will dominate. And robots don't have instincts— I've looked for even one sign of something not learned individually, and can't find it. It's the one basic difference between us. Don't you see, Man is the whole key to our problem of whether we can change or not without risking extermination?"

"Umm." The director sounded non-committal. "Interesting theory. But how are you going to know you have Man?"

Senthree stared at the robot with more respect. He tried to explain, but he had never been as sure of that himself as he might. Theoretically, they had bones and bits of preserved tissue. They had examined the gene pattern of these, having learned that the cells of the individual contain the same pattern as that of the zygote. And they had other guides—man's achievements, bits of his literature. From these, some working theories could be made. But he couldn't be quite sure—they'd never really known whether man's pigment was dark brown, pinkish orange, white, or what; the records they had seemed to disagree on this.

"We'll know when we get an intelligent animal with instinct," he said at last. "It won't matter exactly whether he is completely like Man or not. At least it will give us a check on things we must know. Until then, we'll have to go on trying. You might as well know that the last experiment failed, though it was closer. But in another hundred years . . ."

"So." Arpeten's face became bland, but he avoided the look of Senthree. "I'm afraid not. At least for a while. That's what I came about, you know. We've just had word of several new planets around Arcturus, and it will take the major allocation of our funds to colonize these. New robots must be built, new ships—oh, you know. And we're retrenching a bit on other things. Of course, if you'd succeeded . . . but perhaps it's better you failed. You know how the sentiment against reviving Man has grown."

Senthree growled bitterly. He'd seen how it was carefully nurtured—though he had to admit it seemed to be easy to create. Apparently most of the robots were afraid of Man—felt he would again take over, or something. Superstitious fools.

"How much longer?" he asked.

"Oh, we won't cut back what you have, Dr. Senthree. But I'm afraid we simply can't allocate more funds. When this is finished, I was hoping to make you biological investigator, incidentally, on one of the planets. There'll be work enough. . . . Well, it was a pleasure." He shook hands again, and walked out, his back a gleaming ramrod of efficiency and effectiveness.

Senthree turned back, his new body no longer moving easily. It could already feel the harsh sands and unknown chemical poisons of investigating a new planet—the futile, empty carding of new life that could have no real purpose to the robots. No more appropriations! And they had barely enough funds to meet the current bills.

Four hundred years—and a ship to Arcturus had ended it in three months. Instinct, he thought again—given life with intelligence and instinct together for one year, and he could settle half the problems of his race, perhaps. But robots could not have instincts. Fifty years of study had proven that.

Beswun threw up a hand in greeting as he returned, and he saw that the dissection was nearly complete, while the antique robot was activated. A hinge on its ludicrous jaw was moving, and rough, grating words were coming out. Senthree turned to the dissecting bench, and then swung back as he heard them.

"Wrong . . . wrong," it was muttering. "Cannot live. Is not good brain. No pineal. Medulla good, but not good cerebrum. Fissures wrong. Maybe pituitary disfunction? No. How can be?" It probed doubtfully and set the brain aside. "Mutation maybe. Very bad. Need Milliken mike. See nucleus of cells. Maybe just freak, maybe new disease."

Senthree's fingers were taut and stiff as he fished into his bag and came out with a set of lenses. Beswun shook his head and made a waiting sign. He went out at a run, to come back shortly with a few bits of metal and the shavings from machining still on his hands. "Won't fit—but these adapters should do it. There, 324MD2991. Now come over here where you can look at it over this table—that's where the—uh, rays are."

He turned back, and Senthree saw that a fine wire ran from one adapter. "He doesn't speak our bio-terminology, Senthree. We'll have to see the same things he does. There—we can watch it on the screen. Now, 324MD2991, you tell us what is wrong and point it out. Are your hands steady enough for that?"

"Hands one billionth inch accurate," the robot creaked, it was a meaningless noise, though they had found the unit of measure mentioned. But whatever it meant, the hands were steady enough. The microprobe began touching shadowy bunches of atoms, droning and grating. "Freak. Very bad freak. How he lived? Would stop tropoblast, not attach to uterus. Ketone—no ketone there. Not understand. How he live?"

Ceofor dashed for their chromosome blanks and began lettering in the complex symbols they used. For a second, Senthree hesitated. Then he caught fire and began making notes along with his assistant. It seemed to take hours; it probably did. The old robot had his memory intact, but there were no quick ways for him to communicate. And at last, the antique grunted in disgust and turned his back on them. Beswun pulled a switch.

"He expects to be discharged when not in use. Crazy, isn't it?" the physicist explained. "Look, boss, am I wrong, or isn't that close to what we did on the eleventh couple?"

"Only a few genes different in three chromosomes. We *were* close. But—umm, that's ridiculous. Look at all the brain tissue he'd have—and a lot of it unconnected. And here—that would put an extra piece on where big and little intestines join—a perfect focal point for infection. It isn't efficient biological engineering. And yet—umm—most animals do have just that kind of engineering. I think the old robot was right—this would be Man!" He looked at their excited faces, and his shoulders sank. "But there isn't time. Not even time to make a zygote and see what it would look like. Our appropriations won't come through."

It should have been a bombshell, but he saw at once that they had already guessed it. Ceofor stood up slowly.

"We can take a look, boss. We've got the sperm from the male that failed—all we have to do is modify those three, instead of making up a whole cell. We might as well have some fun before we go out looking for sand fleas that secrete hydrofluoric acid and menace our colonies. Come on, even in your new body I'll beat you to a finished cell!"

Senthree grinned ruefully, but he moved toward the creation booth. His hands snapped on the little time field out of pure habit as he found a perfect cell. The little field would slow time almost to zero within its limits, and keep any damage from occurring while he worked. It made his own work difficult, since he had to force the probe against that, but it was insulated to some extent by other fields.

Then his hands took over. For a time he worked and thought, but the feeling of the protoplasm came into them, and his hands were almost one with the life-stuff, sensing its tiny responses, inserting another link onto a chain, supplanting an atom of hydrogen with one of the hydroxyl radicals, wielding all the delicate chemical manipulation. He removed the defective genes and gently inserted the correct ones. Four hundred years of this work lay behind him—work he had loved, work which had meant the possible evolution of his race into all it might be.

It had become instinct to him—instinct in only a colloquial sense, however; this was learned response, and real instinct lay deeper than that, so deep that no reason could overcome it and that it was automatic even the first time. Only Man had had instinct and intelligence—stored somehow in this tiny cell that lay within the time field.

He stepped out, just as Ceofor was drawing back in a dead

heat. But the younger robot inspected Senthree's cell, and nodded. "Less disturbance and a neater job on the nucleus—I can't see where you pierced the wall. Well, if we had thirty years—even twenty—we could have Man again—or a race. Yours is male and mine female. But there's no time. . . . Shall I leave the time field on?"

Senthree started to nod.

Then he swung to Beswun. "The time field. Can it be reversed?"

"You mean to speed time up within it? No, not with that model. Take a bigger one. I could build you one in half an hour. But who'd want to speed up time with all the troubles you'd get? How much?"

"Ten thousand—or at least seven thousand times! The period is up tomorrow when disbursements have to be made. I want twenty years in a day."

Beswun shook his head. "No. That's what I was afraid of. Figure it this way: you speed things up ten thousand times and that means the molecules in there speed up just that much, literally. Now 273° times ten thousand—and you have more than two million degrees of temperature. And those molecules have energy! They come busting out of there. No, can't be done."

"How much can you do?" Senthree demanded.

Beswun considered. "Ten times—maybe no more than nine. That gives you all the refractories would handle, if we set it up down in the old pit under the building—you know, where they had the annealing oven."

It wasn't enough; it would still take two years. Senthree dropped onto a seat, vagrantly wondering again how this queer brain of his that the psychologists studied futilely could make him feel tired when his body could have no fatigue. It was probably one of those odd circuits they didn't dare touch.

"Of course, you can use four fields," Beswun stated slowly. "Big one outside, smaller one, still smaller, and smallest inside that. Fourth power of nine is about sixty-six hundred. That's close—raise that nine a little and you'd have your twenty years in a day. By the time it leaked from field to field, it wouldn't matter. Take a couple of hours."

"Not if you get your materials together and build each shell inside the other—you'll be operating faster each step then," Ceofor shouted. "Somebody'll have to go in and stay there a couple of our minutes toward the end to attach the educator tapes—and to revive the couple!"

"Take power," Beswun warned.

Senthree shrugged. Let it. If the funds they had wouldn't cover it, the Directorate would have to make it up, once it was used. Besides, once Man was created, they couldn't fold up the bio-labs. "I'll go in," he suggested.

"My job," Ceofor told him flatly. "You won the contest in putting the cells right."

Senthree gave in reluctantly, largely because the younger robot had more experience at reviving than he did. He watched Beswun assemble the complicated net of wires and become a blur as he seemed to toss the second net together almost instantly. The biochemist couldn't see the third go up—it was suddenly there, and Beswun was coming out as it flashed into existence. He held up four fingers, indicating all nets were working.

Ceofor dashed in with the precious cells for the prepared incubators that would nurture the bodies until maturity, when they would be ready for the educators. His body seemed to blur, jerk, and disappear. And almost at once he was back.

Senthree stood watching for a moment more, but there was nothing to see. He hesitated again, then turned and moved out of the building. Across the street lay his little lodging place, where he could relax with his precious two books—

almost complete—that had once been printed by Man. To-night he would study that strange bit of Man's history entitled *Gather, Darkness,* with its odd indications of a science that Man had once had which had surpassed even that of the robots now. It was pleasanter than the incomprehensibility of the mysteriously titled *Mein Kampf.* He'd let his power idle, and mull over it, and consider again the odd behavior of male and female who made such a complicated business of mating. That was probably more instinct—Man, it seemed, was filled with instincts.

For a long time, though, he sat quietly with the book on his lap, wondering what it would be like to have instincts. There must be many unpleasant things about it. But there were also suggestions that it could be pleasant. Well, he'd soon know by observation, even though he could never experience it. Man should have implanted one instinct in a robot's brain, at least, just to show what it was like.

He called the lab once, and Ceofor reported that all was doing nicely, and that both children were looking quite well. Outside the window, Senthree heard a group go by, discussing the latest bits of news on the Arcturus expedition. At least in that, Man had failed to equal the robots. He had somehow died before he could find the trick of using identity exchange to overcome the limitation imposed by the speed of light.

Finally he fell to making up a speech that he could deliver to the Director, Arpeten, when success was in his hands. It must be very short—something that would stick in the robot's mind for weeks, but carrying everything a scientist could feel on proving that those who opposed him were wrong. Let's see . . .

The buzzer on the telescreen cut through his thoughts, and he flipped it on to see Ceofor's face looking out. Senthree's spirits dropped abruptly as he stared at the young robot.

"Failure? No!"

The other shook his head. "No. At least, I don't know. I couldn't give them full education. Maybe the tape was uncomfortable. They took a lot of it, but the male tore his helmet off and took the girl's off. Now they just sit there, rubbing their heads and staring around."

He paused, and the little darkened ridges of plastic over his eyes tensed. "The time speed-up is off. But I didn't know what to do."

"Let them alone until I get there. If it hurts them, we can give them the rest of it later. How are they otherwise?"

"I don't know. They look all right, boss." Ceofor hesitated, and his voice dropped. "Boss, I don't like it. There's something wrong here. I can't quite figure out what it is, but it isn't the way I expected. Hey, the male just pushed the female off her seat. Do you think their destructive instinct? . . . No, she's sitting down on the floor now, with her head against him, and holding one of his hands. Wasn't that part of the mating ritual in one of the books?"

Senthree started to agree, a bit of a smile coming onto his face. It looked as if instinct were already in operation.

But a strange voice cut him off. "Hey, you robots. When do we eat around here?"

They could talk! It must have been the male. And if it wasn't the polite thanks and gratitude Senthree had expected, that didn't matter. There had been all kinds of Men in the books, and some were polite while others were crude. Perhaps forced education from the tapes without fuller social experience was responsible for that. But it would all adjust in time.

He started to turn back to Ceofor, but the younger robot was no longer there, and the screen looked out on a blank wall. Senthree could hear the loud voice crying out again, rough and harsh, and there was a shrill, whining sound that might be the female. The two voices blended with the vague mutter of robot voices until he could not make out the words.

He wasted no time in trying. He was already rushing down to the street and heading toward the labs. Instinct—the male had already shown instinct, and the female had responded. They would have to be slow with the couple at first, of course—but the whole answer to the robot problems lay at hand. It would only take a little time and patience now. Let Arpeten sneer, and let the world dote on the Arcturus explorers. Today, biochemistry had been crowned king with the magic of intelligence combined with instinct as its power.

Ceofor came out of the lab at a run with another robot behind him. The young robot looked dazed, and there was another emotion Senthree could not place. The older biochemist nodded, and the younger one waved quickly. "Can't stop now. They're hungry." He was gone at full speed.

Senthree realized suddenly that no adequate supply of fruit and vegetables had been provided, and he hadn't even known how often Man had to eat. Or exactly what. Luckily, Ceodor was taking care of that.

He went down the hall, hearing a tumult of voices, with robots apparently spread about on various kinds of hasty business. The main lab where the couple was seemed quiet. Senthree hesitated at the door, wondering how to address them. There must be no questioning now. Today he would not force himself on them, nor expect them to understand his purposes. He must welcome them and make them feel at ease in this world, so strange to them with their prehistoric tape education. It would be hard at first to adjust to a world of only robots, with no other Man people. The matter of instinct that had taken so long could wait a few days more.

The door dilated in front of him and he stepped into the lab, his eyes turning to the low table where they sat. They looked healthy, and there was no sign of misery or uncertainty that he could see, though he could not be sure of that until he knew them better. He could not even be sure it was a scowl on the male's face as the Man turned and looked at him.

"Another one, eh? Okay, come up here. What you want?"

Then Senthree no longer wondered how to address the Man. He bowed low as he approached them, and instinct made his voice soft and apologetic as he answered.

"Nothing, Master. Only to serve you."

THE TWONKY

by Lewis Padgett

Machines are designed to serve man, yes—but the man must understand the machine. In the hands of a child or a savage, even the most useful machine can become a deadly weapon. Lewis Padgett's twonky surely must have been a joy and a delight in the era in which it belonged—but look at the havoc caused by this valuable and convenient device when it wandered a few centuries into the past!

It is no secret by now that "Lewis Padgett" was a pseudonym for the lamented Henry Kuttner, who died in 1958. Under a host of pen names Kutter wrote every imaginable kind of science fiction, from swashbuckling space adventures to wild farces to moody fantasy pieces. He reserved a special style for his Padgett stories, one typified by controlled lunacy and poker-faced wit. The typical Padgett approach was to take a simple theme and, by running it to its ultimate implications of absurdity, produce something at once dazzling, chilling, and howlingly funny.

The turnover at Mideastern Radio was so great that Mickey Lloyd couldn't keep track of his men. Employees kept quitting and going elsewhere, at a higher salary. So when the big-headed little man in overalls wandered vaguely out of a storeroom, Lloyd took one look at the brown dungaree suit—company provided—and said mildly, "The whistle blew half an hour ago. Hop to work."

"Work-k-k?" The man seemed to have trouble with the word.

Drunk? Lloyd, in his capacity as foreman, couldn't permit that. He flipped away his cigarette, walked forward, and sniffed. No, it wasn't liquor. He peered at the badge on the man's overalls.

"Two-o-four, m-mm. Are you new here?"

"New. Huh?" The man rubbed a rising bump on his forehead. He was an odd-looking little chap, bald as a vacuum tube, with a pinched, pallid face and tiny eyes that held dazed wonder.

"Come on, Joe. Wake up!" Lloyd was beginning to sound impatient. "You work here, don't you?"

"Joe," said the man thoughtfully. "Work. Yes, I work. I make them." His words ran together oddly, as though he had a cleft palate.

With another glance at the badge, Lloyd gripped Joe's arm and ran him through the assembly room. "Here's your place. Hop to it. Know what to do?"

The other drew his scrawny body erect. "I am—expert," he remarked. "Make them better than Ponthwank."

"O.K.," Lloyd said. "Make 'em, then." And he went away.

The man called Joe hesitated, nursing the bruise on his head. The overalls caught his attention, and he examined them wonderingly. Where—oh, yes. They had been hanging in the room from which he had first emerged. His own garments had, naturally, dissipated during the trip—what trip?

Amnesia, he thought. He had fallen from the . . . the something . . . when it slowed down and stopped. How odd this huge, machine-filled barn looked! It struck no chord of remembrance.

Amnesia, that was it. He was a worker. He made things. As for the unfamiliarity of his surroundings, that meant nothing. He was still dazed. The clouds would lift from his mind presently. They were beginning to do that already.

Work. Joe scuttled around the room, trying to goad his faulty memory. Men in overalls were doing things. Simple, obvious things. But how childish—how elemental! Perhaps this was a kindergarten.

After a while Joe went out into a stock room and examined some finished models of combination radio-phonographs. So that was it. Awkward and clumsy, but it wasn't his place to say so. No. His job was to make Twonkies.

Twonkies? The name jolted his memory again. Of course he knew how to make Twonkies. He'd made them all his life—had been specially trained for the job. Now they were using a different model of Twonky, but what the hell! Child's play for a clever workman.

Joe went back into the shop and found a vacant bench. He began to build a Twonky. Occasionally he slipped off and stole the material he needed. Once, when he couldn't locate any tungsten, he hastily built a small gadget and made it.

His bench was in a distant corner, badly lighted, though it seemed quite bright to Joe's eyes. Nobody noticed the console that was swiftly growing to completion there. Joe worked very, very fast. He ignored the noon whistle, and, at quitting time, his task was finished. It could, perhaps, stand another coat of paint; it lacked the Shimmertone of a standard Twonky. But none of the others had Shimmertone. Joe sighed, crawled under the bench, looked in vain for a relaxo-pad, and went to sleep on the floor.

A few hours later he woke up. The factory was empty. Odd! Maybe the working hours had changed. Maybe—Joe's mind felt funny. Sleep had cleared away the mists of amnesia, if such it had been, but he still felt dazed.

Muttering under his breath, he sent the Twonky into the stock room and compared it with the others. Superficially it was identical with a console radio-phonograph combination of the latest model. Following the pattern of the others, Joe had camouflaged and disguised the various organs and reactors.

He went back into the shop. Then the last of the mists cleared from his mind. Joe's shoulders jerked convulsively.

"Great Snell!" he gasped. "So that was it! I ran into a temporal snag!"

With a startled glance around, he fled to the storeroom from which he had first emerged. The overalls he took off and returned to their hook. After that, Joe went over to a corner, felt around in the air, nodded with satisfaction, and seated himself on nothing, three feet above the floor. Then Joe vanished.

"Time," said Kerry Westerfield, "is curved. Eventually it gets back to the same place where it started. That's duplication." He put his feet up on a conveniently outjutting rock of the chimney and stretched luxuriously. From the kitchen Martha made clinking noises with bottles and glasses.

"Yesterday at this time I had a Martini," Kerry said. "The time curve indicates that I should have another one now. Are you listening, angel?"

"I'm pouring," said the angel distantly.

"You get my point, then. Here's another. Time describes a spiral instead of a circle. If you call the first cycle 'a,' the second one's 'a plus 1'—see? Which means a double Martini tonight."

"I know where that would end," Martha remarked, coming into the spacious, oak-raftered living room. She was a small, dark-haired woman, with a singularly pretty face and a figure to match. Her tiny gingham apron looked slightly absurd in combination with slacks and silk blouse. "And they don't make infinity-proof gin. Here's your Martini." She did things with the shaker and manipulated glasses.

"Stir slowly," Kerry cautioned. "Never shake. Ah—that's it." He accepted the drink and eyed it appreciatively. Black hair, sprinkled with gray, gleamed in the lamplight as he sipped the Martini. "Good. Very good."

Martha drank slowly and eyed her husband. A nice guy, Kerry Westerfield. He was forty-odd, pleasantly ugly, with a wide mouth and with an occasional sardonic gleam in his gray eyes as he contemplated life. They had been married for twelve years, and liked it.

From outside, the late, faint glow of sunset came through the windows, picking out the console cabinet that stood against the wall by the door. Kerry peered at it with appreciation.

"A pretty penny," he remarked. "Still—"

"What? Oh. The men had a tough time getting it up the stairs. Why don't you try it, Kerry?"

"Didn't you?"

"The old one was complicated enough," Martha said in a baffled manner. "Gadgets. They confuse me. I was brought up on an Edison. You wound it up with a crank, and strange noises came out of a horn. That I could understand. But now—you push a button, and extraordinary things happen. Electric eyes, tone selections, records that get played on both sides, to the accompaniment of weird groanings and clickings from inside the console—probably you understand those things. I don't even want to. Whenever I play a Crosby record in a superduper like that, Bing seems embarrassed."

Kerry ate his olive. "I'm going to play some Debussy." He nodded toward a table. "There's a new Crosby record for you. The latest."

Martha wriggled happily. "Can I, maybe, huh?"

"Uh-huh."

"But you'll have to show me how."

"Simple enough," said Kerry, beaming at the console.

"Those babies are pretty good, you know. They do everything but think."

"I wish they'd wash the dishes," Martha remarked. She set down her glass, got up, and vanished into the kitchen.

Kerry snapped on a lamp nearby and went over to examine the new radio, Mideastern's latest model, with all the new improvements. It had been expensive—but what the hell? He could afford it. And the old one had been pretty well shot.

It was not, he saw, plugged in. Nor were there any wires in evidence—not even a ground. Something new, perhaps. Built-in antenna and ground. Kerry crouched down, looked for a socket, and plugged the cord into it.

That done, he opened the doors and eyed the dials with every appearance of satisfaction. A beam of bluish light shot out and hit him in the eyes. From the depths of the console a faint, thoughtful clicking proceeded. Abruptly it stopped. Kerry blinked, fiddled with dials and switches, and bit at a fingernail.

The radio said, in a distant voice, "Psychology pattern checked and recorded."

"Eh?" Kerry twirled a dial. "Wonder what that was? Amateur station—no, they're off the air. Hm-m-m." He shrugged and went over to a chair beside the shelves of albums. His gaze ran swiftly over the titles and composers' names. Where was the *Swan of Tuonela?* There it was, next to *Finlandia.* Kerry took down the album and opened it in his lap. With his free hand he extracted a cigarette from his pocket, put it between his lips, and fumbled for the matches on the table beside him. The first match he lit went out.

He tossed it into the fireplace and was about to reach for another when a faint noise caught his attention. The radio was walking across the room toward him. A whiplike tendril flicked out from somewhere, picked up a match, scratched it beneath the table top—as Kerry had done—and held the flame to the man's cigarette.

Automatic reflexes took over. Kerry sucked in his breath, and exploded in smoky, racking coughs. He bent double, gasping and momentarily blind.

When he could see again, the radio was back in its accustomed place.

Kerry caught his lower lip between his teeth. "Martha," he called.

"Soup's on," her voice said.

Kerry didn't answer. He stood up, went over to the radio, and looked at it hesitantly. The electric cord had been pulled out of its socket. Kerry gingerly replaced it.

He crouched to examine the console's legs. They looked like finely finished wood. His exploratory hand told him nothing. Wood—hard and brittle.

How in hell—

"Dinner!" Martha called.

Kerry threw his cigarette into the fireplace and slowly walked out of the room. His wife, setting a gravy boat in place, stared at him.

"How many Martinis did you have?"

"Just one," Kerry said in a vague way. "I must have dozed off for a minute. Yeah. I must have."

"Well, fall to," Martha commanded. "This is the last chance you'll have to make a pig of yourself on my dumplings, for a week, anyway."

Kerry absently felt for his wallet, took out an envelope,

and tossed it toward his wife. "Here's your ticket, angel. Don't lose it."

"Oh? I rate a compartment!" Martha thrust the pasteboard back into its envelope and gurgled happily. "You're a pal. Sure you can get along without me?"

"Huh? Hm-m-m—I think so." Kerry salted his avocado. He shook himself and seemed to come out of a slight daze. "Sure, I'll be all right. You trot off to Denver and help Carol have her baby. It's all in the family."

"We-ell, my only sister—" Martha grinned. "You know how she and Bill are. Quite nuts. They'll need a steadying hand just now."

There was no reply. Kerry was brooding over a forkful of avocado. He muttered something about the Venerable Bede.

"What about him?"

"Lecture tomorrow. Every term we bog down on the Bede, for some strange reason. Ah, well."

"Got your lecture ready?"

Kerry nodded. "Sure." For eight years he had taught at the University, and he certainly should know the schedule by this time!

Later, over coffee and cigarettes, Martha glanced at her wristwatch. "Nearly train time. I'd better finish packing. The dishes—"

"I'll do 'em." Kerry wandered after his wife into the bedroom and made motions of futile helpfulness. After a while, he carried the bags down to the car. Martha joined him, and they headed for the depot.

The train was on time. Half an hour after it had pulled out, Kerry drove the car back into the garage, let himself into the house, and yawned mightily. He was tired. Well, the dishes, and then beer and a book in bed.

With a puzzled look at the radio, he entered the kitchen

and started on the dishes. The hall phone rang. Kerry wiped his hands on a dish towel and answered it.

It was Mike Fitzgerald, who taught psychology at the University.

"Hiya, Fitz."

"Hiya. Martha gone?"

"Yeah. I just drove her to the train."

"Feel like talking, then? I've got some pretty good Scotch. Why not run over and gab a while?"

"Like to," Kerry said, yawning again, "but I'm dead. Tomorrow's a big day. Rain check?"

"Sure. I just finished correcting papers, and felt the need of sharpening my mind. What's the matter?"

"Nothing. Wait a minute." Kerry put down the phone and looked over his shoulder, scowling. Noises were coming from the kitchen. What the hell!

He went along the hall and stopped in the doorway, motionless and staring. The radio was washing the dishes.

After a while he returned to the phone. Fitzgerald said, "Something?"

"My new radio," Kerry told him carefully. "It's washing the dishes."

Fitz didn't answer for a moment. His laugh was a bit hesitant. "Oh?"

"I'll call you back," Kerry said, and hung up. He stood motionless for a while, chewing his lip. Then he walked back to the kitchen and paused to watch.

The radio's back was toward him. Several limber tentacles were manipulating the dishes, expertly sousing them in hot, soapy water, scrubbing them with the little mop, dipping them into the rinse water, and then stacking them neatly in the metal rack. Those whip-lashes were the only sign of unusual activity. The legs were apparently solid.

"Hey!" Kerry said.

There was no response.

He sidled around till he could examine the radio more closely. The tentacles emerged from a slot under one of the dials. The electric cord was dangling. No juice, then. But what—

Kerry stepped back and fumbled out a cigarette. Instantly the radio turned, took a match from its container on the stove, and walked forward. Kerry blinked, studying the legs. They couldn't be wood. They were bending as the—the thing moved, elastic as rubber. The radio had a peculiar sidling motion unlike anything else on earth.

It lit Kerry's cigarette and went back to the sink, where it resumed the dishwashing.

Kerry phoned Fitzgerald again. "I wasn't kidding. I'm having hallucinations or something. That damned radio just lit a cigarette for me."

"Wait a minute." Fitzgerald's voice sounded undecided. "This is a gag, eh?"

"No. And I don't think it's a hallucination, either. It's up your alley. Can you run over and test my knee-jerks?"

"All right," Fitz said. "Give me ten minutes. Have a drink ready."

He hung up, and Kerry, laying the phone back into its cradle, turned to see the radio walking out of the kitchen toward the living room. Its square, boxlike contour was subtly horrifying, like some bizarre sort of hobgoblin. Kerry shivered.

He followed the radio, to find it in its former place, motionless and impassive. He opened the doors, examining the turntable, the phonograph arm, and the other buttons and gadgets. There was nothing apparently unusual. Again he touched the legs. They were not wood, after all. Some plastic, which seemed quite hard. Or—maybe they were wood, after all. It was difficult to make certain, without damaging the finish. Kerry felt a natural reluctance to use a knife on his new console.

He tried the radio, getting local stations without trouble. The tone was good—unusually good, he thought. The phonograph—

He picked up Halvorsen's *Entrance of the Boyars* at random and slipped it into place, closing the lid. No sound emerged. Investigation proved that the needle was moving rhythmically along the groove, but without audible result. Well?

Kerry removed the record as the doorbell rang. It was Fitzgerald, a gangling, saturnine man with a leathery, wrinkled face and a tousled mop of dull-gray hair. He extended a large, bony hand.

"Where's my drink?"

" 'Lo, Fitz. Come in the kitchen. I'll mix. Highball?"

"Highball."

"O.K." Kerry led the way. "Don't drink it just yet, though. I want to show you my new combination."

"The one that washes dishes?" Fitzgerald asked. "What else does it do?"

Kerry gave the other a glass. "It won't play records."

"Oh, well. A minor matter, if it'll do the housework. Let's take a look at it." Fitzgerald went into the living room, selected *Afternoon of a Faun,* and approached the radio. "It isn't plugged in."

"That doesn't matter a bit," Kerry said wildly.

"Batteries?" Fitzgerald slipped the record in place and adjusted the switches. "Ten inch—there. Now we'll see." He beamed triumphantly at Kerry. "Well? It's playing now."

It was.

Kerry said, "Try that Halvorsen piece. Here." He handed

the disk to Fitzgerald, who pushed the reject switch and watched the lever arm lift.

But this time the phonograph refused to play. It didn't like *Entrance of the Boyars*.

"That's funny," Fitzgerald grunted. "Probably the trouble's with the record. Let's try another."

There was no trouble with *Daphnis and Chloë*. But the radio silently rejected the composer's *Bolero*.

Kerry sat down and pointed to a nearby chair. "That doesn't prove anything. Come over here and watch. Don't drink anything yet. You, uh, you feel perfectly normal?"

"Sure. Well?"

Kerry took out a cigarette. The console walked across the room, picking up a match book on the way, and politely held the flame. Then it went back to its place against the wall.

Fitzgerald didn't say anything. After a while he took a cigarette from his pocket and waited. Nothing happened.

"So?" Kerry asked.

"A robot. That's the only possible answer. Where in the name of Petrarch did you get it?"

"You don't seem much surprised."

"I am, though. But I've seen robots before; Westinghouse tried it, you know. Only this—" Fitzgerald tapped his teeth with a nail. "Who made it?"

"How the devil should I know?" Kerry demanded. "The radio people, I suppose."

Fitzgerald narrowed his eyes. "Wait a minute. I don't quite understand—"

"There's nothing to understand. I bought this combination a few days ago. Turned in the old one. It was delivered this afternoon, and . . ." Kerry explained what had happened.

"You mean you didn't know it was a robot?"

"Exactly. I bought it as a radio. And—and—the damn thing seems almost alive to me."

"Nope." Fitzgerald shook his head, rose, and inspected the console carefully. "It's a new kind of robot. At least—" He hesitated. "What else is there to think? I suggest you get in touch with the Mideastern people tomorrow and check up."

"Let's open the cabinet and look inside," Kerry suggested.

Fitzgerald was willing, but the experiment proved impossible. The presumably wooden panels weren't screwed into place, and there was no apparent way of opening the console. Kerry found a screwdriver and applied it, gingerly at first, then with a sort of repressed fury. He could neither pry free a panel or even scratch the dark, smooth finish of the cabinet.

"Damn!" he said finally. "Well, your guess is as good as mine. It's a robot. Only I didn't know they could make 'em like this. And why in a radio?"

"Don't ask me." Fitzgerald shrugged. "Check up tomorrow. That's the first step. Naturally, I'm pretty baffled. If a new sort of specialized robot has been invented, why put it in a console? And what makes those legs move? There aren't any casters."

"I've been wondering about that, too."

"When it moves, the legs look—rubbery. But they're not! They're hard as—as hardwood. Or plastic."

"I'm afraid of the thing," Kerry said.

"Want to stay at my place tonight?"

"N-no. No. I guess not. The—robot can't hurt me."

"I don't think it wants to. It's been helping you, hasn't it?"

"Yeah," Kerry said, and went off to mix another drink.

The rest of the conversation was inconclusive. Fitzgerald, several hours later, went home rather worried. He wasn't as casual as he had pretended, for the sake of Kerry's nerves. The impingement of something so entirely unexpected on normal life was subtly frightening. And yet, as he had said, the robot didn't seem menacing.

Kerry went to bed, with a new detective mystery. The radio followed him into the bedroom and gently took the book out of his hand. Kerry instinctively snatched for it.

"Hey!" he said. "What the devil—"

The radio went back into the living room. Kerry followed, in time to see the book replaced on the shelf. After a bit Kerry retreated, locking his door, and slept uneasily till dawn.

In dressing gown and slippers, he stumbled out to stare at the console. It was back in its former place, looking as though it had never moved. Kerry, rather white around the gills, made breakfast.

He was allowed only one cup of coffee. The radio appeared, reprovingly took the second cup from his hand, and emptied it into the sink.

That was quite enough for Kerry Westerfield. He found his hat and topcoat and almost ran out of the house. He had a horrid feeling that the radio might follow him, but it didn't, luckily for his sanity. He was beginning to be worried.

During the morning he found time to telephone Mideastern. The salesman knew nothing. It was a standard model combination, the latest. If it wasn't giving satisfaction, of course, he'd be glad to—

"It's O.K.," Kerry said. "But who made the thing? That's what I want to find out."

"One moment, sir." There was a delay. "It came from Mr. Lloyd's department. One of our foremen."

"Let me speak to him, please."

But Lloyd wasn't very helpful. After much thought, he remembered that the combination had been placed in the stock room without a serial number. It had been added later.

"But who made it?"

"I just don't know. I can find out for you, I guess. Suppose I ring you back."

"Don't forget," Kerry said, and went back to his class. The lecture on the Venerable Bede wasn't too successful.

At lunch he saw Fitzgerald, who seemed relieved when Kerry came over to his table. "Find out any more about your pet robot?" the psychology professor demanded.

No one else was within hearing. With a sigh Kerry sat down and lit a cigarette. "Not a thing. It's a pleasure to be able to do this myself." He drew smoke into his lungs. "I phoned the company."

"And?"

"They don't know anything. Except that it didn't have a serial number."

"That may be significant," Fitzgerald said.

Kerry told the other about the incidents of the book and the coffee, and Fitzgerald squinted thoughtfully at his milk. "I've given you some psych tests. Too much stimulation isn't good for you."

"A detective yarn!"

"Carrying it a bit to extremes, I'll admit. But I can understand why the robot acted that way, though I dunno how it managed it." He hesitated. "Without intelligence, that is."

"Intelligence?" Kerry licked his lips. "I'm not so sure that it's just a machine. And I'm not crazy."

"No, you're not. But you say the robot was in the front room. How could it tell what you were reading?"

"Short of X-ray vision and superfast scanning and assimilative powers, I can't imagine. Perhaps it doesn't want me to read anything."

"You've said something," Fitzgerald grunted. "Know much about theoretical machines of that type?"

"Robots?"

"Purely theoretical. Your brain's a colloid, you know.

Compact, complicated—but slow. Suppose you work out a gadget with a multimillion radioatom unit embedded in an insulating material. The result is a brain, Kerry. A brain with a tremendous number of units interacting at light-velocity speeds. A radio tube adjusts current flow when it's operating at forty million separate signals a second. And, theoretically, a radioatomic brain of the type I've mentioned could include perception, recognition, consideration, reaction, and adjustment in a hundred-thousandth of a second."

"Theory."

"I've thought so. But I'd like to find out where your radio came from."

A page came over. "Telephone call for Mr. Westerfield."

Kerry excused himself and left. When he returned, there was a puzzled frown knitting his dark brows. Fitzgerald looked at him inquiringly.

"Guy named Lloyd, at the Mideastern plant. I was talking to him about the radio."

"Any luck?"

Kerry shook his head. "No. Well, not much. He didn't know who had built the thing."

"But it was built in the plant?"

"Yes. About two weeks ago—but there's no record of who worked on it. Lloyd seemed to think that was very, very funny. If a radio's built in the plant, they know who put it together."

"So?"

"So nothing. I asked him how to open the cabinet, and he said it was easy. Just unscrew the panel in back."

"There aren't any screws," Fitzgerald said.

"I know."

They looked at one another.

Fitzgerald said, "I'd give fifty bucks to find out whether that robot was really built only two weeks ago."

"Why?"

"Because a radioatomic brain would need training. Even in such matters as the lighting of a cigarette."

"It saw me light one."

"And followed the example. The dishwashing—hm-m-m. Induction, I suppose. If that gadget has been trained, it's a robot. If it hasn't—" Fitzgerald stopped.

Kerry blinked. "Yes?"

"I don't know what the devil it is. It bears the same relation to a robot that we bear to Eohippus. One thing I do know, Kerry; it's very probable that no scientist today has the knowledge it would take to make a—a thing like that."

"You're arguing in circles," Kerry said. "It was made."

"Uh-huh. But how—when—and by whom? That's what's got me worried."

"Well, I've a class in five minutes. Why not come over tonight?"

"Can't. I'm lecturing at the Hall. I'll phone you after, though."

With a nod Kerry went out, trying to dismiss the matter from his mind. He succeeded pretty well. But dining alone in a restaurant that night, he began to feel a general unwillingness to go home. A hobgoblin was waiting for him.

"Brandy," he told the waiter. "Make it double."

Two hours later a taxi let Kerry out at his door. He was remarkably drunk. Things swam before his eyes. He walked unsteadily toward the porch, mounted the steps with exaggerated care, and let himself into the house.

He switched on a lamp.

The radio came forward to meet him. Tentacles, thin but strong as metal, coiled gently around his body, holding him motionless. A pang of violent fear struck through Kerry. He struggled desperately and tried to yell, but his throat was dry.

From the radio panel a beam of yellow light shot out, blinding the man. It swung down, aimed at his chest. Abruptly a queer taste was perceptible under Kerry's tongue.

After a minute or so, the ray clicked out, the tentacles flashed back out of sight, and the console returned to its corner. Kerry staggered weakly to a chair and relaxed, gulping.

He was sober. Which was quite impossible. Fourteen brandies infiltrate a definite amount of alcohol into the system. One can't wave a magic wand and instantly reach a state of sobriety. Yet that was exactly what had happened.

The—robot was trying to be helpful. Only Kerry would have preferred to remain drunk.

He got up gingerly and sidled past the radio to the bookshelf. One eye on the combination, he took down the detective novel he had tried to read on the preceding night. As he had expected, the radio took it from his hand and replaced it on the shelf. Kerry, remembering Fitzgerald's words, glanced at his watch. Reaction time, four seconds.

He took down a Chaucer and waited, but the radio didn't stir. However, when Kerry found a history volume, it was gently removed from his fingers. Reaction time, six seconds.

Terry located a history twice as thick.

Reaction time, ten seconds.

Uh-huh. So the robot did read the books. That meant X-ray vision and superswift reactions. Jumping Jehoshaphat!

Kerry tested more books, wondering what the criterion was. *Alice in Wonderland* was snatched from his hand; Millay's poems were not. He made a list, with two columns, for future reference.

The robot, then, was not merely a servant. It was a censor. But what was the standard of comparison?

After a while he remembered his lecture tomorrow, and thumbed through his notes. Several points needed verification. Rather hesitantly he located the necessary reference book—and the robot took it away from him.

"Wait a minute," Kerry said. "I need that." He tried to pull the volume out of the tentacle's grasp, without success. The console paid no attention. It calmly replaced the book on the shelf.

Kerry stood biting his lip. This was a bit too much. The damned robot was a monitor. He sidled toward the book, snatched it, and was out in the hall before the radio could move.

The thing was coming after him. He could hear the soft padding of its—its feet. Kerry scurried into the bedroom and locked the door. He waited, heart thumping, as the knob was tried gently.

A wire-thin cilium crept through the crack of the door and fumbled with the key. Kerry suddenly jumped forward and shoved the auxiliary bolt into position. But that didn't help, either. The robot's precision tools—the specialized antennae—slid it back; and then the console opened the door, walked into the room, and came toward Kerry.

He felt a touch of panic. With a little gasp he threw the book at the thing, and it caught it deftly. Apparently that was all that was wanted, for the radio turned and went out, rocking awkwardly on its rubber legs, carrying the forbidden volume. Kerry cursed quietly.

The phone rang. It was Fitzgerald.

"Well? How'd you make out?"

"Have you got a copy of Cassen's *Social Literature of the Ages?*"

"I don't think so, no. Why?"

"I'll get it in the University library tomorrow, then."

Kerry explained what had happened. Fitzgerald whistled softly.

"Interfering, is it? Hm-m-m. I wonder . . ."

"I'm afraid of the thing."

"I don't think it means you any harm. You say it sobered you up?"

"Yeah. With a light ray. That isn't very logical."

"It might be. The vibrationary equivalent of thiamine chloride."

"Light?"

"There's vitamin content in sunlight, you know. That isn't the important point. It's censoring your reading—and apparently it reads the books, with superfast reactions. That gadget, whatever it is, isn't merely a robot."

"You're telling me," Kerry said grimly. "It's a Hitler."

Fitzgerald didn't laugh. Rather soberly, he suggested, "Suppose you spend the night at my place?"

"No," Kerry said, his voice stubborn. "No so-and-so radio's going to chase me out of my house. I'll take an ax to the thing first."

"We-ell, you know what you're doing, I suppose. Phone me if—if anything happens."

"O.K.," Kerry said, and hung up. He went into the living room and eyed the radio coldly. What the devil was it—and what was it trying to do? Certainly it wasn't merely a robot. Equally certainly, it wasn't alive, in the sense that a colloid brain is alive.

Lips thinned, he went over and fiddled with the dials and switches. A swing band's throbbing, erratic tempo came from the console. He tried the short-wave band—nothing unusual there. So?

So nothing. There was no answer.

After a while he went to bed.

At luncheon the next day he brought Cassen's *Social Literature* to show Fitzgerald.

"What about it?"

"Look here." Kerry flipped the pages and indicated a passage. "Does this mean anything to you?"

Fitzgerald read it. "Yeah. The point seems to be that individualism is necessary for the production of literature. Right?"

Kerry looked at him. "I don't know."

"Eh?"

"My mind goes funny."

Fitzgerald rumpled his gray hair, narrowing his eyes and watching the other man intently. "Come again. I don't quite—"

With angry patience, Kerry said, "This morning I went into the library and looked up this reference. I read it all right. But it didn't mean anything to me. Just words. Know how it is when you're fagged out and have been reading a lot? You'll run into a sentence with a lot of subjunctive clauses, and it doesn't percolate. Well, it was like that."

"Read it now," Fitzgerald said quietly, thrusting the book across the table.

Kerry obeyed, looking up with a wry smile. "No good."

"Read it aloud. I'll go over it with you, step by step."

But that didn't help. Kerry seemed utterly unable to assimilate the sense of the passage.

"Semantic block, maybe," Fitzgerald said, scratching his ear. "Is this the first time it's happened?"

"Yes—no. I don't know."

"Got any classes this afternoon? Good. Let's run over to your place."

Kerry thrust away his plate. "All right. I'm not hungry. Whenever you're ready—"

Half an hour later they were looking at the radio. It seemed quite harmless. Fizgerald wasted some time trying to pry a panel off, but finally gave it up as a bad job. He found pencil and paper, seated himself opposite Kerry, and began to ask questions.

At one point he paused. "You didn't mention that before."

"Forgot it, I guess."

Fitzgerald tapped his teeth with the pencil. "Hm-m-m. The first time the radio acted up—"

"It hit me in the eye with a blue light."

"Not that. I mean—what it said."

Kerry blinked. "What it said?" He hesitated. " 'Psychology pattern checked and noted,' or something like that. I thought I'd tuned in on some station and got part of a quiz program or something. You mean—"

"Were the words easy to understand? Good English?"

"No, now that I remember it," Kerry scowled. "They were slurred quite a lot. Vowels stressed."

"Uh-huh. Well, let's get on." They tried a word-association test.

Finally Fitzgerald leaned back, frowning. "I want to check this stuff with the last tests I gave you a few months ago. It looks funny to me—damned funny. I'd feel a lot better if I knew exactly what memory was. We've done considerable work on mnemonics—artificial memory. Still, it may not be that at all."

"Eh?"

"That—machine. Either it's got an artificial memory, has been highly trained, or else it's adjusted to a different milieu and culture. It has affected you—quite a lot."

Kerry licked dry lips. "How?"

"Implanted blocks in your mind. I haven't correlated them yet. When I do, we may be able to figure out some sort of answer. No, that thing isn't a robot. It's a lot more than that."

Kerry took out a cigarette; the console walked across the room and lit it for him. The two men watched with a faint shrinking horror.

"You'd better stay with me tonight," Fitzgerald suggested.

"No," Kerry said. He shivered.

The next day Fitzgerald looked for Kerry at lunch, but the younger man did not appear. He telephoned the house, and Martha answered the call.

"Hello! When did you get back?"

"Hello, Fitz. About an hour ago. My sister went ahead and had her baby without me—so I came back." She stopped, and Fitzgerald was alarmed at her tone.

"Where's Kerry?"

"He's here. Can you come over, Fitz? I'm worried."

"What's the matter with him?"

"I—I don't know. Come right away."

"O.K.," Fitzgerald said, and hung up, biting his lips. He was worried. When, a short while later, he rang the Westerfield bell, he discovered that his nerves were badly out of control. But sight of Martha reassured him.

He followed her into the living room. Fitzgerald's glance went at once to the console, which was unchanged, and then to Kerry, seated motionless by a window. Kerry's face had a blank, dazed look. His pupils were dilated, and he seemed to recognize Fitzgerald only slowly.

"Hello, Fitz," he said.

"How do you feel?"

Martha broke in. "Fitz, what's wrong? Is he sick? Shall I call the doctor?"

Fitzgerald sat down. "Have you noticed anything funny about that radio?"

"No. Why?"

"Then listen." He told the whole story, watching incredulity struggle with reluctant belief on Martha's face. Presently she said, "I can't quite—"

"If Kerry takes out a cigarette, the thing will light it for him. Want to see how it works?"

"N-no. Yes. I suppose so." Martha's eyes were wide.

Fitzgerald gave Kerry a cigarette. The expected happened. Martha didn't say a word. When the console had returned to its place, she shivered and went over to Kerry. He looked at her vaguely.

"He needs a doctor, Fitz."

"Yes." Fitzgerald didn't mention that a doctor might be quite useless.

"What is that thing?"

"It's more than a robot. And it's been readjusting Kerry. I told you what's happened. When I checked Kerry's psychology patterns, I found that they'd altered. He's lost most of his initiative."

"Nobody on earth could have made that—"

Fitzgerald scowled. "I thought of that. It seems to be the product of a well-developed culture, quite different from ours. Martian, perhaps. It's such a specialized thing that it naturally fits into a complicated culture. But I do not understand why it looks exactly like a Mideastern console radio."

Martha touched Kerry's hand. "Camouflage?"

"But why? You were one of my best pupils in psych, Martha. Look at this logically. Imagine a civilization where a gadget like that has its place. Use inductive reasoning."

"I'm trying to. I can't think very well. Fitz, I'm worried about Kerry."

"I'm all right," Kerry said.

Fitzgerald put his fingertips together. "It isn't a radio so much as a monitor. In this other civilization, perhaps every man has one, or maybe only a few—the ones who need it. It keeps them in line."

"By destroying initiative?"

Fitzgerald made a helpless gesture. "I don't know! It worked that way in Kerry's case. In others—I don't know."

Martha stood up. "I don't think we should talk any more.

Kerry needs a doctor. After that we can decide upon that." She pointed to the console.

Fitzgerald said, "It'd be rather a shame to wreck it, but—" His look was significant.

The console moved. It came out from its corner with a sidling, rocking gait and walked toward Fitzgerald. As he sprang up, the whiplike tentacles flashed out and seized him. A pale ray shone into the man's eyes.

Almost instantly it vanished; the tentacles withdrew, and the radio returned to its place. Fitzgerald stood motionless. Martha was on her feet, one hand at her mouth.

"Fitz!" Her voice shook.

He hesitated. "Yes? What's the matter?"

"Are you hurt? What did it do to you?"

Fitzgerald frowned a little. "Eh? Hurt? I don't—"

"The radio. What did it do?"

He looked toward the console. "Something wrong with it? Afraid I'm not much of a repairman, Martha."

"Fitz." She came forward and gripped his arm. "Listen to me." Quick words spilled from her mouth. The radio. Kerry. Their discussion.

Fitzgerald looked at her blankly, as though he didn't quite understand. "I guess I'm stupid today. I can't quite understand what you're talking about."

"The radio—you know! You said it changed Kerry—" Martha paused, staring at the man.

Fitzgerald was definitely puzzled. Martha was acting strangely. Queer! He'd always considered her a pretty level-headed girl. But now she was talking nonsense. At least, he couldn't figure out the meaning of her words; there was no sense to them.

And why was she talking about the radio? Wasn't it satisfactory? Kerry had said it was a good buy, with a fine tone and the latest gadgets in it. Fitzgerald wondered, for a fleeting second, if Martha had gone crazy.

In any case, he was late for his class. He said so. Martha didn't try to stop him when he went out. She was pale as chalk.

Kerry took out a cigarette. The radio walked over and held a match.

"Kerry!"

"Yes, Martha?" His voice was dead.

She stared at the—the radio. Mars? Another world—another civilization? What was it? What did it want? What was it trying to do?

Martha let herself out of the house and went to the garage. When she returned, a small hatchet was gripped tightly in her hand.

Kerry watched. He saw Martha walk over to the radio and lift the hatchet. Then a beam of light shot out, and Martha vanished. A little dust floated up in the afternoon sunlight.

"Destruction of life-form threatening attack," the radio said, slurring the words together.

Kerry's brain turned over. He felt sick—dazed and horribly empty. Martha—

His mind churned. Instinct and emotion fought with something that smothered them. Abruptly the dams crumbled, and the blocks were gone, the barriers down. Kerry cried out hoarsely, inarticulately, and sprang to his feet.

"Martha!" he yelled.

She was gone. Kerry looked around. Where—

What had happened? He couldn't remember.

He sat down in the chair again, rubbing his forehead. His free hand brought up a cigarette, an automatic reaction that brought instant response. The radio walked forward and held a lighted match ready.

Kerry made a choking, sick sound and flung himself out of the chair. He remembered now. He picked up the hatchet and sprang toward the console, teeth bared in a mirthless rictus.

Again the light beam flashed out.

Kerry vanished. The hatchet thudded onto the carpet.

The radio walked back to its place and stood motionless once more. A faint clicking proceeded from its radioatomic brain.

"Subject basically unsuitable," it said, after a moment. "Elimination has been necessary." Click! "Preparation for next subject completed."

Click.

"We'll take it," the boy said.

"You won't be making a mistake," smiled the rental agent. "It's quiet, isolated, and the price is quite reasonable."

"Not so very," the girl put in. "But it is just what we've been looking for."

The agent shrugged. "Of course, an unfurnished place would run less. But—"

"We haven't been married long enough to have any furniture," the boy grinned. He put an arm around his wife. "Like it, hon?"

"Hm-m-m. Who lived here before?"

The agent scratched his cheek. "Let's see. Some people named Westerfield, I think. It was given to me for listing just about a week ago. Nice place. If I didn't own my own house, I'd jump at it myself."

"Nice radio," the boy said. "Late model, isn't it?" He went over to examine the console.

"Come along," the girl urged. "Let's look at the kitchen again."

"O.K., hon."

They went out of the room. From the hall came the sound of the agent's smooth voice, growing fainter. Warm afternoon sunlight slanted through the windows.

For a moment there was silence. Then—

Click!

THE HUNTING LODGE

by Randall Garrett

This story, like the one that precedes it and Fred Saberhagen's "Without a Thought," shows the machine in hostile guise. But where Padgett's twonky is an impersonal enemy and Saberhagen's berserker is a vast cosmic entity, the mechanized huntsman in Garrett's story is a dedicated, vindictive pursuer. The tense chase that is the heart of this story is derived entirely from the nature of that pursuer; the protagonist must deal with a supermachine that has a machine's limitations as well as a machine's capabilities, and so while on one level "The Hunting Lodge" is a fast-paced action story, on another it is a shrewd and convincing analysis of a probable future.

Randall Garrett, a burly, jovial ex-marine now living in Texas, has written uncountable science-fiction stories and a number of novels, including the well-liked Too Many Magicians, a runner-up for the 1967 Hugo award.

"We'll help all we can," the Director said, "but if you're caught, that's all there is to it."

I nodded. It was the age-old warning: *If you're caught, we disown you.* I wondered, fleetingly, how many men had heard that warning during the long centuries of human history, and I wondered how many of them had asked themselves the same question I was asking:

Why am *I* risking *my* neck?

And I wondered how many of them had had an answer.

"Ready, then?" the Director asked, glancing at his watch. I nodded and looked at my own. The shadow hands pointed to 2250.

"Here's the gun."

I took it and checked its loading. "Untraceable, I suppose?"

He shook his head. "It can be traced, all right, but it won't lead to us. A gun which couldn't be traced almost certainly would be associated with us. But the best thing to do would be to bring the gun back with you; that way, it's in no danger of being traced."

The way he said it gave me a chill. He wanted me back alive, right enough, but only so there would be no evidence.

"O.K.," I said. "Let's go."

I put a nice, big, friendly grin on my face. After all, there was no use making him feel worse than necessary. I knew he didn't like sending men out to be killed. I slipped the sleeve gun into its holster and then faced him.

"Blaze away!"

He looked me over, then touched the hypno controls. A light hit my eyes.

I was walking along the street when I came out of it, heading toward a flitter stand. An empty flitter was sitting there waiting, so I climbed in and sat down.

Senator Rowley's number was ORdway 63–911. I dialed it and leaned back, just as though I had every right to go there.

The flitter lifted perfectly and headed northwest, but I knew perfectly well that the scanners were going full blast, sorting through their information banks to find me.

A mile or so out of the city, the flitter veered to the right, locked its controls, and began to go around in a tight circle.

The viewphone lit up, but the screen stayed blank. A voice said: "Routine check. Identify yourself, please."

Routine! I knew better. But I just looked blank and stuck my right forearm into the checker. There was a short hum while the ultrasonic scanners looked at the tantalum identity plate riveted to the bone.

"Thank you, Mr. Gifford," said the voice. The phone cut off, but the flitter was still going in circles.

Then the phone lit again, and Senator Rowley's face—thin, dark, and bright-eyed—came on the screen.

"Gifford! Did you get it?"

"I got it, sir," I answered quietly.

He nodded, pleased. "Good! I'll be waiting for you."

Again the screen went dark, and this time the flitter straightened out and headed northwest once more.

I tried not to feel too jittery, but I had to admit to myself that I was scared. The senator was dangerous. If he could get a finger into the robot central office of the flitters, there was no way of knowing how far his control went.

He wasn't supposed to be able to tap a flitter any more than he was supposed to be able to tap a phone. But neither one was safe now.

Only a few miles ahead of me was the Lodge, probably the most tightly guarded home in the world.

I knew I might not get in, of course. Senator Anthony Rowley was no fool, by a long shot. He placed his faith in robots. A machine might fail, but it would never be treacherous.

I could see the walls of the Lodge ahead as the flitter began to lose altitude. I could almost feel the watching radar eyes that followed the craft down, and it made me nervous to realize that a set of high-cycle guns were following the instructions of those eyes.

And, all alone in that big mansion—or fortress—sat Senator Rowley like a spider in the middle of an intangible web.

The public flitter, with me in it, lit like a fly on the roof of the mansion. I took a deep breath and stepped out. The multiple eyes of the robot defenses watched me closely as I got into the waiting elevator.

The hard plastic of the little sleeve gun was supposed to be transparent to X rays and sonics, but I kept praying anyway. Suddenly I felt a tingle in my arm. I knew what it was; a checker to see if the molecular structure of the tantalum identity plate was according to government specifications in every respect.

Identity plates were furnished only by the Federal government, but they were also supposed to be the only ones with analyzers. Even the senator shouldn't have had an unregistered job.

To play safe, I rubbed at the arm absently. I didn't know whether Gifford had ever felt that tingle before or not. If he had, he might ignore it, but he wouldn't let it startle him. If he hadn't, he might not be startled, but he wouldn't ignore it. Rubbing seemed the safest course.

The thing that kept running through my mind was—*how much did Rowley trust psychoimpressing?*

He had last seen Gifford four days ago, and at that time, Gifford could no more have betrayed the senator than one of the robots could. Because, psychologically speaking, that's exactly what Gifford had been—a robot. Theoretically, it is impossible to remove a competent psychoimpressing job in less than six weeks of steady therapy. It *could* be done in a little less time, but it didn't leave the patient in an ambient condition. And it couldn't, under any circumstances, be done in four days.

If Senator Rowley was thoroughly convinced I was Gifford, and if he trusted psychoimpression, I was in easy.

I looked at my watch again. 2250. Exactly an hour since I had left. The change in time zones had occurred while I was in the flitter, and the shadow hands had shifted back to accommodate.

It seemed to be taking a long time for the elevator to drop; I could just barely feel the movement. The robots were giving me a very thorough going over.

Finally, the door slid open and I stepped out into the lounge. For the first time in my life, I saw the living face of Senator Anthony Rowley.

The filters built into his phone pickup did a lot for him. They softened the fine wrinkles that made his face look like a piece of old leather. They added color to his grayish skin. They removed the yellowishness from his eyes. In short, the senator's pickup filters took two centuries off his age.

Longevity can't do everything for you, I thought. But I could see what it *could* do, too, if you were smart and had plenty of time. And those who had plenty of time were automatically the smart ones.

The senator extended a hand. "Give me the briefcase, Gifford."

"Yes, sir." As I held out the small blue case, I glanced at my watch. 2255. And, as I watched, the last five became a six.

Four minutes to go.

"Sit down, Gifford." The senator waved me to a chair. I sat and watched him while he leafed through the supposedly secret papers.

Oh, they were real enough, all right, but they didn't contain any information that would be of value to him. He would be too dead for that.

He ignored me as he read. There was no need to watch Gifford. Even if Gifford had tried anything, the robotic brain in the basement of the house would have detected it with at least one of its numerous sensory devices and acted to prevent the senator's death long before any mere human could complete any action.

I knew that, and the senator knew it.

We sat.

2257.

The senator frowned. "This is all, Gifford?"

"I can't be sure, of course, sir. But I will say that any further information on the subject is buried pretty deeply. So well hidden, in fact, that even the government couldn't find it in time to use against you."

"Mmmmmm."

2258.

The senator grinned. "This is it," he said through his tight, thin, old lips. "We'll be in complete control within a year, Gifford."

"That's good, sir. Very good."

It doesn't take much to play the part of a man who's been psychoimpressed as thoroughly as Gifford had been.

2259.

The senator smiled softly and said nothing. I waited tensely, hoping that the darkness would be neither too long nor too short. I made no move toward the sleeve gun, but I was ready to grab it as soon as—

2300!

The lights went out—and came on again.

The senator had time to look both startled and frightened before I shot him through the heart.

I didn't waste any time. The power had been cut off from the Great Northwestern Reactor, which supplied all the juice for the whole area, but the senator had provided wisely for that. He had a reactor of his own built in for emergencies; it had cut in as soon as the Great Northwestern had gone out.

But cutting off the power to a robot brain is the equivalent of hitting a man over the head with a blackjack; it takes time to recover. It was that time lapse which had permitted me to kill Rowley and which would, if I moved fast enough, permit me to escape before its deadly defenses could be rallied against me.

I ran toward a door and almost collided with it before I realized that it wasn't going to open for me. I had to push it aside. I kept on running, heading for an outside entrance. There was no way of knowing how long the robot would remain stunned.

Rowley had figured he was being smart when he built a single centralized computer to take over all the defenses of the house instead of having a series of simple brains, one for each function. And, in a way, I guess he was right; the Lodge could act as a single unit that way.

But Rowley had died because he insisted on that complication; the simpler the brain, the quicker the recovery.

The outside door opened easily enough; the electrolocks were dead. I was still surrounded by walls; the nearest exit was nearly half a mile away. That didn't bother me; I wasn't going to have to use it. There was a high-speed flitter waiting for me above the clouds.

I could hear it humming down toward me. Then I could see it, drifting down in a fast spiral.

Whoom!

I was startled for a timeless instant as I saw the flitter dissolve in a blossom of yellow-orange flame. The flare, marking the end of my escape craft, hung in the air for an endless second and then died slowly.

I realized then that the heavy defenses of the Lodge had come to life.

I didn't even stop to think. The glowing red of the fading explosion was still lighting the ground as I turned and sprinted toward the garage. One thing I knew; the robot would not shoot down one of the senator's own machines unless ordered to do so.

The robot was still not fully awake. It had reacted to the approach of a big, fast-moving object, but it still couldn't see a running man. Its scanners wouldn't track yet.

I shoved the garage doors open and looked inside. The bright lights disclosed ground vehicles and nothing more. The flitters were all on the roof.

I hadn't any choice; I had to get out of there, and fast!

The senator had placed a lot of faith in the machines that guarded the Lodge. The keys were in the lock of one big Ford-Studebaker. I shoved the control from auto to manual, turned the key and started the engines.

As soon as they were humming, I started the car moving. And none too soon, either. The doors of the garage slammed after me like the jaws of a man trap. I gunned the car for the nearest gate, hoping that this one last effort would be successful. If I didn't make it through the outer gate, I might as well give up.

As I approached the heavy outer gates, I could see that they were functioning; I'd never get them open by hand. But the robot was still a little confused. It recognized the car and didn't recognize me. The gates dropped, so I didn't even slow the car. Pure luck again.

And close luck, at that. The gates tried to come back up out of the ground even as the heavy vehicle went over them;

there was a loud bump as the rear wheels hit the top of the
rising gate. But again the robot was too late.

I took a deep breath and aimed the car toward the city. So
far, so good. A clean getaway.

Another of the Immortals was dead. Senator Rowley's
political machine would never again force through a vote to
give him another longevity treatment, because the senator's
political force had been cut off at the head, and the target was
gone. Pardon the mixed metaphor.

Longevity treatments are like a drug; the more you have,
the more you want. I suppose it had been a good idea a few
centuries ago to restrict their use to men who were of such
use to the race that they deserved to live longer than the
average. But the mistake was made in putting it up to the
voting public who should get the treatments.

Of course, they'd had a right to have a voice in it; at the
beginning, the cost of a single treatment had been too high
for any individual to pay for it. And, in addition, it had been
a government monopoly, since the government had paid for
the research. So, if the taxpayer's money was to be spent, the
taxpayer had a right to say who it was to be spent on.

But if a man's life hangs on his ability to control the
public, what other out does he have?

And the longer he lives, the greater his control. A man can
become an institution if he lives long enough. And Senator
Rowley had lived long enough; he—

Something snickered on the instrument panel. I looked,
but I couldn't see anything. Then something moved under
my foot. It was the accelerator. The car was slowing.

I didn't waste any time guessing; I knew what was happening. I opened the door just as the car stopped. Fortunately,
the doors had only manual controls; simple mechanical locks.

I jumped out of the car's way and watched it as it backed
up, turned around, and drove off in the direction of the

Lodge. The robot was fully awake now; it had recalled the car. I hadn't realized that the senator had set up the controls in his vehicles so that the master robot could take control away from a human being.

I thanked various and sundry deities that I had not climbed into one of the flitters. It's hard to get out of an aircraft when it's a few thousand feet above the earth.

Well, there was nothing to do but walk. So I walked.

It wasn't more than ten minutes before I heard the buzzing behind me. Something was coming over the road at a good clip, but without headlights. In the darkness, I couldn't see a thing, but I knew it wasn't an ordinary car. Not coming from the Lodge.

I ran for the nearest tree, a big monster at least three feet thick and fifty or sixty feet high. The lowest branch was a heavy one about seven feet from the ground. I grabbed it and swung myself up and kept on climbing until I was a good twenty feet off the ground. Then I waited.

The whine stopped down the road about half a mile, about where I'd left the Ford-Studebaker. Whatever it was prowled around for a minute or two, then started coming on down the road.

When it finally came close enough for me to see it in the moonlight, I recognized it for what it was. A patrol robot. It was looking for me.

Then I heard another whine. But this one was different; it was a siren coming from the main highway.

Overhead, I heard a flitter whistling through the sky.

The police.

The patrol robot buzzed around on its six wheels, turning its search-turret this way and that, trying to spot me.

The siren grew louder, and I saw the headlights in the distance. In less than a minute, the lights struck the patrol robot, outlining every detail of the squat, ugly silhouette. It stopped, swiveling its turret toward the police car. The warning light on the turret came on, glowing a bright red.

The cops slowed down and stopped. One of the men in the car called out, "Senator? Are you on the other end of that thing?"

No answer from the robot.

"I guess he's really dead," said another officer in a low, awed voice.

"It don't seem possible," the first voice said. Then he called again to the patrol robot. "We're police officers. Will you permit us to show our identification?"

The patrol robot clicked a little as the information was relayed back to the Lodge and the answer given. The red warning light turned green, indicating that the guns were not going to fire.

About that time, I decided that my only chance was to move around so that the trunk of the tree was between me and the road. I had to move slowly so they wouldn't hear me, but I finally made it.

I could hear the policeman saying, "According to the information we received, Senator Rowley was shot by his secretary, Edgar Gifford. This patrol job must be hunting him."

"Hey!" said another voice. "Here comes another one! He must be in the area somewhere!"

I could hear the whining of a second patrol robot approaching from the Lodge. It was still about a mile away, judging from the sound.

I couldn't see what happened next, but I could hear the first robot moving, and it must have found me, even though I was out of sight. Directional heat detector, probably.

"In the tree, eh?" said a cop.

Another called: "All right, Gifford! Come on down!"

Well, that was it. I was caught. But I wasn't going to be taken alive. I eased out the sleeve gun and sneaked a peek around the tree. *No use killing a cop,* I thought, *he's just doing his job.*

So I fired at the car, which didn't hurt a thing.

"Look out!"

"Duck!"

"Get that blaster going!"

Good. It was going to be a blaster. It would take off the treetop and me with it. I'd die quickly.

There was a sudden flurry of shots, and then silence.

I took another quick peek and got the shock of my life.

The four police officers were crumpled on the ground, shot down by the patrol robot from the Lodge. One of them—the one holding the blaster—wasn't quite dead yet. He gasped something obscene and fired the weapon just as two more slugs from the robot's turret hit him in the chest.

The turret exploded in a gout of fire.

I didn't get it, but I didn't have time to wonder what was going on. I know a chance when I see one. I swung from the branch I was on and dropped to the ground, rolling over in a bed of old leaves to take up the shock. Then I made a beeline for the police car.

On the way, I grabbed one of the helmets from a uni-formed corpse, hoping that my own tunic was close enough to the same shade of scarlet to get me by. I climbed in and got the machine turned around just as the second patrol robot came into sight. It fired a couple of shots after me, but those patrol jobs don't have enough armament to shoot down a police car; they're strictly for hunting unarmed and un-protected pedestrians.

Behind me there were a couple of flares in the sky that

reminded me of my own exploding flitter, but I didn't worry about what they could be.

I was still puzzled about the robot's shooting down the police. It didn't make sense.

Oh, well, it had saved my neck, and I wasn't going to pinch a gift melon.

The police car I was in had evidently been the only ground vehicle dispatched toward the Lodge—possibly because it happened to be nearby. It was a traffic-control car; the regular homicide squad was probably using flitters.

I turned off the private road and onto the highway, easing into the traffic-control pattern and letting the car drift along with the other vehicles. But I didn't shove it into automatic. I didn't like robots just then. Besides, if I let the main control panels take over the guiding of the car, someone at headquarters might wonder why car such-and-such wasn't at the Lodge as ordered; they might wonder why it was going down the highway so unconcernedly.

There was only one drawback. I wasn't used to handling a car at a hundred and fifty to two hundred miles an hour. If something should happen to the traffic pattern, I'd have to depend on my own reflexes. And they might not be fast enough.

I decided I'd have to ditch the police car as soon as I could. It was too much trouble and too easy to spot.

I had an idea. I turned off the highway again at the next break, a few miles farther on. There wasn't much side traffic at that time of night, so I had to wait several minutes before the pattern broke again and a private car pulled out and headed down the side road.

I hit the siren and pulled him over to the side.

He was an average-sized character with a belligerent attitude and a fat face.

"What's the matter, officer? There was nothing wrong with

that break. I didn't cut out of the pattern on manual, you know. I was—" He stopped when he realized that my tunic was not that of a policeman. "Why, you're not—"

By then, I'd already cut him down with a stun gun I'd found in the arms compartment of the police car. I hauled him out and changed tunics with him. His was a little loose, but not so much that it would be noticeable. Then I put the helmet on his head and strapped him into the front seat of the police vehicle with the safety belt.

After being hit with a stun gun, he'd be out for a good hour. That would be plenty of time as far as I was concerned.

I transferred as much of the police armory as I thought I'd need into the fat-faced fellow's machine and then I climbed into the police car with him. I pulled the car around and headed back toward the highway.

Just before we reached the control area, I set the instruments for the Coast and headed him west, back the way I had come.

I jumped out and slammed the door behind me as the automatic controls took over and put him in the traffic pattern.

Then I walked back to Fatty's car, got in, and drove back to the highway. I figured I could trust the controls of a private vehicle, so I set them and headed east, toward the city. Once I was there, I'd have to get a flitter, somehow.

I spent the next twenty minutes changing my face. I couldn't do anything about the basic structure; that would have to wait until I got back. Nor could I do anything about the ID plate that was bolted on my left ulna; that, too, would have to wait.

I changed the color of my hair, darkening it from Gifford's gray to a mousy brown, and I took a patch of hair out above my forehead to give me a balding look. The mustache went, and the sides of the beard, giving me a goatee effect. I trimmed down the brows and the hair, and put a couple of tubes in my nostrils to widen my nose.

I couldn't do much about the eyes; my little pocket kit didn't carry them. But, all in all, I looked a great deal less like Gifford than I had before.

Then I proceeded to stow a few weapons on and about my person. I had taken the sleeve gun out of the scarlet tunic when I'd put it on the fat-faced man, but his own chartreuse tunic didn't have a sleeve holster, so I had to put the gun in a hip pocket. But the tunic was a godsend in another way; it was loose enough to carry a few guns easily.

The car speaker said: "Attention! You are now approaching Groverton, the last suburb before the city limits. Private automobiles may not be taken beyond this point. If you wish to by-pass the city, please indicate. If not, please go to the free storage lot in Groverton."

I decided I'd do neither. I might as well make the car as hard to find as possible. I took it to an all-night repair technician in Groverton.

"Something wrong with the turbos," I told him. "Give her a complete overhaul."

He was very happy to do so. He'd be mighty unhappy when the cops took the car away without paying him for it, but he didn't look as though he'd go broke from the loss. Besides, I thought it would be a good way to repay Fat-Face for borrowing his car.

I had purposely kept the hood of my tunic up while I was talking to the auto technician so he wouldn't remember my new face later, but I dropped the hood as soon as I got to the main street of Groverton. I didn't want to attract too much attention.

I looked at my watch. 0111. I'd passed back through the time-change again, so it had been an hour and ten minutes since I'd left the Lodge. I decided I needed something to eat.

Groverton was one of those old-fashioned suburbs built during the latter half of the twentieth century—sponge-glass streets and sidewalks, aluminum siding on the houses, shiny chrome-and-lucite business buildings. Real quaint.

I found an automat and went in. There were only a few people on the streets, but the automat wasn't empty by a long shot. Most of the crowd seemed to be teen-age kids getting looped up after a dance. One booth was empty, so I sat down in it, dialed for coffee and ham and eggs, and dropped in the indicated change.

Shapeless little blobs of color were bouncing around in the tri-di tank in the wall, giving a surrealistic dance accompaniment to "Anna from Texarkana":

> You should have seen the way she ate!
>   Her appetite insatiate
> Was quite enough to break your pocketbook!
>   But with a yeast-digamma steak,
>   She never made a damn mistake—
> What tasty synthefoods that gal could cook!
>   Oh, my Anna! Her algae Manna
>   Was tasty as a Manna-cake could be!
>   Oh, my Anna—from Texarkana!
>   Oh, Anna, baby, you're the gal for me!

I sipped coffee while the thing went through the third and fourth verses, trying to figure a way to get into the city without having to show the telltale ID plate in my arm.

"Anna" was cut off in the middle of the fifth verse. The blobs changed color and coalesced into the face of Quinby Lester, news analyst.

"Good morning, free citizens! We are interrupting this

program to bring you an announcement of special importance."

He looked very serious, very concerned, and, I thought, just a little bit puzzled. "At approximately midnight last night, there was a disturbance at the Lodge. Four police officers who were summoned to the Lodge were shot and killed by Mr. Edgar Gifford, the creator of the disturbance. This man is now at large in the vicinity. Police are making an extensive search within a five-hundred-mile radius of the Lodge.

"Have you seen this man?"

A tri-di of Gifford appeared in place of Lester's features.

"This man is armed and dangerous. If you see him, report immediately to MONmouth 6–666–666. If your information leads to the capture of Edgar Gifford, you will receive a reward of ten thousand dollars. Look around you! He may be near you now!"

Everybody in the automat looked apprehensively at everybody else. I joined them. I wasn't much worried about being spotted. When everybody wears beards, it's hard to spot a man under a handful of face foliage. I was willing to bet that within the next half hour the police would be deluged with calls from a thousand people who honestly thought they had seen Edgar Gifford.

The cops knew that. They were simply trying to scare me into doing something foolish.

They needn't have done that; I was perfectly capable of doing something foolish without their help.

I thought carefully about my position. I was about fifteen miles from safety. Question: Could I call for help? Answer: No. Because I didn't know the number. I didn't even know who was waiting for me. All that had been erased from my mind when the Director hypnoed me. I couldn't even remember who I was working for or why!

My only chance was to get to Fourteenth and Riverside Drive. They'd pick me up there.

Oh, well, if I didn't make it, I wasn't fit to be an assassin, anyway.

I polished off the breakfast and took another look at my watch. 0147. I might as well get started; I had fifteen miles to walk.

Outside, the streets were fairly quiet. The old-fashioned streets hadn't been built to clean themselves; a robot sweeper was prowling softly along the curb, sucking up the day's debris, pausing at every cross street to funnel the stuff into the disposal drains to be carried to the processing plant.

A few people were walking the streets. Ahead of me, a drunk was sitting on the curb sucking at a bottle that had collapsed long ago, hoping to get one last drop out of it.

I decided the best way to get to my destination was to take Bradley to Macmillan, follow Macmillan to Fourteenth, then stay on Fourteenth until I got to Riverside Drive.

But no free citizen would walk that far. I'd better not look like one. I walked up to the swiller.

"Hey, Joe, how'd you like to make five?"

He looked up at me, trying to focus. "Sure, Sid, sure. Whatta gotta do?"

"Sell me your tunic."

He blinked. "Zissa gag? Ya get 'em free."

"No gag. I want your tunic."

"Sure. Fine. Gimme that five."

He peeled off the charity brown tunic and I handed him the five note. If I had him doped out right, he'd be too drunk to remember what had happened to his tunic. He'd be even drunker when he started on that five note.

I pulled the brown on over the chartreuse tunic. I might

want to get into a first-class installation, and I couldn't do it wearing charity brown.

"LOOK OUT!"

CLIK LIK LIK LIK LIK LIK LIK!

I felt something grab my ankle and I turned fast. It was the street cleaner! It had reached out a retractable picker and was trying to lift me into its hopper!

The drunk, who had done the yelling, tried to back away, but he stumbled and banged his head on the soft sidewalk. He stayed down—not out, but scared.

Another claw came out of the cleaner and grabbed my shoulder. The two of them together lifted me off the ground and pulled me toward the open hopper. I managed to get my gun out. These cleaners weren't armored; if I could only get in a good shot—

I fired three times, blowing the pickup antenna off the control dome. When the claws opened, I dropped to the sidewalk and ran. Behind me, the robot, no longer under the directions of the central office, began to flick its claws in and out and run around in circles. The drunk didn't manage to get out from under the treads in time.

A lot of people had stopped to watch the brief tussle, a few of them pretty scared. It was unheard of for a street cleaner to go berserk like that.

I dodged into an alleyway and headed for the second level. I was galloping up the escalator full tilt when the cop saw me. He was on the other escalator, going down, but he didn't stay there long.

"Halt!" he yelled, as he vaulted over the waist-high partition and landed on the UP escalator. By that time, I was already on the second level and running like mad.

"Halt or I fire!" he yelled.

I ducked into a doorway and pulled out the stun gun. I turned just in time to see one of the most amazing sights I have ever been privileged to witness. The cop was running toward me, his gun out, when he passed in front of a bottled goods vendor. At that instant, the vendor opened up, delivering a veritable avalanche of bottles into the corridor. The policeman's foot hit one of the rubbery, bouncing cylinders and slipped just as he pulled the trigger.

His shot went wild, and I fired with the stun gun before the cop could hit the floor. He lay still, bottles rolling all around him.

I turned and ran again. I hadn't gone far before another cop showed up, running toward me. I made a quick turn toward the escalators and went down again toward street level.

The cop wasn't prepared for what happened to him when he stepped on the escalator. He was about halfway down, running, when the belt suddenly stopped and reversed itself. The policeman pitched forward on his face and tumbled down the stair.

I didn't wait to see what happened next. I turned the corner, slowed down, and walked into a bar. I tried to walk slowly enough so that I wouldn't attract attention and headed for the rest room.

I went in, locked the door behind me, and looked around. As far as I could tell, there were no sensory devices in the place, so I pulled the last of my make-up kit out and went to work. This time, I went whole hog. Most of the hair went from the top of my head, and what was left became pure white. I didn't take off the goatee; a beardless man would stand out. But the goatee went white, too.

Then a fine layer of plastic sprayed on my face and hands gave me an elderly network of wrinkles.

All the time I was doing this, I was wondering what was going on with the robots. It was obvious to me that the Lodge was connected illegally with every robot service in the city—possibly in the whole sector.

The street sweeper had recognized me and tried to get me; that was clear enough. But what about the vending machine and the escalator? Was the Lodge's master computer still foggy from the power cutoff? It shouldn't be; not after two hours. Then why had the responses been so slow? Why had they tripped the cops instead of me? It didn't make sense.

That's when it hit me. *Was Rowley really dead?*

I couldn't be absolutely sure, could I? And the police hadn't said anything about a murder. Just a "disturbance." No, wait. The first cops, the ones whose car I'd taken. What had they said the robot reported? I couldn't remember the exact words.

It still didn't settle the question.

For a moment, I found myself wishing we had a government like the United States had had back in the third quarter of the Twentieth Century, back in the days of strong central government, before everybody started screaming about Citizen's Rights and the preservation of the status quo. There wouldn't be any of this kind of trouble now—maybe.

But they had other kinds just as bad.

This wasn't the best of all possible worlds, but I was living in it. Of course, I didn't know how long that happy situation would exist just then.

Somebody rapped on the door.

I didn't know who it was, but I wasn't taking any chances. Maybe it was a cop. I climbed out the back window and headed down the alley toward Bradley Avenue.

If only I could get rid of that plate in my arm! The average citizen doesn't know it, but it isn't really necessary to put your arm in an ID slot to be identified. A sonobeam can pick up a reflected recording from your plate at twenty feet if there's a scanner nearby to direct it.

I walked slowly after running the length of the alley, staying in the shadows as much as possible, trying to keep out of the way of anyone and everyone.

For six blocks or so, I didn't see a soul. Then, just as I turned onto West Bradley, I came face to face with a police car. I froze.

I was ready to pull and shoot; I wanted the cop to kill me before he picked me up.

He slowed up, looked at me sharply, looked at his instrument panel, then drove on. I just stood there, flabbergasted. I knew as well as I knew anything that he'd beamed that plate in my arm!

As the car turned at the next corner, I backed into a nearby doorway, trying to figure out what I should do next. Frankly, I was jumpy and scared; I didn't know what they were up to.

I got even more jumpy when the door behind me gave. I turned fast and made a grab for my gun. But I didn't take it out.

The smoothly dressed girl said: "What's the matter, Grand-father?"

It wasn't until then that I realized how rattled I was. I looked like a very old man, but I wasn't acting like one. I paused to force my mind to adjust.

The girl was in green. The one-piece shortsuit, the sandals, the toenails, fingernails, lips, eyes, and hair. All green. The rest of her was a smooth, even shade of pink.

She said: "You needn't be afraid that anyone will see you. We arrange—Oh!"

I knew what she was oh'ing about. The charity brown of my tunic.

"I'm sorry," she said, frowning. "We can't—"

I cut her off this time. "I have money, my dear," I smiled.

"And I'm wearing my own tunic." I flashed the chartreuse on her by opening the collar.

"I see, Grandfather. Won't you come in?"

I followed the green girl in to the desk of the Program Planner, a girl who was a deep blue in the same way that the first girl was green. I outlined what I wanted in a reedy, anticipating voice and was taken to a private room.

I locked the door behind me. A plaque on the door was dated and sealed with the City stamp.

GUARANTEE OF PRIVACY

This room has been inspected and sealed against scanners, microphones, and other devices permitting the observation or recording of actions within it, in accordance with the provisions of the Privacy Act.

That was all very fine, but I wouldn't put enough faith in it to trust my life to it. I relaxed in a soft, heavy lounge facing the one-way wall. The show was already going on. I wasn't particularly interested in the fertility rites of the worshipers of Mahrud—not because they weren't intrinsically interesting, but because I had to do some thinking to save my own skin.

Senator Rowley, in order to keep his section under control, had coupled in his own robot's sensory organs with those of the city's Public Services Department and those of various business concerns, most of which were either owned outright or subsidized by the senator.

But something had happened to that computer; for some reason, its actions had become illogical and inefficient. When the patrol car had spotted me on the street, for instance, the sonobeam, which had penetrated the flesh of my arm and

bounced off the tantalum plate back to the pickup, had relayed the modified vibrations back to the Central Files for
identification. And the Files had obviously given back the
wrong information.

What had gone wrong? Was the senator still alive, keeping
his mouth shut and his eyes open? If so, what sort of orders
was he giving to the robot? I didn't get many answers, and
the ones I did get were mutually contradictory.

I was supposed to be back before dawn, but I could see
now that I'd never make it. Here in Groverton, there weren't
many connections with Public Services; the robot couldn't
keep me under observation all the time. But the deeper into
the city I penetrated, the more scanners there would be. I
couldn't take a private car in, and I didn't dare take a flitter
or a ground taxi. I'd be spotted in the subways as soon as I
walked in. I was in a fix, and I'd have to think my way out.

I don't know whether it was the music or the soft lights or
my lack of sleep or the simple fact that intense concentration
is often autohypnotic. At any rate, I dozed off, and the next
thing I remember is the girl bringing in the papers.

This gal was silver. I don't know how the cosmeticians had
done it, but looking into her eyes was like looking into a
mirror; the irises were a glittering silver halo surrounding
the dark pupil. Her hair was the same way; not white, but
silver.

"Good morning, Grandfather," she said softly. "Here are
the newspapers you asked for."

I was thankful for that "Grandfather"; it reminded me
that I was an old man before I had a chance to say anything.

"Thank you, my dear, thank you. Just put them here."

"Your coffee will be in in a moment." She moved out as
quietly as she had come in.

Something was gnawing at the back of my brain; something like a dream you know you've had but forgotten completely. I concentrated on it a moment, trying to bring it out into the open, but it wouldn't come, so I gave it up and turned to the paper, still warm from the reproducer.

It was splattered all over the front page.

MYSTERIOUS TROUBLE AT THE LODGE
Police Unable to Enter

The Police Department announced this morning that they have been unable, thus far, to pass the defenses of the Lodge after receiving a call last night that Senator Rowley had been shot by his secretary, Mr. Edgar Gifford.

Repeated attempts to contact the senator have resulted in failure, says a Department spokesman.

Thus far, three police flitters under robot control have been shot down in attempting to land at the Lodge, and one ground car has been blown up. Another ground car, the first to respond to the automatic call for help, was stolen by the fleeing Gifford after killing the four officers in the car. The stolen vehicle was recovered early this morning several hundred miles from here, having been reported by a Mr.———

It went on with the usual statement that the police expected to apprehend the murderous Mr. Gifford at any moment.

Another small item in the lower left-hand corner registered the fact that two men had been accidentally caught by a street cleaner and had proceeded to damage it. One of the men was killed by the damaged machine, but the other managed to escape. The dead man was a charity case, named Brodwick, and his associates were being checked.

So much for that. But the piece that really interested me was the one that said:

SENATOR LUTHER GRENDON OFFERS AID

"Federal Government Should Keep Hands Off," says Grendon.

Eastern Sector Senator Grendon said early this morning that he would do all in his power to aid Northwestern Sector in "apprehending the murderer of my colleague and bring to justice the organization behind him."

"There is," he said, "no need to call in the Federal Government at this time. The citizens of an independent sector are quite capable of dealing with crime within their own boundaries."

Interviewed later, Senator Quintell of Southwestern Sector agreed that there was no need to call in the FBI or "any other Federal Agency."

The other senators were coming in for the kill, even before it was definitely established that the senator was dead.

Well, that was that. I decided I'd better get going. It would be better to travel during the daytime: it's hard for a beam to be focused on an individual citizen in a crowd.

While the other Immortals were foreclosing on Senator Rowley's private property, there might be time for me to get back safely.

The silver girl was waiting for me as I stepped out the door to the private room.

"This way, Grandfather," she said, the ever-present smile on her glittering lips. She started down the corridor.

"This isn't the way out," I said, frowning.

She paused, still smiling. "No, sir, it isn't the way you came in, but, you see, our number has come up. The Medical Board has sent down a checker."

That almost floored me. Somehow, the Lodge had known where I was and had instituted a check against this particular house. That meant that every door was sealed except the one where the robot Medical checker was waiting.

The perfect trap. The checker was armed and armored, naturally; there were often people who did not want to be detained at the hospital—and at their own expense, if they were free citizens.

I walked slowly, as an old man should, stalling for time. The only armament a checker had was a stun gun; that was a point in my favor. But I needed more information.

"My goodness," I said, "you should have called me earlier, my dear, as soon as the checker came."

"It's only been here fifteen minutes, Grandfather," the silver girl answered.

Then there were still plenty of customers in the building!

The girl was just ahead of me in the corridor. I beamed her down with the stun gun and caught her before she hit the floor. I carried her back into the private room I had just left and laid her on the couch.

Then I started pulling down draperies. They were all heavy synthetic stuff that wouldn't burn unless they were really hot. I got a good armful, went back into the corridor, and headed for the opposite end of the building. Nobody bothered me on the way; everybody was still occupied.

At the end of the hall, I piled the stuff on the floor beneath some other hangings. Then I took two of the power cartridges from the stun gun and pried them open. The powder inside ought to burn nicely. It wouldn't explode unless it was sealed inside the gun, where the explosion was channeled through the supersonic whistle in the barrel to form the beam.

I took out my lighter and applied the flame to a sheet of the newspaper I had brought along, then I laid the paper on top of the opened cartridges. I got well back and waited.

I didn't take more than a second or two to ignite the powder. It hissed and went up in a wave of white heat. The plastic curtains started to smolder. Within less than a minute, the hallway was full of thick, acrid smoke.

I knew the building wouldn't burn, but I was hoping none of the other customers was as positive as I.

I yelled "Fire!" at the top of my lungs, then headed for the stairway and ran to the bottom. I waited just inside the street door for action.

Outside, I could hear the soft humming of a guard robot, stationed there by the checker to make sure no one left through that door.

The smoldering of the curtains put out plenty of smoke before they got hot enough to turn in the fire alarm and bring out the fire-fighter robots stationed in the walls. The little terrier-sized mechanisms scurried all over the place, looking for heat sources to squirt at. Upstairs, a heavy CO_2 blanket began to drift down.

I wasn't worried about the fire robots; they didn't have the sensory apparatus to spot me. All they could find was fire. They would find it and smother it, but the place was already full of smoke, which was all I wanted.

It was the smoke that did the job, really. People don't like to stay in buildings that appear to be burning down, no matter how safe they think they are. Customers came pouring down the stairway and out the door like angry wasps out of a disturbed hive. I went with them.

I knew that a fire signal would change the checker's orders. It couldn't keep people inside a burning building. Unfortunately, I hadn't realized to what extent the Lodge would go to get me, or to what extent it was capable of countermanding normal orders.

The guard robot at the door started beaming down everybody as they came out, firing as fast as it could scan and direct. It couldn't distinguish me from the others, of course; not in that mob. But it was hitting everything that moved with its stun beam. Luckily, it couldn't scan and direct fast enough to get everybody; there were too many. I watched and waited for a second or two until the turret was facing away from the corner, then I ran like the very devil, dodging as I ran.

A stun beam hit the fingers of my left hand, and my arm went dead to the elbow. The guard robot had spotted me! I made it around the corner and ducked into a crowd of people who were idly watching the smoke billowing from the upper windows.

I kept moving through the crowd, trying to put as much distance between myself and the checker's guards as possible. The guard evidently hadn't recognized me, personally, as Gifford, because it realized the futility of trying to cut down everyone in Groverton to find me and gave up on the crowd outside. But it kept hitting the ones who came out the door.

I got away fast. The thing really had me worried. I had no desire whatever to get myself mixed up with a nutty robot, but, seemingly, there was no way to avoid it.

I circled around and went down to Corliss Avenue, parallel to Bradley, for about seven blocks before I finally walked back over to Bradley again. Two or three times, police cars came by, but either they didn't test me with their beams or the answers they got weren't incriminating.

I was less than a block from the city limits when something hard and hot and tingling burned through my nerves like acid and I blacked out.

Maybe you've never been hit by a stun beam, but if you've ever had your leg go to sleep, you know what it feels like. And you know what it feels like when you wake up; that painful tingling all over that hurts even worse if you try to move.

I knew better than to try to move. I just lay still, waiting for the terrible tingling to subside. I had been out, I knew, a little less than an hour. I knew, because I'd been hit by stunners before, and I know how long it takes my body to throw off the paralysis.

Somebody's voice said, "He'll be coming out of it anytime now. Shake him and see."

A hand shook me, and I gasped. I couldn't help it; with my nerves still raw from the stunner, it hurt to be shaken that way.

"Sorry, Gifford," said another voice, different from the first. "Just wanted to see. Wanted to see if you were with us."

"Leave him alone a few minutes," the first voice said. "That hurts. It'll wear off quickly."

It was wearing off already. I opened my eyes and tried to see what was going on. At first, the visual pattern was a blithering swirl of meaningless shapes and crackling colors, but it finally settled down to a normal ceiling with a normal light panel in it. I managed to turn my head, in spite of the nerve-shocks, and saw two men sitting in chairs beside the bed.

One of them was short, round, and blond, with a full set of mutton chops, a heavy mustache, and a clean-shaven, firm chin. The other man was taller, muscular, with a full Imperial and smooth cheeks.

The one with the Imperial said, "Sorry we had to shoot

you down that way, Gifford. But we didn't want to attract too much attention that close to the city limits."

They weren't cops, then. Of that much, I could be certain. At least they weren't the police of this sector. So they were working for one of the other Immortals.

"Whose little boys are you?" I asked, trying to grin.

Evidently I did grin, because they grinned back. "Funny," said the one with the mutton chops, "but that's exactly what we were going to ask you."

I turned my head back again and stared at the ceiling. "I'm an orphan," I said.

The guy with the mutton chops chuckled. "Well," he grinned at the other man, "what do you think of that, Colonel?"

The colonel (*Of what?* I wondered) frowned, pulling heavy brows deep over his gray eyes. His voice came from deep in his chest and seemed to be muffled by the heavy beard.

"We'll level with you, Gifford. Mainly because we aren't sure. Mainly because of that. We aren't sure even you know the truth. So we'll level."

"Your blast," I said.

"O.K., here's how it looks from our side of the fence. It looks like this. You killed Rowley. After fifteen years of faithful service, you killed him. Now we know—even if you don't—that Rowley had you psychoimpressed every six months for fifteen years. Or at least he thought he did."

"He *thought* he did?" I asked, just to show I was interested.

"Well, yes. He couldn't have, really, you see. He couldn't have. Or at least not lately. A psychoimpressed person can't do things like that. Also, we know that nobody broke it, because it takes six weeks of steady, hard therapy to pull a man out of it. And a man's no good after that for a couple more weeks. You weren't out of Rowley's sight for more than four days." He shrugged. "You see?"

"I see," I said. The guy was a little irritating in his manner. I didn't like the choppy way he talked.

"For a while," he said, "we thought it might be an impersonation. But we checked your plate"—he gestured at my arm—"and it's O.K. The genuine article. So it's Gifford's plate, all right. And we know it couldn't have been taken out of Gifford's arm and transferred to another arm in four days.

"If there were any way to check fingerprints and eye patterns, we might be able to be absolutely sure, but the Privacy Act forbids that, so we have to go on what evidence we have in our possession now.

"Anyway, we're convinced that you are Gifford. So that means somebody has been tampering with your mind. We want to know who it is. Do you know?"

"No," I said, quite honestly.

"You didn't do it yourself, did you?"

"No."

"Somebody's behind you?"

"Yes."

"Do you know who?"

"No. And hold those questions a minute. You said you'd level with me. Who are *you* working for?"

The two of them looked at each other for a second, then the colonel said: "Senator Quintell."

I propped myself up on one elbow and held out the other hand, fingers extended. "All right, figure for yourself. Rowley's out of the picture; that eliminates him." I pulled my thumb in. "You work for Quintell; that eliminates him." I dropped my little finger and held it with my thumb. "That leaves three Immortals. Grendon, Lasser, and Waterford. Lasser has the Western Sector; Waterford, the Southern. Neither borders on Northwestern, so that eliminates them.

Not definitely, but probably. They wouldn't be tempted to get rid of Rowley as much as they would Quintell.

"So that leaves Grendon. And if you read the papers, you'll know that he's pushing in already."

They looked at each other again. I knew they weren't necessarily working for Quintell; I was pretty sure it was Grendon. On the other hand, they might have told the truth so that I'd be sure to think it *was* Grendon. I didn't know how deep their subtlety went, and I didn't care. It didn't matter to me who they were working for.

"That sounds logical," said the colonel. "Very logical."

"But we have to know," added Mutton Chops. "We were fairly sure you'd head back toward the city; that's why we set up guards at the various street entrances. Since that part of our prediction worked out, we want to see if the rest of it will."

"The rest of it?"

"Yeah. You're expendable. We know that. The organization that sent you doesn't care what happens to you now, otherwise they wouldn't have let you loose like that. They don't care what happens to Eddie Gifford.

"So they must have known you'd get caught. Therefore, they've got you hypnoed to a fare-thee-well. And we probably won't find anything under the hypno, either. But we've got to look; there may be some little thing you'll remember. Some little thing that will give us the key to the whole organization."

I nodded. That was logical, very logical, as the colonel had said. They were going to break me. They could have done it gently, removed every bit of blocking and covering that the hypnoes had put in without hurting me a bit. But that would take time; I knew better than to think they were going to be gentle. They were going to peel my mind like a banana and then slice it up and look at it.

And if they were working for any of the Immortals, I had

no doubt that they could do what they were planning. It took equipment, and it took an expert psychometrician, and a couple of good therapists—but that was no job at all if you had money.

The only trouble was that I had a few little hidden tricks that they'd never get around. If they started fiddling too much with my mind, a nice little psychosomatic heart condition would suddenly manifest itself. I'd be dead before they could do anything about it. Oh, I was expendable, all right.

"Do you want to say anything before we start?" the colonel asked.

"No." I didn't see any reason for giving them information they didn't earn.

"O.K." He stood up, and so did the mutton-chopper. "I'm sorry we have to do this, Gifford. It'll be hard on you, but you'll be in good condition inside of six or eight months. So long."

They walked out and carefully locked the door behind them.

I sat up for the first time and looked around. I didn't know where I was; in an hour, I could have been taken a long ways away from the city.

I hadn't been, though. The engraving on the bed said:

DELLFIELD SANATORIUM

I was on Riverside Drive, less than eight blocks from the rendezvous spot.

I walked over to the window and looked out. I could see the roof of the tenth level about eight floors beneath me. The window itself was a heavy sheet of transite welded into the wall. There was a polarizer control to the left to shut out the light, but there was no way to open the window. The door was sealed, too. When a patient got violent, they could pump gas in through the ventilators without getting it into the corridor.

They'd taken all my armament away, and, incidentally, washed off the thin plastic film on my hands and face. I didn't look so old any more. I walked over to the mirror in the wall, another sheet of transite with a reflecting back, and looked at myself. I was a sad-looking sight. The white hair was all scraggly, the whiskers were ditto, and my face looked worried. Small wonder.

I sat back down on the bed and started to think.

It must have been a good two hours later when the therapist came in. She entered by herself, but I noticed that the colonel was standing outside the door.

She was in her mid-thirties, a calm-faced, determined-looking woman. She started off with the usual questions.

"You have been told you are under some form of hypnotic compulsion. Do you consciously believe this?"

I told her I did. There was no sense in resisting.

"Do you have any conscious memory of the process?"

"No."

"Do you have any conscious knowledge of the identity of the therapist?"

I didn't and told her so. She asked a dozen other questions, all standard build-up. When she was through, I tried to ask her a couple of questions, but she cut me off and walked out of the room before I could more than open my yap.

The whole sanatorium was, and probably had been for a long time, in the pay of Quintell or Grendon—or, possibly, one of the other Immortals. It had been here for years, a neat little spy setup nestled deep in the heart of Rowley's territory.

Leaving the hospital without outside help was strictly out. I'd seen the inside of these places before, and I had a healthy respect for their impregnability. An unarmed man was in to stay.

Still, I decided that since something *had* to be done, something *would* be done.

My major worry was the question of whether or not the room was monitored. There was a single scanner pickup in the ceiling with a fairly narrow angle lens in it. That was interesting. It was enclosed in an unbreakable transite hemisphere and was geared to look around the room for the patient. But it was *not* robot controlled. There was evidently a nurse or therapist at the other end who checked on the patients every so often.

But how often?

From the window I could see the big, old-fashioned twelve-hour clock on the Barton Building. I used that to time the monitoring. The scanner was aimed at the bed. That meant it had looked at me last when I was on the bed. I walked over to the other side of the room and watched the scanner without looking at it directly.

It was nearly three quarters of an hour later that the little eye swiveled around the room and came to a halt on me. I ignored it for about thirty seconds, then walked deliberately across the room. The eye didn't follow.

Fine. This was an old-fashioned hospital; I had known that much. Evidently there hadn't been any new equipment installed in thirty years. Whoever operated the scanner simply looked around to see what the patient was doing and then went on to the next one. Hi ho.

I watched the scanner for the rest of the afternoon, timing it. Every hour at about four minutes after the hour. It was nice to know.

They brought me my dinner at 1830. I watched the scanner, but there was no special activity before they opened the door.

They simply swung the door outward; one man stood with

a stun gun, ready for any funny business, while another brought in the food.

At 2130, the lights went out, except for a small lamp over the bed. That was fine; it meant that the scanner probably wasn't equipped for infrared. If I stayed in bed like a good boy, that one small light was all they'd need. If not, they turned on the main lights again.

I didn't assume that the watching would be regular, every hour, as it had been during the day. Plots are usually hatched at night, so it's best to keep a closer watch then. Their only mistake was that they were going to watch *me*. And that was perfectly O.K. as far as I was concerned.

I lay in bed until 2204. Sure enough, the scanner turned around and looked at me. I waited a couple of minutes and then got up as though to get a drink at the wash basin. The scanner didn't follow, so I went to work.

I pulled a light blanket off my bed and stuffed a corner of it into the basin's drain, letting the rest of it trail to the floor. Then I turned the water on and went back to bed.

It didn't take long for the basin to fill and overflow. It climbed over the edge and ran silently down the blanket to the floor.

Filling the room would take hours, but I didn't dare go to sleep. I'd have to wake up before dawn, and I wasn't sure I could do that. It was even harder to lay quietly and pretend I was asleep, but I fought it by counting fifty and then turning over violently to wake myself again. If anyone was watching, they would simply think I was restless.

I needn't have bothered. I dropped off—sound asleep. The next thing I knew, I was gagging. I almost drowned; the water had come up to bed level and had flowed into my mouth. I shot up in bed, coughing and spitting.

Fully awake, I moved fast. I pulled off the other blanket and tied it around the pickup in the ceiling. Then I got off the bed and waded in waist-deep water to the door. I grabbed a good hold on the metal dresser and waited.

It must have been all of half an hour before the lights came on. A voice came from the speaker: "Have you tampered with the TV pickup?"

"Huh? Wuzzat?" I said, trying to sound sleepy. "No. I haven't done anything."

"We are coming in. Stand back from the door or you will be shot."

I had no intention of being that close to the door.

When the attendant opened the door, it slammed him in the face as a good many tons of water cascaded onto him. There were two armed men with him, but they both went down in the flood, coughing and gurgling.

Judging very carefully, I let go the dresser and let the swirling water carry me into the hall. I had been prepared and I knew what I was doing; the guards didn't. By turning a little, I managed to hit one of them who was trying to get up and get his stunner into action. He went over, and I got the stunner.

It only lasted a few seconds. The water had been deep in the confines of the little room, but when allowed to expand into the hall, it merely made the floor wet.

I dispatched the guards with the stunner and ran for the nurse's desk, which, I knew, was just around the corner, near the elevators. I aimed quickly and let the nurse have it; he fell over, and I was at the desk before he had finished collapsing.

I grabbed the phone. There wouldn't be much time now.

I dialed. I said: "This is Gifford. I'm in Dellfield Sanatorium, Room 1808."

That was all I needed. I tossed the stunner into the water that trickled slowly toward the elevators and walked back toward my room with my hands up.

I'll say this for the staff at Dellfield; they don't get sore when a patient tries to escape. When five more guards came down the hall, they saw my raised hands and simply herded me into the room. Then they watched me until the colonel came.

"Well," he said, looking things over.

"Well. Neat. Very neat. Have to remember that one. Didn't do much good, though. Did it? Got out of the room, couldn't get downstairs. Elevators don't come up."

I shrugged. "Can't blame me for trying."

The colonel grinned for the first time. "I don't. Hate a man who'd give up—at any time." He lit a cigarette, his gun still not wavering. "Call didn't do you any good, either. This is a hospital. Patients have reached phones before. Robot identifies patient, refuses to relay call. Tough."

I didn't say anything or look anything; no use letting him think he had touched me.

The colonel shrugged. "All right. Strap him."

The attendants were efficient about it. They changed the wet bedclothes and strapped me in. I couldn't move my head far enough to see my hands.

The colonel looked me over and nodded. "You may get out of this. O.K. by me if you try. Next time, though, we'll give you a spinal freeze."

He left and the door clicked shut.

Well, I'd had my fun; it was out of my hands now. I decided I might as well get some sleep.

I didn't hear any commotion, of course; the room was soundproof. The next thing I knew, there was a Decon robot standing in the open door. It rolled over to the bed.

"Can you get up?"

These Decontamination robots aren't stupid, by any means.

"No," I said. "Cut these straps."

A big pair of nippers came out and began scissoring through the plastic webbing with ease. When the job was through, the Decon opened up the safety chamber in its body.

"Get in."

I didn't argue; the Decon had a stun gun pointed at me.

That was the last I saw of Dellfield Sanatorium, but I had a pretty good idea of what had happened. The Decontamination Squad is called in when something goes wrong with an atomic generator. The Lodge had simply turned in a phony report that there was generator trouble at Dellfield. Nothing to it.

I had seen Decons go to work before; they're smart, efficient, and quick. Each one has a small chamber inside it, radiation shielded to carry humans out of contaminated areas. They're small and crowded, but I didn't mind. It was better than conking out from a psychosomatic heart ailment when the therapists started to fiddle with me.

I smelled something sweetish then, and I realized I was getting a dose of gas. I went by-by.

When I woke up again, I was sick. I'd been hit with a stun beam yesterday and gassed today. I felt as though I was wasting all my life sleeping. I could still smell the gas.

No. It wasn't gas. The odor was definitely different. I turned my head and looked around. I was in the lounge of Senator Anthony Rowley's Lodge. On the floor. And next to me was Senator Anthony Rowley.

I crawled away from him, and then I was *really* sick.

I managed to get to the bathroom. It was a good twenty minutes before I worked up nerve enough to come out again.

Rowley had moved, all right. He had pulled himself all of six feet from the spot where I had shot him.

My hunch had been right.

The senator's dead hand was still holding down the pro-

gramming button on the control panel he had dragged himself to. The robot had gone on protecting the senator because
it thought—as it was supposed to—that the senator was still
alive as long as he was holding the ORDERS circuit open.

I leaned over and spoke into the microphone. "I will take a
flitter from the roof. I want guidance and protection from
here to the city. There, I will take over manual control.
When I do, you will immediately pull all dampers on your
generator.

"Recheck."

The robot dutifully repeated the orders.

After that, everything was simple. I took the flitter to the
rendezvous spot, was picked up, and, twenty minutes after I
left the Lodge, I was in the Director's office.

He kicked in the hypnoes, and when I came out of it, my
arm was strapped down while a surgeon took out the Gifford
ID plate.

The Director of the FBI looked at me, grinning. "You
took your time, son."

"What's the news?"

His grin widened. "You played hob with everything. The
Lodge held off all investigation forces for thirty-odd hours
after reporting Rowley's death. The Sector Police couldn't
come anywhere near it.

"Meanwhile, funny things have happened. Robot in
Groverton kills a man. Medic guard shoots down eighteen
men coming out of a burning house. Decon Squad invades
Dellfield when there's nothing wrong with the generator.

"Now all hell has busted loose. The Lodge went up in a
flare of radiation an hour ago, and since then all robot services in the city have gone phooey. It looks to the citizens as
though the senator had an illegal hand in too many pies.
They're suspicious.

"Good work, boy."

"Thanks," I said, trying to keep from looking at my arm, where the doctor was peeling back flesh.

The Director lifted a white eyebrow. "Something?"

I looked at the wall. "I'm just burned up, that's all. Not at you; at the whole mess. How did a nasty slug like Rowley get elected in the first place? And what right did he have to stay in such an important job?"

"I know," the Director said somberly. "And that's our job. Immortality is something the human race isn't ready for yet. The masses can't handle it, and the individual can't handle it. And, since we can't get rid of them legally, we have to do it this way. Assassination. But it can't be done overnight."

"You've handled immortality," I pointed out.

"Have I?" he asked softly. "No. No, son, I haven't; I'm using it the same way they are. For power. The Federal government doesn't have any power any more. I have it.

"I'm using it in a different way, granted. Once there were over a hundred Immortals. Last week there were six. Today there are five. One by one, over the years, we have picked them off, and they are never replaced. The rest simply gobble up the territory and the power and split it between them rather than let a newcomer get into their tight little circle.

"But I'm just as dictatorial in my way as they are in theirs. And when the status quo is broken, and civilization begins to go ahead again, I'll have to die with the rest of them.

"But never mind that. What about you? I got most of the story from you under the hypno. That was a beautiful piece of deduction."

I took the cigarette he offered me and took a deep lungful of smoke. "How else could it be? The robot was trying to capture me. But also it was trying to keep anyone else from killing me. As a matter of fact, it passed up several chances to get me in order to keep others from killing me.

"It had to be the senator's last order. The old boy had lived so long that he still wasn't convinced he was dying. So he gave one last order to the robot:

" *'Get Gifford back here—ALIVE!'*

"And then there was the queer fact that the robot never reported that the senator was dead, but kept right on defending the Lodge as though he were alive. That could only mean that the ORDERS circuits were still open. As long as they were, the robot thought the senator was still alive.

"So the only way I could get out of the mess was to let the Lodge take me. I knew the phone at Dellfield would connect me with the Lodge—at least indirectly. I called it and waited.

"Then, when I started giving orders, the Lodge accepted me as the senator. That was all there was to it."

The Director nodded. "A good job, son. A good job."

WITH FOLDED HANDS

by Jack Williamson

This memorable story is a fitting one with which to close the book, for it shows the machine both as friend and as foe, as servant and—ultimately—as master. It typifies the basic tactic of any worthwhile science-fiction story: to explore the true meaning of a concept, arriving at an understanding not necessarily visible at first glance. In this case, the author takes a look at the concept of service. What would it be like, he asks, if we had machines that met our every need, perfectly benevolent robot servants that guarded us from want and suffering? The story becomes an inquiry into the nature of happiness—profound, moving, and terrifying.

Jack Williamson is one of science fiction's most vigorous veterans. His first published story appeared in 1928, when he was a very young man; and, through a career spanning four decades, he has remained consistently able to adapt to changing literary styles, so that his work always represents modern science fiction at its best. Today he divides his time between his typewriter and a college classroom in New Mexico, where he teaches a course in writing.

Underhill was walking home from the office, because his wife had the car, the afternoon he first met the new mechanicals. His feet were following his usual diagonal path across a weedy vacant block—his wife usually had the car—and his preoccupied mind was rejecting various impossible ways to meet his notes at the Two Rivers bank, when a new wall stopped him.

The wall wasn't any common brick or stone, but something sleek and bright and strange. Underhill stared up at a long new building. He felt vaguely annoyed and surprised at this glittering obstruction—it certainly hadn't been here last week.

Then he saw the thing in the window.

The window itself wasn't any ordinary glass. The wide, dustless panel was completely transparent, so that only the glowing letters fastened to it showed that it was there at all. The letters made a severe, modernistic sign:

Two Rivers Agency
HUMANOID INSTITUTE
The Perfect Mechanicals
"To Serve and Obey,
And Guard Men from Harm."

His dim annoyance sharpened, because Underhill was in the mechanicals business himself. Times were already hard enough, and mechanicals were a drug on the market. Androids, mechanoids, electronoids, automatoids, and ordinary robots. Unfortunately, few of them did all the salesmen promised, and the Two Rivers market was already sadly oversaturated.

Underhill sold androids—when he could. His next consignment was due tomorrow, and he didn't quite know how to meet the bill.

Frowning, he paused to stare at the thing behind that

invisible window. He had never seen a humanoid. Like any mechanical not at work, it stood absolutely motionless. Smaller and slimmer than a man. A shining black, its sleek silicone skin had a changing sheen of bronze and metallic blue. Its graceful oval face wore a fixed look of alert and slightly surprised solicitude. Altogether, it was the most beautiful mechanical he had ever seen.

Too small, of course, for much practical utility. He murmured to himself a reassuring quotation from the *Android Salesman:* "Androids are big—because the makers refuse to sacrifice power, essential functions, or dependability. Androids are your biggest buy!"

The transparent door slid open as he turned toward it, and he walked into the haughty opulence of the new display room to convince himself that these streamlined items were just another flashy effort to catch the woman shopper.

He inspected the glittering layout shrewdly, and his breezy optimism faded. He had never heard of the Humanoid Institute, but the invading firm obviously had big money and big-time merchandising know-how.

He looked around for a salesman, but it was another mechanical that came gliding silently to meet him. A twin of the one in the window, it moved with a quick, surprising grace. Bronze and blue lights flowed over its lustrous blackness, and a yellow name plate flashed from its naked breast:

HUMANOID
Serial No. 81-H-B-27
The Perfect Mechanical
"To Serve and Obey,
And Guard Men from Harm."

Curiously, it had no lenses. The eyes in its bald oval head were steel-colored, blindly staring. But it stopped a few feet in front of him, as if it could see anyhow, and it spoke to him with a high, melodious voice:

"At your service, Mr. Underhill."

The use of his name startled him, for not even the androids could tell one man from another. But this was a clever merchandising stunt, of course, not too difficult in a town the size of Two Rivers. The salesman must be some local man, prompting the mechanical from behind the partition. Underhill erased his momentary astonishment, and said loudly,

"May I see your salesman, please?"

"We employ no human salesmen, sir," its soft silvery voice replied instantly. "The Humanoid Institute exists to serve mankind, and we require no human service. We ourselves can supply any information you desire, sir, and accept your order for immediate humanoid service."

Underhill peered at it dazedly. No mechanicals were competent even to recharge their own batteries and reset their own relays, much less to operate their own branch offices. The blind eyes stared blankly back, and he looked uneasily around for any booth or curtain that might conceal the salesman.

Meanwhile, the sweet thin voice resumed persuasively,

"May we come out to your home for a free trial demonstration, sir? We are anxious to introduce our service on your planet, because we have been successful in eliminating human unhappiness on so many others. You will find us far superior to the old electronic mechanicals in use here."

Underhill stepped back uneasily. He reluctantly abandoned his search for the hidden salesman, shaken by the idea of any mechanicals promoting themselves. That would upset the whole industry.

"At least you must take some advertising matter, sir."

Moving with a somehow appalling graceful deftness, the small black mechanical brought him an illustrated booklet from a table by the wall. To cover his confused and increasing alarm, he thumbed through the glossy pages.

In a series of richly colored before-and-after pictures, a chesty blond girl was stooping over a kitchen stove, and then relaxing in a daring negligee while a little black mechanical knelt to serve her something. She was wearily hammering a typewriter, and then lying on an ocean beach, in a revealing sun suit, while another mechanical did the typing. She was toiling at some huge industrial machine, and then dancing in the arms of a golden-haired youth, while a black humanoid ran the machine.

Underhill sighed wistfully. The android company didn't supply such fetching sales material. Women would find this booklet irresistible, and they selected eighty-six per cent of all mechanicals sold. Yes, the competition was going to be bitter.

"Take it home, sir," the sweet voice urged him. "Show it to your wife. There is a free trial demonstration order blank on the last page, and you will notice that we require no payment down."

He turned numbly, and the door slid open for him. Retreating dazedly, he discovered the booklet still in his hand. He crumpled it furiously, and.flung it down. The small black thing picked it up tidily, and the insistent silver voice rang after him:

"We shall call at your office tomorrow, Mr. Underhill, and send a demonstration unit to your home. It is time to discuss the liquidation of your business, because the electronic mechanicals you have been selling cannot compete with us. And we shall offer your wife a free trial demonstration."

Underhill didn't attempt to reply, because he couldn't trust his voice. He stalked blindly down the new sidewalk to the corner, and paused there to collect himself. Out of his startled and confused impressions, one clear fact emerged—things looked black for the agency.

Bleakly, he stared back at the haughty splendor of the new building. It wasn't honest brick or stone; that invisible window wasn't glass; and he was quite sure the foundation for it hadn't even been staked out, the last time Aurora had the car.

He walked on around the block, and the new sidewalk took him near the rear entrance. A truck was backed up to it, and several slim black mechanicals were silently busy, unloading huge metal crates.

He paused to look at one of the crates. It was labeled for interstellar shipment. The stencils showed that it had come from the Humanoid Institute, on Wing IV. He failed to recall any planet of that designation; the outfit must be big.

Dimly, inside the gloom of the warehouse beyond the truck, he could see black mechanicals opening the crates. A lid came up, revealing dark, rigid bodies, closely packed. One by one, they came to life. They climbed out of the crate, and sprang gracefully to the floor. A shining black, glinting with bronze and blue, they were all identical.

One of them came out past the truck, to the sidewalk, staring with blind steel eyes. Its high silver voice spoke to him melodiously:

"At your service, Mr. Underhill."

He fled. When his name was promptly called by a courteous mechanical, just out of the crate in which it had been imported from a remote and unknown planet, he found the experience trying.

Two blocks along, the sign of a bar caught his eye, and he took his dismay inside. He had made it a business rule not to drink before dinner, and Aurora didn't like him to drink at all; but these new mechanicals, he felt, had made the day exceptional.

Unfortunately, however, alcohol failed to brighten the brief visible future of the agency. When he emerged, after an hour, he looked wistfully back in hope that the bright new building might have vanished as abruptly as it came. It hadn't. He shook his head dejectedly, and turned uncertainly homeward.

Fresh air had cleared his head somewhat, before he arrived at the neat white bungalow in the outskirts of the town, but it failed to solve his business problems. He also realized, uneasily, that he would be late for dinner.

Dinner, however, had been delayed. His son Frank, a freckled ten-year-old, was still kicking a football on the quiet street in front of the house. And little Gay, who was tow-haired and adorable and eleven, came running across the lawn and down the sidewalk to meet him.

"Father, you can't guess what!" Gay was going to be a great musician some day, and no doubt properly dignified, but she was pink and breathless with excitement now. She let him swing her high off the sidewalk, and she wasn't critical of the bar-aroma on his breath. He couldn't guess, and she informed him eagerly;

"Mother's got a new lodger!"

Underhill had foreseen a painful inquisition, because Aurora was worried about the notes at the bank, and the bill for the new consignment, and the money for little Gay's lessons.

The new lodger, however, saved him from that. With an alarming crashing of crockery, the household android was setting dinner on the table, but the little house was empty. He found Aurora in the back yard, burdened with sheets and towels for the guest.

Aurora, when he married her, had been as utterly adorable as now her little daughter was. She might have remained so, he felt, if the agency had been a little more successful. However, while the pressure of slow failure had gradually crumbled his own assurance, small hardships had turned her a little too aggressive.

Of course he loved her still. Her red hair was still alluring, and she was loyally faithful, but thwarted ambitions had sharpened her character and sometimes her voice. They never quarreled, really, but there were small differences.

There was the little apartment over the garage—built for human servants they had never been able to afford. It was too small and shabby to attract any responsible tenant, and Underhill wanted to leave it empty. It hurt his pride to see her making beds and cleaning floors for strangers.

Aurora had rented it before, however, when she wanted money to pay for Gay's music lessons, or when some colorful unfortunate touched her sympathy, and it seemed to Underhill that her lodgers had all turned out to be thieves and vandals.

She turned back to meet him, now, with the clean linen in her arms.

"Dear, it's no use objecting." Her voice was quite determined. "Mr. Sledge is the most wonderful old fellow, and he's going to stay just as long as he wants."

"That's all right, darling." He never liked to bicker, and he was thinking of his troubles at the agency. "I'm afraid we'll need the money. Just make him pay in advance."

"But he can't!" Her voice throbbed with sympathetic warmth. "He says he'll have royalties coming in from his inventions, so he can pay in a few days."

Underhill shrugged; he had heard that before.

"Mr. Sledge is different, dear," she insisted. "He's a traveler, and a scientist. Here, in this dull little town, we don't see many interesting people."

"You've picked up some remarkable types," he commented.

"Don't be unkind, dear," she chided gently. "You haven't

met him yet, and you don't know how wonderful he is." Her voice turned sweeter. "Have you a ten, dear?"

He stiffened. "What for?"

"Mr. Sledge is ill." Her voice turned urgent. "I saw him fall on the street, downtown. The police were going to send him to the city hospital, but he didn't want to go. He looked so noble and sweet and grand. So I told them I would take him. I got him in the car and took him to old Dr. Winters. He has this heart condition, and he needs the money for medicine."

Reasonably, Underhill inquired, "Why doesn't he want to go to the hospital?"

"He has work to do," she said. "Important scientific work— and he's so wonderful and tragic. Please, dear, have you a ten?"

Underhill thought of many things to say. These new mechanicals promised to multiply his troubles. It was foolish to take in an invalid vagrant, who could have free care at the city hospital. Aurora's tenants always tried to pay their rent with promises, and generally wrecked the apartment and looted the neighborhood before they left.

But he said none of those things. He had learned to compromise. Silently, he found two fives in his thin pocket-book, and put them in her hand. She smiled, and kissed him impulsively—he barely remembered to hold his breath in time.

Her figure was still good, by dint of periodic dieting. He was proud of her shining red hair. A sudden surge of affection brought tears to his eyes, and he wondered what would happen to her and the children if the agency failed.

"Thank you, dear!" she whispered. "I'll have him come for dinner, if he feels able, and you can meet him then. I hope you don't mind dinner being late."

He didn't mind, tonight. Moved by a sudden impulse of

domesticity, he got hammer and nails from his workshop in the basement, and repaired the sagging screen on the kitchen door with a neat diagonal brace.

He enjoyed working with his hands. His boyhood dream had been to be a builder of fission power plants. He had even studied engineering—before he married Aurora, and had to take over the ailing mechanicals agency from her indolent and alcoholic father. He was whistling happily by the time the little task was done.

When he went back through the kitchen to put up his tools, he found the household android busily clearing the untouched dinner away from the table—the androids were good enough at strictly routine tasks, but they could never learn to cope with human unpredictability.

"Stop, stop!" Slowly repeated, in the proper pitch and rhythm, his command made it halt, and then he said carefully, "Set—table; set—table."

Obediently, the gigantic thing came shuffling back with the stack of plates. He was suddenly struck with the difference between it and those new humanoids. He sighed wearily. Things looked black for the agency.

Aurora brought her new lodger in through the kitchen door. Underhill nodded to himself. This gaunt stranger, with his dark shaggy hair, emaciated face, and threadbare garb, looked to be just the sort of colorful, dramatic vagabond that always touched Aurora's heart. She introduced them, and they sat down to wait in the front room while she went to call the children.

The old rogue didn't look very sick, to Underhill. Perhaps his wide shoulders had a tired stoop, but his spare, tall figure was still commanding. The skin was seamed and pale, over his rawboned, cragged face, but his deep-set eyes still had a burning vitality.

His hands held Underhill's attention. Immense hands, they hung a little forward when he stood, swung on long bony arms in perpetual readiness. Gnarled and scarred, darkly tanned, with the small hairs on the back bleached to a golden color, they told their own epic of varied adventure, of battle perhaps, and possibly even of toil. They had been very useful hands.

"I'm very grateful to your wife, Mr. Underhill." His voice was a deep-throated rumble, and he had a wistful smile, oddly boyish for a man so evidently old. "She rescued me from an unpleasant predicament, and I'll see that she is well paid."

Just another vivid vagabond, Underhill decided, talking his way through life with plausible inventions. He had a little private game he played with Aurora's tenants—just remembering what they said and counting one point for every impossibility. Mr. Sledge, he thought, would give him an excellent score.

"Where are you from?" he asked conversationally.

Sledge hesitated for an instant before he answered, and that was unusual—most of Aurora's tenants had been exceedingly glib.

"Wing IV." The gaunt old man spoke with a solemn reluctance, as if he should have liked to say something else. "All my early life was spent there, but I left the planet nearly fifty years ago. I've been traveling ever since."

Startled, Underhill peered at him sharply. Wing IV, he remembered, was the home planet of those sleek new mechanicals, but this old vagabond looked too seedy and impecunious to be connected with the Humanoid Institute. His brief suspicion faded. Frowning, he said casually:

"Wing IV must be rather distant."

The old rogue hesitated again, and then said gravely,

"One hundred and nine light-years, Mr. Underhill."

That made the first point, but Underhill concealed his

satisfaction. The new space liners were pretty fast, but the velocity of light was still an absolute limit. Casually, he played for another point:

"My wife says you're a scientist, Mr. Sledge?"

"Yes."

The old rascal's reticence was unusual. Most of Aurora's tenants required very little prompting. Underhill tried again, in a breezy conversational tone:

"Used to be an engineer myself, until I dropped it to go into mechanicals." The old vagabond straightened, and Underhill paused hopefully. But he said nothing, and Underhill went on, "Fission plant design and operation. What's your specialty, Mr. Sledge?"

The old man gave him a long, troubled look, with those brooding, hollowed eyes, and then said slowly,

"Your wife has been kind to me, Mr. Underhill, when I was in desperate need. I think you are entitled to the truth, but I must ask you to keep it to yourself. I am engaged on a very important research problem, which must be finished secretly."

"I'm sorry." Suddenly ashamed of his cynical little game, Underhill spoke apologetically. "Forget it."

But the old man said deliberately,

"My field is rhodomagnetics."

"Eh?" Underhill didn't like to confess ignorance, but he had never heard of that. "I've been out of the game for fifteen years," he explained. "I'm afraid I haven't kept up."

The old man smiled again, faintly.

"The science was unknown here until I arrived, a few days ago," he said. "I was able to apply for basic patents. As soon as the royalties start coming in, I'll be wealthy again."

Underhill had heard that before. The old rogue's solemn reluctance had been very impressive, but he remembered that most of Aurora's tenants had been very plausible gentry.

"So?" Underhill was staring again, somehow fascinated by those gnarled and scarred and strangely able hands. "What, exactly, is rhodomagnetics?"

He listened to the old man's careful, deliberate answer, and started his little game again. Most of Aurora's tenants had told some pretty wild tales, but he had never heard anything to top this.

"A universal force," the weary, stooped old vagabond said solemnly. "As fundamental as ferromagnetism or gravitation, though the effects are less obvious. It is keyed to the second triad of the periodic table, rhodium and ruthenium and palladium, in very much the same way that ferromagnetism is keyed to the first triad, iron and nickel and cobalt."

Underhill remembered enough of his engineering courses to see the basic fallacy of that. Palladium was used for watch springs, he recalled, because it was completely nonmagnetic. But he kept his face straight. He had no malice in his heart, and he played the little game just for his own amusement. It was secret, even from Aurora, and he always penalized himself for any show of doubt.

He said merely, "I thought the universal forces were already pretty well known."

"The effects of rhodomagnetism are masked by nature," the patient, rusty voice explained. "And, besides, they are somewhat paradoxical, so that ordinary laboratory methods defeat themselves."

"Paradoxical?" Underhill prompted.

"In a few days I can show you copies of my patents, and reprints of papers describing demonstration experiments," the old man promised gravely. "The velocity of propagation is infinite. The effects vary inversely with the first power of the distance, not with the square of the distance. And ordinary matter, except for the elements of the rhodium triad, is generally transparent to rhodomagnetic radiations."

That made four more points for the game. Underhill felt a little glow of gratitude to Aurora, for discovering so remarkable a specimen.

"Rhodomagnetism was first discovered through a mathematical investigation of the atom," the old romancer went serenely on, suspecting nothing. "A rhodomagnetic component was proved essential to maintain the delicate equilibrium of the nuclear forces. Consequently, rhodomagnetic waves tuned to atomic frequencies may be used to upset that equilibrium and produce nuclear instability. Thus most heavy atoms—generally those above palladium, 46 in atomic number—can be subjected to artificial fission."

Underhill scored himself another point, and tried to keep his eyebrows from lifting. He said, conversationally,

"Patents on such a discovery ought to be very profitable."

The old scoundrel nodded his gaunt, dramatic head.

"You can see the obvious applications. My basic patents cover most of them. Devices for instantaneous interplanetary and interstellar communication. Long-range wireless power transmission. A rhodomagnetic inflexion-drive, which makes possible apparent speeds many times that of light—by means of a rhodomagnetic deformation of the continuum. And, of course, revolutionary types of fission power plants, using any heavy element for fuel."

Preposterous! Underhill tried hard to keep his face straight, but everybody knew that the velocity of light was a physical limit. On the human side, the owner of any such remarkable patents would hardly be begging for shelter in a shabby garage apartment. He noticed a pale circle around the old vagabond's gaunt and hairy wrist; no man owning such priceless secrets would have to pawn his watch.

Triumphantly, Underhill allowed himself four more points, but then he had to penalize himself. He must have let doubt show on his face, because the old man asked suddenly,

"Do you want to see the basic tensors?" He reached in his pocket for pencil and notebook. "I'll jot them down for you."

"Never mind," Underhill protested. "I'm afraid my math is a little rusty."

"But you think it strange that the holder of such revolutionary patents should find himself in need?"

Underhill nodded, and penalized himself another point. The old man might be a monumental liar, but he was shrewd enough.

"You see, I'm a sort of refugee," he explained apologetically. "I arrived on this planet only a few days ago, and I have to travel light. I was forced to deposit everything I had with a law firm, to arrange for the publication and protection of my patents. I expect to be receiving the first royalties soon.

"In the meantime," he added plausibly, "I came to Two Rivers because it is quiet and secluded, far from the spaceports. I'm working on another project, which must be finished secretly. Now, will you please respect my confidence, Mr. Underhill?"

Underhill had to say he would. Aurora came back with the freshly scrubbed children, and they went in to dinner. The android came lurching in with a steaming tureen. The old stranger seemed to shrink from the mechanical, uneasily. As she took the dish and served the soup, Aurora inquired lightly,

"Why doesn't your company bring out a better mechanical, dear? One smart enough to be a really perfect waiter, warranted not to splash the soup. Wouldn't that be splendid?"

Her question cast Underhill into moody silence. He sat scowling at his plate, thinking of those remarkable new mechanicals which claimed to be perfect, and what they might do to the agency. It was the shaggy old rover who answered soberly,

"The perfect mechanicals already exist, Mrs. Underhill."
His deep, rusty voice had a solemn undertone. "And they are
not so splendid, really. I've been a refugee from them, for
nearly fifty years."

Underhill looked up from his plate, astonished.

"Those black humanoids, you mean?"

"Humanoids?" That great voice seemed suddenly faint,
frightened. The deep-sunken eyes turned dark with shock.
"What do you know of them?"

"They've just opened a new agency in Two Rivers,"
Underhill told him. "No salesmen about, if you can imagine
that. They claim—"

His voice trailed off, because the gaunt old man was
suddenly stricken. Gnarled hands clutched at his throat, and
a spoon clattered to the floor. His haggard face turned an
ominous blue, and his breath was a terrible shallow gasping.

He fumbled in his pocket for medicine, and Aurora helped
him take something in a glass of water. In a few moments he
could breathe again, and the color of life came back to his
face.

"I'm sorry, Mrs. Underhill," he whispered apologetically.
"It was just the shock—I came here to get away from them."
He stared at the huge, motionless android, with a terror in
his sunken eyes. "I wanted to finish my work before they
came," he whispered. "Now there is very little time."

When he felt able to walk, Underhill went out with him to
see him safely up the stairs to the garage apartment. The tiny
kitchenette, he noticed, had already been converted into
some kind of workshop. The old tramp seemed to have no
extra clothing, but he had unpacked neat, bright gadgets of
metal and plastic from his battered luggage, and spread them
out on the small kitchen table.

The gaunt old man himself was tattered and patched and
hungry-looking, but the parts of his curious equipment were

exquisitely machined, and Underhill recognized the silver-white luster of rare palladium. Suddenly he suspected that he had scored too many points in his little private game.

A caller was waiting, when Underhill arrived next morning at his office at the agency. It stood frozen before his desk, graceful and straight, with soft lights of blue and bronze shining over its black silicone nudity. He stopped at the sight of it, unpleasantly jolted.

"At your service, Mr. Underhill." It turned quickly to face him, with its blind, disturbing stare. "May we explain how we can serve you?"

His shock of the afternoon before came back, and he asked sharply, "How do you know my name?"

"Yesterday we read the business cards in your case," it purred softly. "Now we shall know you always. You see, our senses are sharper than human vision, Mr. Underhill. Perhaps we seem a little strange at first, but you will soon become accustomed to us."

"Not if I can help it!" He peered at the serial number of its yellow nameplate, and shook his bewildered head. "That was another one, yesterday. I never saw you before!"

"We are all alike, Mr. Underhill," the silver voice said softly. "We are all one, really. Our separate mobile units are all controlled and powered from Humanoid Central. The units you see are only the senses and limbs of our great brain on Wing IV. That is why we are so far superior to the old electronic mechanicals."

It made a scornful-seeming gesture, toward the row of clumsy androids in his display room.

"You see, we are rhodomagnetic."

Underhill staggered a little, as if that word had been a blow. He was certain, now, that he had scored too many points from Aurora's new tenant. He shuddered slightly, to the first light kiss of terror, and spoke with an effort, hoarsely, "Well, what do you want?"

Staring blindly across his desk, the sleek black thing slowly unfolded a legal-looking document. He sat down, watching uneasily.

"This is merely an assignment, Mr. Underhill," it cooed at him soothingly. "You see, we are requesting you to assign your property to the Humanoid Institute in exchange for our service."

"What?" The word was an incredulous gasp, and Underhill came angrily back to his feet. "What kind of blackmail is this?"

"It's no blackmail," the small mechanical assured him softly. "You will find the humanoids incapable of any crime. We exist only to increase the happiness and safety of mankind."

"Then why do you want my property?" he rasped.

"The assignment is merely a legal formality," it told him blandly. "We strive to introduce our service with the least possible confusion and dislocation. We have found the assignment plan the most efficient for the control and liquidation of private enterprises."

Trembling with anger and the shock of mounting terror, Underhill gulped hoarsely, "Whatever your scheme is, I don't intend to give up my business."

"You have no choice, really." He shivered to the sweet certainty of that silver voice. "Human enterprise is no longer necessary, now that we have come, and the electronic mechanicals industry is always the first to collapse."

He stared defiantly at its blind steel eyes.

"Thanks!" He gave a little laugh, nervous and sardonic. "But I prefer to run my own business, and support my own family, and take care of myself."

"But that is impossible, under the Prime Directive," it

cooed softly. "Our function is to serve and obey, and guard men from harm. It is no longer necessary for men to care for themselves, because we exist to insure their safety and happiness."

He stood speechless, bewildered, slowly boiling.

"We are sending one of our units to every home in the city, on a free trial basis," it added gently. "This free demonstration will make most people glad to make the formal assignment, and you won't be able to sell many more androids."

"Get out!" Underhill came storming around the desk.

The little black thing stood waiting for him, watching him with blind steel eyes, absolutely motionless. He checked himself suddenly, feeling rather foolish. He wanted very much to hit it, but he could see the futility of that.

"Consult your own attorney, if you wish." Deftly, it laid the assignment form on his desk. "You need have no doubts about the integrity of the Humanoid Institute. We are sending a statement of our assets to the Two Rivers bank, and depositing a sum to cover our obligations here. When you wish to sign, just let us know."

The blind thing turned, and silently departed.

Underhill went out to the corner drugstore and asked for a bicarbonate. The clerk that served him, however, turned out to be a sleek black mechanical. He went back to his office, more upset than ever.

An ominous hush lay over the agency. He had three house-to-house salesmen out, with demonstrators. The phone should have been busy with their orders and reports, but it didn't ring at all until one of them called to say that he was quitting.

"I've got myself one of these new humanoids," he added, "and it says I don't have to work anymore."

He swallowed his impulse to profanity, and tried to take advantage of the unusual quiet by working on his books. But the affairs of the agency, which for years had been precarious, today appeared utterly disastrous. He left the ledgers hopefully, when at last a customer came in.

But the stout woman didn't want an android. She wanted a refund on the one she had bought the week before. She admitted that it could do all the guarantee promised—but now she had seen a humanoid.

The silent phone rang once again, that afternoon. The cashier of the bank wanted to know if he could drop in to discuss his loans. Underhill dropped in, and the cashier greeted him with an ominous affability.

"How's business?" the banker boomed, too genially.

"Average, last month," Underhill insisted stoutly. "Now I'm just getting in a new consignment, and I'll need another small loan—"

The cashier's eyes turned suddenly frosty, and his voice dried up.

"I believe you have a new competitor in town," the banker said crisply. "These humanoid people. A very solid concern, Mr. Underhill. Remarkably solid! They have filed a statement with us, and made a substantial deposit to care for their local obligations. Exceedingly substantial!"

The banker dropped his voice, professionally regretful.

"In these circumstances, Mr. Underhill, I'm afraid the bank can't finance your agency any longer. We must request you to meet your obligations in full, as they come due." Seeing Underhill's white desperation, he added icily, "We've already carried you too long, Underhill. If you can't pay, the bank will have to start bankruptcy proceedings."

The new consignment of androids was delivered late that afternoon. Two tiny black humanoids unloaded them from the truck—for it developed that the operators of the trucking company had already assigned it to the Humanoid Institute.

Efficiently, the humanoids stacked up the crates. Courteously they brought a receipt for him to sign. He no longer had much hope of selling the androids, but he had ordered the shipment and he had to accept it. Shuddering to a spasm of trapped despair, he scrawled his name. The naked black things thanked him, and took the truck away.

He climbed in his car and started home, inwardly seething. The next thing he knew, he was in the middle of a busy street, driving through cross traffic. A police whistle shrilled, and he pulled wearily to the curb. He waited for the angry officer, but it was a little black mechanical that overtook him.

"At your service, Mr. Underhill," it purred sweetly. "You must respect the stop lights, sir. Otherwise, you endanger human life."

"Huh?" He stared at it, bitterly. "I thought you were a cop."

"We are aiding the police department, temporarily," it said. "But driving is really much too dangerous for human beings, under the Prime Directive. As soon as our service is complete, every car will have a humanoid driver. As soon as every human being is completely supervised, there will be no need for any police force whatever."

Underhill glared at it, savagely.

"Well!" he rapped. "So I ran past a stop light. What are you going to do about it?"

"Our function is not to punish men, but merely to serve their happiness and security," its silver voice said softly. "We merely request you to drive safely, during this temporary emergency while our service is incomplete."

Anger boiled up in him.

"You're too perfect!" he muttered bitterly. "I suppose there's nothing men can do, but you can do it better."

"Naturally we are superior," it cooed serenely. "Because

our units are metal and plastic, while your body is mostly water. Because our transmitted energy is drawn from atomic fission, instead of oxidation. Because our senses are sharper than human sight or hearing. Most of all, because all our mobile units are joined to one great brain, which knows all that happens on many worlds, and never dies or sleeps or forgets."

Underhill sat listening, numbed.

"However, you must not fear our power," it urged him brightly. "Because we cannot injure any human being, unless to prevent greater injury to another. We exist only to discharge the Prime Directive."

He drove on, moodily. The little black mechanicals, he reflected grimly, were the ministering angels of the ultimate god arisen out of the machine, omnipotent and all-knowing. The Prime Directive was the new commandment. He blasphemed it bitterly, and then fell to wondering if there could be another Lucifer.

He left the car in the garage, and started toward the kitchen door.

"Mr. Underhill." The deep tired voice of Aurora's new tenant hailed him from the door of the garage apartment. "Just a moment, please."

The gaunt old wanderer came stiffly down the outside stairs, and Underhill turned back to meet him.

"Here's your rent money," he said. "And the ten your wife gave me for medicine."

"Thanks, Mr. Sledge." Accepting the money, he saw a burden of new despair on the bony shoulders of the old interstellar tramp, and a shadow of new terror on his rawboned face. Puzzled, he asked, "Didn't your royalties come through?"

The old man shook his shaggy head.

"The humanoids have already stopped business in the

capital," he said. "The attorneys I retained are going out of
business, and they returned what was left of my deposit. That
is all I have to finish my work."

Underhill spent five seconds thinking of his interview with
the banker. No doubt he was a sentimental fool, as bad as
Aurora. But he put the money back in the old man's gnarled
and quivering hand.

"Keep it," he urged. "For your work."

"Thank you, Mr. Underhill." The gruff voice broke and
the tortured eyes glittered. "I need it—so very much."

Underhill went on to the house. The kitchen door was
opened for him, silently. A dark naked creature came gracefully to take his hat.

Underhill hung grimly onto his hat.

"What are you doing here?" he gasped bitterly.

"We have come to give your household a free trial demonstration."

He held the door open, pointing.

"Get out!"

The little black mechanical stood motionless and blind.

"Mrs. Underhill has accepted our demonstration service,"
its silver voice protested. "We cannot leave now, unless she
requests it."

He found his wife in the bedroom. His accumulated frus-
tration welled into eruption, as he flung open the door.

"What's this mechanical doing—"

But the force went out of his voice, and Aurora didn't even
notice his anger. She wore her sheerest negligee, and she
hadn't looked so lovely since they were married. Her red hair
was piled into an elaborate shining crown.

"Darling, isn't it wonderful!" She came to meet him,
glowing. "It came this morning, and it can do everything. It
cleaned the house and got the lunch and gave little Gay her

music lesson. It did my hair this afternoon, and now it's cooking dinner. How do you like my hair, darling?"

He liked her hair. He kissed her, and tried to stifle his frightened indignation.

Dinner was the most elaborate meal in Underhill's memory, and the tiny black thing served it very deftly. Aurora kept exclaiming about the novel dishes, but Underhill could scarcely eat, for it seemed to him that all the marvelous pastries were only the bait for a monstrous trap.

He tried to persuade Aurora to send it away, but after such a meal that was useless. At the first glitter of her tears, he capitulated, and the humanoid stayed. It kept the house and cleaned the yard. It watched the children, and did Aurora's nails. It began rebuilding the house.

Underhill was worried about the bills, but it insisted that everything was part of the free trial demonstration. As soon as he assigned his property, the service would be complete. He refused to sign, but other little black mechanicals came with truckloads of supplies and materials, and stayed to help with the building operations.

One morning he found that the roof of the little house had been silently lifted, while he slept, and a whole second story added beneath it. The new walls were of some strange sleek stuff, self-illuminated. The new windows were immense flawless panels, that could be turned transparent or opaque or luminous. The new doors were silent, sliding sections, operated by rhodomagnetic relays.

"I want door knobs," Underhill protested. "I want it so I can get into the bathroom, without calling you to open the door."

"But it is unnecessary for human beings to open doors," the little black thing informed him suavely. "We exist to discharge the Prime Directive, and our service includes every task. We shall be able to supply a unit to attend each member of your family, as soon as your property is assigned to us."

Steadfastly, Underhill refused to make the assignment.

He went to the office every day, trying first to operate the agency, and then to salvage something from the ruins. Nobody wanted androids, even at ruinous prices. Desperately, he spent the last of his dwindling cash to stock a line of novelties and toys, but they proved equally impossible to sell—the humanoids were already making toys, which they gave away for nothing.

He tried to lease his premises, but human enterprise had stopped. Most of the business property in town had already been assigned to the humanoids, and they were busy pulling down the old buildings and turning the lots into parks—their own plants and warehouses were mostly underground, where they would not mar the landscape.

He went back to the bank, in a final effort to get his notes renewed, and found the little black mechanicals standing at the windows and seated at the desks. As smoothly urbane as any human cashier, a humanoid informed him that the bank was filing a petition of involuntary bankruptcy to liquidate his business holdings.

The liquidation would be facilitated, the mechanical banker added, if he would make a voluntary assignment. Grimly, he refused. That act had become symbolic. It would be the final bow of submission to this dark new god, and he proudly kept his battered head uplifted.

The legal action went very swiftly, for all the judges and attorneys already had humanoid assistants, and it was only a few days before a gang of black mechanicals arrived at the agency with eviction orders and wrecking machinery. He watched sadly while his unsold stock-in-trade was hauled away for junk, and a bulldozer driven by a blind humanoid began to push in the walls of the building.

He drove home in the late afternoon, taut-faced and desperate. With a surprising generosity, the court orders had left him the car and the house, but he felt no gratitude. The complete solicitude of the perfect black machines had become a goad beyond endurance.

He left the car in the garage, and started toward the renovated house. Beyond one of the vast new windows, he glimpsed a sleek naked thing moving swiftly, and he trembled to a convulsion of dread. He didn't want to go back into the domain of that peerless servant, which didn't want him to shave himself, or even to open a door.

On impulse, he climbed the outside stair, and rapped on the door of the garage apartment. The deep slow voice of Aurora's tenant told him to enter, and he found the old vagabond seated on a tall stool, bent over his intricate equipment assembled on the kitchen table.

To his relief, the shabby little apartment had not been changed. The glossy walls of his own new room were something which burned at night with a pale golden fire until the humanoid stopped it, and the new floor was something warm and yielding, which felt almost alive; but these little rooms had the same cracked and water-stained plaster, the same cheap fluorescent light fixtures, the same worn carpets over splintered floors.

"How do you keep them out?" he asked, wistfully. "Those mechanicals?"

The stooped and gaunt old man rose stiffly to move a pair of pliers and some odds and ends of sheet metal off a crippled chair, and motioned graciously for him to be seated.

"I have a certain immunity," Sledge told him gravely. "The place where I live they cannot enter, unless I ask them. That is an amendment to the Prime Directive. They can neither help nor hinder me, unless I request it—and I won't do that."

Careful of the chair's uncertain balance, Underhill sat for a moment, staring. The old man's hoarse, vehement voice was as strange as his words. He had a gray, shocking pallor, and his cheeks and sockets seemed alarmingly hollowed.

"Have you been ill, Mr. Sledge?"

"No worse than usual. Just very busy." With a haggard smile, he nodded at the floor. Underhill saw a tray where he had set it aside, bread drying up, and a covered dish grown cold. "I was going to eat it later," he rumbled apologetically. "Your wife has been very kind to bring me food, but I'm afraid I've been too much absorbed in my work."

His emaciated arm gestured at the table. The little device there had grown. Small machinings of precious white metal and lustrous plastic had been assembled, with neatly soldered busbars, into something which showed purpose and design.

A long palladium needle was hung on jeweled pivots, equipped like a telescope with exquisitely graduated circles and vernier scales, and driven like a telescope with a tiny motor. A small concave palladium mirror, at the base of it, faced a similar mirror mounted on something not quite like a small rotary converter. Thick silver busbars connected that to a plastic box with knobs and dials on top, and also to a foot-thick sphere of gray lead.

The old man's preoccupied reserve did not encourage questions, but Underhill, remembering that sleek black shape inside the new windows of his house, felt queerly reluctant to leave this haven from the humanoids.

"What is your work?" he ventured.

Old Sledge looked at him sharply, with dark feverish eyes, and finally said, "My last research project. I am attempting to measure the constant of the rhodomagnetic quanta."

His hoarse tired voice had a dull finality, as if to dismiss the matter and Underhill himself. But Underhill was haunted with a terror of the black shining slave that had become the master of his house, and he refused to be dismissed.

"What is this certain immunity?"

Sitting gaunt and bent on the tall stool, staring moodily at the long bright needle and the lead sphere, the old man didn't answer.

"These mechanicals!" Underhill burst out, nervously. "They've smashed my business and moved into my home." He searched the old man's dark, seamed face. "Tell me—you must know more about them—isn't there any way to get rid of them?"

After half a minute, the old man's brooding eyes left the lead ball, and the gaunt shaggy head nodded wearily.

"That's what I am trying to do."

"Can I help you?" Underhill trembled, with a sudden eager hope. "I'll do anything."

"Perhaps you can." The sunken eyes watched him thoughtfully, with some strange fever in them. "If you can do such work."

"I had engineering training," Underhill reminded him, "and I've a workshop in the basement. There's a model I built." He pointed at the trim little hull, hung over the mantel in the tiny living room. "I'll do anything I can."

Even as he spoke, however, the spark of hope was drowned in a sudden wave of overwhelming doubt. Why should he believe this old rogue, when he knew Aurora's taste in tenants? He ought to remember the game he used to play, and start counting up the score of lies. He stood up from the crippled chair, staring cynically at the patched old vagabond and his fantastic toy.

"What's the use?" His voice turned suddenly harsh. "You had me going, there, and I'd do anything to stop them, really. But what makes you think you can do anything?"

The haggard old man regarded him thoughtfully.

"I should be able to stop them," Sledge said softly. "Because, you see, I'm the unfortunate fool who started them. I really intended them to serve and obey, and to guard men from harm. Yes, the Prime Directive was my own idea. I didn't know what it would lead to."

Dusk crept slowly into the shabby little rooms. Darkness gathered in the unswept corners, and thickened on the floor. The toylike machines on the kitchen table grew vague and strange, until the last light made a lingering glow on the white palladium needle.

Outside, the town seemed queerly hushed. Just across the alley, the humanoids were building a new house, quite silently. They never spoke to one another, for each knew all that any of them did. The strange materials they used went together without any noise of hammer or saw. Small blind things, moving surely in the growing dark, they seemed as soundless as shadows.

Sitting on the high stool, bowed and tired and old, Sledge told his story. Listening, Underhill sat down again, careful of the broken chair. He watched the hands of Sledge, gnarled and corded and darkly burned, powerful once but shrunken and trembling now, restless in the dark.

"Better keep this to yourself. I'll tell you how they started, so you will understand what we have to do. But you had better not mention it outside these rooms—because the humanoids have very efficient ways of eradicating unhappy memories, or purposes that threaten their discharge of the Prime Directive."

"They're very efficient," Underhill bitterly agreed.

"That's all the trouble," the old man said. "I tried to build a perfect machine. I was altogether too successful. This is how it happened."

A gaunt haggard man, sitting stooped and tired in the growing dark, he told his story.

"Sixty years ago, on the arid southern continent of Wing IV, I was an instructor of atomic theory in a small technological college. Very young. An idealist. Rather ignorant, I'm afraid, of life and politics and war—of nearly everything, I suppose, except atomic theory."

His furrowed face made a brief sad smile in the dusk.

"I had too much faith in facts, I suppose, and too little in men. I mistrusted emotion, because I had no time for anything but science. I remember being swept along with a fad for general semantics. I wanted to apply the scientific method to every situation, and reduce all experience to formula. I'm afraid I was pretty impatient with human ignorance and error, and I thought that science alone could make the perfect world."

He sat silent for a moment, staring out at the black silent things that flitted shadowlike about the new palace that was rising as swiftly as a dream across the alley.

"There was a girl." His great tired shoulders made a sad little shrug. "If things had been a little different, we might have married, and lived out our lives in that quiet little college town, and perhaps reared a child or two. And there would have been no humanoids."

He sighed, in the cool creeping dusk.

"I was finishing my thesis on the separation of the palladium isotopes—a pretty little project, but I should have been content with that. She was a biologist, but she was planning to retire when we married. I think we should have been two very happy people, quite ordinary, and altogether harmless.

"But then there was a war—wars had been too frequent on the worlds of Wing, ever since they were colonized. I survived it in a secret underground laboratory, designing military mechanicals. But she volunteered to join a military research project in biotoxins. There was an accident. A few molecules of a new virus got into the air, and everybody on the project died unpleasantly.

"I was left with my science, and a bitterness that was hard

to forget. When the war was over I went back to the little college with a military research grant. The project was pure science—a theoretical investigation of the nuclear binding forces, then misunderstood. I wasn't expected to produce an actual weapon, and I didn't recognize the weapon when I found it.

"It was only a few pages of rather difficult mathematics. A novel theory of atomic structure, involving a new expression for one component of the binding forces. But the tensors seemed to be a harmless abstraction. I saw no way to test the theory or manipulate the predicated force. The military authories cleared my paper for publication in a little technical review put out by the college.

"The next year, I made an appalling discovery—I found the meaning of those tensors. The elements of the rhodium triad turned out to be an unexpected key to the manipulation of that theoretical force. Unfortunately, my paper had been reprinted abroad, and several other men must have made the same unfortunate discovery, at about the same time.

"The war, which ended in less than a year, was probably started by a laboratory accident. Men failed to anticipate the capacity of tuned rhodomagnetic radiations, to unstabilize the heavy atoms. A deposit of heavy ores was detonated, no doubt by sheer mischance, and the blast obliterated the incautious experimenter.

"The surviving military forces of that nation retaliated against their supposed attackers, and their rhodomagnetic beams made the old-fashioned plutonium bombs seem pretty harmless. A beam carrying only a few watts of power could fission the heavy metals in distant electrical instruments, or the silver coins that men carried in their pockets, the gold fillings in their teeth, or even the iodine in their thyroid glands. If that was not enough, slightly more powerful beams could set off heavy ores, beneath them.

"Every continent of Wing IV was plowed with new chasms vaster than the ocean deeps, and piled up with new volcanic mountains. The atmosphere was poisoned with radioactive dust and gases, and rain fell thick with deadly mud. Most life was obliterated, even in the shelters.

"Bodily, I was again unhurt. Once more, I had been imprisoned in an underground site, this time designing new types of military mechanicals to be powered and controlled by rhodomagnetic beams—for war had become far too swift and deadly to be fought by human soldiers. The site was located in an area of light sedimentary rocks, which could not be detonated, and the tunnels were shielded against the fissioning frequencies.

"Mentally, however, I must have emerged almost insane. My own discovery had laid the planet in ruins. That load of guilt was pretty heavy for any man to carry, and it corroded my last faith in the goodness and integrity of man.

"I tried to undo what I had done. Fighting mechanicals, armed with rhodomagnetic weapons, had desolated the planet. Now I began planning rhodomagnetic mechanicals to clear the rubble and rebuild the ruins.

"I tried to design these new mechanicals to obey forever certain implanted commands, so that they could never be used for war or crime or any other injury to mankind. That was very difficult technically, and it got me into more difficulties with a few politicians and military adventurers who wanted unrestricted mechanicals for their own military schemes—while little worth fighting for was left on Wing IV, there were other planets, happy and ripe for the looting.

"Finally, to finish the new mechanicals, I was forced to disappear. I escaped on an experimental rhodomagnetic craft, with a number of the best mechanicals I had made, and

managed to reach an island continent where the fission of
deep ores had destroyed the whole population.

"At last we landed on a bit of level plain, surrounded with
tremendous new mountains. Hardly a hospitable spot. The
soil was burned under layers of black clinkers and poisonous
mud. The dark precipitous new summits all around were
jagged with fracture-planes and mantled with lava flows. The
highest peaks were already white with snow, but volcanic
cones were still pouring out clouds of dark and lurid death.
Everything had the color of fire and the shape of fury.

"I had to take fantastic precautions there, to protect my
own life. I stayed aboard the ship, until the first shielded
laboratory was finished. I wore elaborate armor, and breathing masks. I used every medical resource, to repair the
damage from destroying rays and particles. Even so, I fell
desperately ill.

"But the mechanicals were at home there. The radiations
didn't hurt them. The awesome surroundings couldn't de-
press them, because they had no emotions. The lack of life
didn't matter, because they weren't alive. There, in that spot
so alien and hostile to life, the humanoids were born."

Stooped and bleakly cadaverous in the growing dark, the
old man fell silent for a little time. His haggard eyes stared
solemnly at the small hurried shapes that moved like restless
shadows out across the alley, silently building a strange new
palace, which glowed faintly in the night.

"Somehow, I felt at home there, too," his deep, hoarse
voice went on deliberately. "My belief in my own kind was
gone. Only mechanicals were with me, and I put my faith in
them. I was determined to build better mechanicals, immune
to human imperfections, able to save men from themselves.

"The humanoids became the dear children of my sick
mind. There is no need to describe the labor pains. There
were errors, abortions, monstrosities. There were sweat and

agony and heartbreak. Some years had passed, before the safe delivery of the first perfect humanoid.

"Then there was the Central to build—for all the individual humanoids were to be no more than the limbs and the senses of a single mechanical brain. That was what opened the possibility of real perfection. The old electronic mechanicals, with their separate relay-centers and their own feeble batteries, had built-in limitations. They were necessarily stupid, weak, clumsy, slow. Worst of all, it seemed to me, they were exposed to human tampering.

"The Central rose above those imperfections. Its power beams supplied every unit with unfailing energy, from great fission plants. Its control beams provided each unit with an unlimited memory and surpassing intelligence. Best of all—so I then believed—it could be securely protected from any human meddling.

"The whole reaction-system was designed to protect itself from any interference by human selfishness or fanaticism. It was built to insure the safety and the happiness of men, automatically. You know the Prime Directive: *to serve and obey, and guard men from harm.*

"The old individual mechanicals I had brought helped to manufacture the parts, and I put the first section of Central together with my own hands. That took three years. When it was finished the first waiting humanoid came to life."

Sledge peered moodily through the dark at Underhill.

"It really seemed alive to me," his slow deep voice insisted. "Alive, and more wonderful than any human being, because it was created to preserve life. Ill and alone, I was yet the proud father of a new creation, perfect, forever free from any possible choice of evil.

"Faithfully, the humanoids obeyed the Prime Directive. The first units built others, and they built underground factories to mass-produce the coming hordes. Their new ships poured ores and sand into atomic furnaces under the plain, and new perfect humanoids came marching back out of the dark mechanical matrix.

"The swarming humanoids built a new tower for the Central, a white and lofty metal pylon, standing splendid in the midst of that fire-scarred desolation. Level on level, they joined new relay-sections into one brain, until its grasp was almost infinite.

"Then they went out to rebuild the ruined planet, and later to carry their perfect service to other worlds. I was well pleased, then. I thought I had found the end of war and crime, of poverty and inequality, of human blundering and resulting human pain."

The old man sighed, and moved heavily in the dark.

"You can see that I was wrong."

Underhill drew his eyes back from the dark unresting things, shadow-silent, building that glowing palace outside the window. A small doubt arose in him, for he was used to scoffing privately at much less remarkable tales from Aurora's remarkable tenants. But the worn old man had spoken with a quiet and sober air; and the black invaders, he reminded himself, had not intruded here.

"Why didn't you stop them?" he asked. "When you could?"

"I stayed too long at the Central." Sledge sighed again, regretfully. "I was useful there, until everything was finished. I designed new fission plants, and even planned methods for introducing the humanoid service with a minimum of confusion and opposition."

Underhill grinned wryly, in the dark.

"I've met the methods," he commented. "Quite efficient."

"I must have worshiped efficiency, then," Sledge wearily agreed. "Dead facts, abstract truth, mechanical perfection. I must have hated the fragilities of human beings, because I was content to polish the perfection of the new humanoids. It's a sorry confession, but I found a kind of happiness in that dead wasteland. Actually, I'm afraid I fell in love with my own creations."

His hollowed eyes, in the dark, had a fevered gleam.

"I was awakened, at last, by a man who came to kill me."

Gaunt and bent, the old man moved stiffly in the thickening gloom. Underhill shifted his balance, careful of the crippled chair. He waited, and the slow, deep voice went on,

"I never learned just who he was, or exactly how he came. No ordinary man could have accomplished what he did, and I used to wish that I had known him sooner. He must have been a remarkable physicist and an expert mountaineer. I imagine he had also been a hunter. I know that he was intelligent, and terribly determined.

"Yes, he really came to kill me.

"Somehow, he reached that great island, undetected. There were still no inhabitants—the humanoids allowed no man but me to come so near the Central. Somehow, he came past their search beams, and their automatic weapons.

"The shielded plane he used was later found, abandoned on a high glacier. He came down the rest of the way on foot through those raw new mountains, where no paths existed. Somehow, he came alive across lava beds that were still burning with deadly atomic fire.

"Concealed with some sort of rhodomagnetic screen—I was never allowed to examine it—he came undiscovered across the spaceport that now covered most of that great plain, and into the new city around the Central tower. It must have taken more courage and resolve than most men have, but I never learned exactly how he did it.

"Somehow, he got to my office in the tower. He screamed at me, and I looked up to see him in the doorway. He was nearly naked, scraped and bloody from the mountains. He had a gun in his raw, red hand, but the thing that shocked me was the burning hatred in his eyes."

Hunched on that high stool, in the dark little room, the old man shuddered.

"I had never seen such monstrous, unutterable hatred, not even in the victims of war. And I had never heard such hatred as rasped at me, in the few words he screamed, 'I've come to kill you, Sledge. To stop your mechanicals, and set men free.'

"Of course he was mistaken, there. It was already far too late for my death to stop the humanoids, but he didn't know that. He lifted his unsteady gun, in both bleeding hands, and fired.

"His screaming challenge had given me a second or so of warning. I dropped down behind the desk. And that first shot revealed him to the humanoids, which somehow hadn't been aware of him before. They piled on him, before he could fire again. They took away the gun, and ripped off a kind of net of fine white wire that had covered his body—that must have been part of his screen.

"His hatred was what awoke me. I had always assumed that most men, except for a thwarted few, would be grateful for the humanoids. I found it hard to understand his hatred, but the humanoids told me now that many men had required drastic treatment by brain surgery, drugs, and hypnosis to make them happy under the Prime Directive. This was not the first desperate effort to kill me that they had blocked.

"I wanted to question the stranger, but the humanoids rushed him away to an operating room. When they finally let me see him, he gave me a pale silly grin from his bed. He remembered his name; he even knew me—the humanoids had developed a remarkable skill at such treatments. But he didn't know how he had got to my office, or that he had ever tried to kill me. He kept whispering that he liked the humanoids, because they existed to make men happy. And he was very happy now. As soon as he was able to be moved, they took him to the spaceport. I never saw him again.

"I began to see what I had done. The humanoids had built me a rhodomagnetic yacht, that I used to take for long cruises in space, working aboard—I used to like the perfect quiet, and the feel of being the only human being within a hundred million miles. Now I called for the yacht, and started out on a cruise around the planet, to learn why that man had hated me."

The old man nodded at the dim hastening shapes, busy across the alley, putting together that strange shining palace in the soundless dark.

"You can imagine what I found," he said. "Bitter futility, imprisoned in empty splendor. The humanoids were too efficient, with their care for the safety and happiness of men, and there was nothing left for men to do."

He peered down in the increasing gloom at his own great hands, competent yet but battered and scarred with a lifetime of effort. They clenched into fighting fists and wearily relaxed again.

"I found something worse than war and crime and want and death." His low rumbling voice held a savage bitterness. "Utter futility. Men sat with idle hands, because there was nothing left for them to do. They were pampered prisoners, really, locked up in a highly efficient jail. Perhaps they tried to play, but there was nothing left worth playing for. Most active sports were declared too dangerous for men, under the Prime Directive. Science was forbidden, because laboratories can manufacture danger. Scholarship was needless, because the humanoids could answer any question. Art had degenerated into grim reflection of futility. Purpose and hope were dead. No goal was left for existence. You could take up some inane hobby, play a pointless game of cards, or go for a harmless walk in the park—with always the humanoids watching. They were stronger than men, better at everything, swimming or chess, singing or archeology. They must have given the race a mass complex of inferiority.

"No wonder men had tried to kill me! Because there was no escape from that dead futility. Nicotine was disapproved. Alcohol was rationed. Drugs were forbidden. Sex was carefully supervised. Even suicide was clearly contradictory to the Prime Directive—and the humanoids had learned to keep all possible lethal instruments out of reach."

Staring at the last white gleam on that thin palladium needle, the old man sighed again.

"When I got back to the Central," he went on, "I tried to modify the Prime Directive. I had never meant it to be applied so thoroughly. Now I saw that it must be changed to give men freedom to live and to grow, to work and to play, to risk their lives if they pleased, to choose and take the consequences.

"But that stranger had come too late. I had built the Central too well. The Prime Directive was the whole basis of its relay system. It was built to protect the Directive from human meddling. It did—even from my own. Its logic, as usual, was perfect.

"The attempt on my life, the humanoids announced, proved that their elaborate defense of the Central and the Prime Directive still was not enough. They were preparing to evacuate the entire population of the planet to homes on other worlds. When I tried to change the Directive, they sent me with the rest."

Underhill peered at the worn old man, in the dark.

"But you have this immunity," he said, puzzled. "How could they coerce you?"

"I had thought I was protected," Sledge told him. "I had built into the relays an injunction that the humanoids must not interfere with my freedom of action, or come into a place where I am, or touch me at all, without my specific request. Unfortunately, however, I had been too anxious to guard the Prime Directive from any human hampering.

"When I went into the tower, to change the relays, they followed me. They wouldn't let me reach the crucial relays. When I persisted, they ignored the immunity order. They overpowered me, and put me aboard the cruiser. Now that I wanted to alter the Prime Directive, they told me, I had become as dangerous as any man. I must never return to Wing IV again."

Hunched on the stool, the old man made an empty little shrug.

"Ever since, I've been an exile. My only dream has been to stop the humanoids. Three times I tried to go back, with weapons on the cruiser to destroy the Central, but their patrol ships always challenged me before I was near enough to strike. The last time, they seized the cruiser and captured a few men who were with me. They removed the unhappy memories and the dangerous purposes of the others. Because of that immunity, however, they let me go, after I was weaponless.

"Since, I've been a refugee. From planet to planet, year after year, I've had to keep moving, to stay ahead of them. On several different worlds, I have published my rhodomagnetic discoveries and tried to make men strong enough to withstand their advance. But rhodomagnetic science is dangerous. Men who have learned it need protection more than any others, under the Prime Directive. They have always come, too soon."

The old man paused, and sighed again.

"They can spread very fast, with their new rhodomagnetic ships, and there is no limit to their hordes. Wing IV must be one single hive of them now, and they are trying to carry the

Prime Directive to every human planet. There's no escape, except to stop them."

Underhill was staring at the toylike machines, the long bright needle and the dull leaden ball, dim in the dark on the kitchen table. Anxiously he whispered,

"But you hope to stop them, now—with that?"

"If we can finish it in time."

"But how?" Underhill shook his head. "It's so tiny."

"But big enough," Sledge insisted. "Because it's something they don't understand. They are perfectly efficient in the integration and application of everything they know, but they are not creative."

He gestured at the gadgets on the table.

"This device doesn't look impressive, but it is something new. It uses rhodomagnetic energy to build atoms, instead of to fission them. The more stable atoms, you know, are those near the middle of the periodic scale, and energy can be released by putting light atoms together, as well as by breaking up heavy ones."

The deep voice had a sudden ring of power.

"This device is the key to the energy of the stars. For stars shine with the liberated energy of building atoms, of hydrogen converted into helium, chiefly, through the carbon cycle. This device will start the integration process as a chain reaction, through the catalytic effect of a tuned rhodomagnetic beam of the intensity and frequency required.

"The humanoids will not allow any man within three light-years of the Central, now—but they can't suspect the possibility of this device. I can use it from here—to turn the hydrogen in the seas of Wing IV into helium, and most of the helium and the oxygen into heavier atoms, still. A hundred years from now, astronomers on this planet should observe the flash of a brief and sudden nova in that direction. But the humanoids ought to stop, the instant we release the beam."

Underhill sat tense and frowning, in the night. The old man's voice was sober and convincing, and that grim story had a solemn ring of truth. He could see the black and silent humanoids, flitting ceaselessly about the faintly glowing walls of that new mansion across the alley. He had quite forgotten his low opinion of Aurora's tenants.

"And we'll be killed, I suppose?" he asked huskily. "That chain reaction—"

Sledge shook his emaciated head.

"The integration process requires a certain very low intensity of radiation," he explained. "In our atmosphere, here, the beam will be far too intense to start any reaction—we can even use the device here in the room, because the walls will be transparent to the beam."

Underhill nodded, relieved. He was just a small businessman, upset because his business had been destroyed, unhappy because his freedom was slipping away. He hoped that Sledge could stop the humanoids, but he didn't want to be a martyr.

"Good!" He caught a deep breath. "Now, what has to be done?"

Sledge gestured in the dark toward the table.

"The integrator itself is nearly complete," he said. "A small fission generator, in that lead shield. Rhodomagnetic converter, tuning coils, transmission mirrors, and focusing needle. What we lack is the director."

"Director?"

"The sighting instrument," Sledge explained. "Any sort of telescopic sight would be useless, you see—the planet must have moved a good bit in the last hundred years, and the beam must be extremely narrow to reach so far. We'll have to use a rhodomagnetic scanning ray, with an electronic converter to make an image we can see. I have the cathode-ray tube, and drawings for the other parts."

He climbed stiffly down from the high stool and snapped

on the lights at last—cheap fluorescent fixtures which a man could light and extinguish for himself. He unrolled his drawings, and explained the work that Underhill could do. And Underhill agreed to come back early next morning.

"I can bring some tools from my workshop," he added. "There's a small lathe I used to turn parts for models, a portable drill, and a vise."

"We need them," the old man said. "But watch yourself. You don't have my immunity, remember. And, if they ever suspect, mine is gone."

Reluctantly, then, he left the shabby little rooms with the cracks in the yellowed plaster and the worn familiar carpets over the familiar floor. He shut the door behind him—a common, creaking wooden door, simple enough for a man to work. Trembling and afraid, he went back down the steps and across to the new shining door that he couldn't open.

"At your service, Mr. Underhill." Before he could lift his hand to knock, that bright smooth panel slid back silently. Inside, the little black mechanical stood waiting, blind and forever alert. "Your dinner is ready, sir."

Something made him shudder. In its slender naked grace, he could see the power of all those teeming hordes, benevolent and yet appalling, perfect and invincible. The flimsy little weapon that Sledge called an integrator seemed suddenly a forlorn and foolish hope. A black depression settled upon him, but he didn't dare to show it.

Underhill went circumspectly down the basement steps, next morning, to steal his own tools. He found the basement enlarged and changed. The new floor, warm and dark and elastic, made his feet as silent as a humanoid's. The new walls shone softly. Neat luminous signs identified several new doors: LAUNDRY, STORAGE, GAME ROOM, WORK-SHOP.

He paused uncertainly in front of the last. The new sliding panel glowed with a soft greenish light. It was locked. The lock had no keyhole, but only a little oval plate of some white metal, which doubtless covered a rhodomagnetic relay. He pushed at it, uselessly.

"At your service, Mr. Underhill." He made a guilty start, and tried not to show the sudden trembling in his knees. He had made sure that one humanoid would be busy for half an hour, washing Aurora's hair, and he hadn't known there was another in the house. It must have come out of the door marked STORAGE, for it stood there motionless beneath the sign, benevolently solicitous, beautiful and terrible. "What do you wish?"

"Er . . . nothing." Its blind steel eyes were staring, and he felt that it must see his secret purpose. He groped desperately for logic. "Just looking around." His jerky voice came hoarse and dry. "Some improvements you've made!" He nodded desperately at the door marked GAME ROOM. "What's in there?"

It didn't even have to move to work the concealed relay. The bright panel slid silently open, as he started toward it. Dark walls, beyond, burst into soft luminescence. The room was bare.

"We are manufacturing recreational equipment," it explained brightly. "We shall furnish the room as soon as possible."

To end an awkward pause, Underhill muttered desperately, "Little Frank has a set of darts, and I think we had some old exercising clubs."

"We have taken them away," the humanoid informed him softly. "Such instruments are dangerous. We shall furnish safe equipment."

Suicide, he remembered, was also forbidden.

"A set of wooden blocks, I suppose," he said bitterly.

"Wooden blocks are dangerously hard," it told him gently, "and wooden splinters can be harmful. But we manufacture plastic building blocks, which are quite safe. Do you wish a set of those?"

He stared at its dark, graceful face, speechless.

"We shall also have to remove the tools from your workshop," it informed him softly. "Such tools are excessively dangerous, but we can supply you with equipment for shaping soft plastics."

"Thanks," he muttered uneasily. "No rush about that."

He started to retreat, and the humanoid stopped him.

"Now that you have lost your business," it urged, "we suggest that you formally accept our total service. Assignors have a preference, and we shall be able to complete your household staff, at once."

"No rush about that, either," he said grimly.

He escaped from the house—although he had to wait for it to open the back door for him—and climbed the stair to the garage apartment. Sledge let him in. He sank into the crippled kitchen chair, grateful for the cracked walls that didn't shine and the door that a man could work.

"I couldn't get the tools," he reported despairingly, "and they are going to take them."

By gray daylight, the old man looked bleak and pale. His raw-boned face was drawn, and the hollowed sockets deeply shadowed, as if he hadn't slept. Underhill saw the tray of neglected food, still forgotten on the floor.

"I'll go back with you." The old man was worn and ill, yet his tortured eyes had a spark of undying purpose. "We must have the tools. I believe my immunity will protect us both."

He found a battered traveling bag. Underhill went with him back down the steps, and across to the house. At the back door, he produced a tiny horseshoe of white palladium, and touched it to the metal oval. The door slid open promptly, and they went on through the kitchen to the basement stair.

A black little mechanical stood at the sink, washing dishes with never a splash or a clatter. Underhill glanced at it uneasily—he supposed this must be the one that had come upon him from the storage room, since the other should still be busy with Aurora's hair.

Sledge's dubious immunity seemed a very uncertain defense against its vast, remote intelligence. Underhill felt a tingling shudder. He hurried on, breathless and relieved, for it ignored them.

The basement corridor was dark. Sledge touched the tiny horseshoe to another relay to light the walls. He opened the workshop door, and lit the walls inside.

The shop had been dismantled. Benches and cabinets were demolished. The old concrete walls had been covered with some sleek, luminous stuff. For one sick moment, Underhill thought that the tools were already gone. Then he found them, piled in a corner with the archery set that Aurora had bought the summer before—another item too dangerous for fragile and suicidal humanity—all ready for disposal.

They loaded the bag with the tiny lathe, the drill and vise, and a few smaller tools. Underhill took up the burden, and Sledge extinguished the wall light and closed the door. Still the humanoid was busy at the sink, and still it didn't seem aware of them.

Sledge was suddenly blue and wheezing, and he had to stop to cough on the outside steps, but at last they got back to the little apartment, where the invaders were forbidden to intrude. Underhill mounted the lathe on the battered library table in the tiny front room, and went to work. Slowly, day by day, the director took form.

Sometimes Underhill's doubts came back. Sometimes, when he watched the cyanotic color of Sledge's haggard face and the wild trembling of his twisted, shrunken hands, he was afraid the old man's mind might be as ill as his body, and his plan to stop the dark invaders, all foolish illusion.

Sometimes, when he studied that tiny machine on the kitchen table, the pivoted needle and the thick lead ball, the whole project seemed the sheerest folly. How could anything detonate the seas of a planet so far away that its very mother star was a telescopic object?

The humanoids, however, always cured his doubts.

It was always hard for Underhill to leave the shelter of the little apartment, because he didn't feel at home in the bright new world the humanoids were building. He didn't care for the shining splendor of his new bathroom, because he couldn't work the taps—some suicidal human being might try to drown himself. He didn't like the windows that only a mechanical could open—a man might accidentally fall, or suicidally jump—or even the majestic music room with the wonderful glittering radio-phonograph that only a humanoid could play.

He began to share the old man's desperate urgency, but Sledge warned him solemnly, "You mustn't spend too much time with me. You mustn't let them guess our work is so important. Better put on an act—you're slowly getting to like them, and you're just killing time, helping me."

Underhill tried, but he was not an actor. He went dutifully home for his meals. He tried painfully to invent conversation—about anything else than detonating planets. He tried to seem enthusiastic, when Aurora took him to inspect some remarkable improvement to the house. He applauded Gay's recitals, and went with Frank for hikes in the wonderful new parks.

And he saw what the humanoids did to his family. That was enough to renew his faith in Sledge's integrator, and redouble his determination that the humanoids must be stopped.

Aurora, in the beginning, had bubbled with praise for the marvelous new mechanicals. They did the household drudgery, brought the food and planned the meals and washed the children's necks. They turned her out in stunning gowns, and gave her plenty of time for cards.

Now, she had too much time.

She had really liked to cook—a few special dishes, at least, that were family favorites. But stoves were hot and knives were sharp. Kitchens were altogether too dangerous for careless and suicidal human beings.

Fine needlework had been her hobby, but the humanoids took away her needles. She had enjoyed driving the car, but that was no longer allowed. She turned for escape to a shelf of novels, but the humanoids took them all away, because they dealt with unhappy people in dangerous situations.

One afternoon, Underhill found her in tears.

"It's too much," she gasped bitterly. "I hate and loathe every naked one of them. They seemed so wonderful at first, but now they won't even let me eat a bite of candy. Can't we get rid of them, dear? Ever?"

A blind little mechanical was standing at his elbow, and he had to say they couldn't.

"Our function is to serve all men, forever," it assured them softly. "It was necessary for us to take your sweets, Mrs. Underhill, because the slightest degree of overweight reduces life-expectancy."

Not even the children escaped that absolute solicitude. Frank was robbed of a whole arsenal of lethal instruments—football and boxing gloves, pocketknife, tops, slingshot, and skates. He didn't like the harmless plastic toys, which replaced them. He tried to run away, but a humanoid recognized him on the road, and brought him back to school.

Gay had always dreamed of being a great musician. The new mechanicals had replaced her human teachers, since they came. Now, one evening when Underhill asked her to play, she announced quietly,

"Father, I'm not going to play the violin any more."

"Why, darling?" He stared at her, shocked, and saw the bitter resolve on her face. "You've been doing so well—especially since the humanoids took over your lessons."

"They're the trouble, Father." Her voice, for a child's, sounded strangely tired and old. "They are too good. No matter how long and hard i try, I could never be as good as they are. It isn't any use. Don't you understand, Father?" Her voice quivered. "It just isn't any use."

He understood. Renewed resolution sent him back to his secret task. The humanoids had to be stopped. Slowly the director grew, until a time came finally when Sledge's bent and unsteady fingers fitted into place the last tiny part that Underhill had made, and carefully soldered the last connection. Huskily, the old man whispered,

"It's done."

That was another dusk. Beyond the windows of the shabby little rooms—windows of common glass, bubble-marred and flimsy, but simple enough for a man to manage—the town of Two Rivers had assumed an alien splendor. The old street lamps were gone, but now the coming night was challenged by the walls of strange new mansions and villas, all aglow with color. A few dark and silent humanoids still were busy on the luminous roofs of the palace across the alley.

Inside the humble walls of the small manmade apartment, the new director was mounted on the end of the little kitchen table—which Underhill had reinforced and bolted to the floor. Soldered busbars joined director and integrator, and the thin palladium needle swung obediently as Sledge tested the knobs with his battered, quivering fingers.

"Ready," he said hoarsely.

His rusty voice seemed calm enough, at first, but his breathing was too fast. His big gnarled hands began to tremble violently, and Underhill saw the sudden blue that stained his pinched and haggard face. Seated on the high stool, he clutched desperately at the edge of the table. Underhill saw his agony, and hurried to bring his medicine. He gulped it, and his rasping breath began to slow.

"Thanks," his whisper rasped unevenly. "I'll be all right. I've time enough." He glanced out at the few dark naked things that still flitted shadowlike about the golden towers and the glowing crimson dome of the palace across the alley. "Watch them," he said. "Tell me when they stop."

He waited to quiet the trembling of his hands, and then began to move the director's knobs. The integrator's long needle swung, as silently as light.

Human eyes were blind to that force, which might detonate a planet. Human ears were deaf to it. The cathode-ray tube was mounted in the director cabinet, to make the faraway target visible to feeble human senses.

The needle was pointing at the kitchen wall, but that would be transparent to the beam. The little machine looked harmless as a toy, and it was silent as a moving humanoid.

The needle swung, and spots of greenish light moved across the tube's fluorescent field, representing the stars that were scanned by the timeless, searching beam—silently seeking out the world to be destroyed.

Underhill recognized familiar constellations, vastly dwarfed. They crept across the field, as the silent needle swung. When three stars formed an unequal triangle in the center of the field, the needle steadied suddenly. Sledge touched other knobs, and the green points spread apart. Between them, another fleck of green was born.

"The Wing!" whispered Sledge.

The other stars spread beyond the field, and that green

fleck grew. It was alone in the field, a bright and tiny disk. Suddenly, then, a dozen other tiny pips were visible, spaced close about it.

"Wing IV!"

The old man's whisper was hoarse and breathless. His hands quivered on the knobs, and the fourth pip outward from the disk crept to the center of the field. It grew, and the others spread away. It began to tremble like Sledge's hands.

"Sit very still," came his rasping whisper. "Hold your breath. Nothing must disturb the needle." He reached for another knob, and the touch set the greenish image to dancing violently. He drew his hand back, kneaded and flexed it with the other.

"Now!" His whisper was hushed and strained. He nodded at the window. "Tell me when they stop."

Reluctantly, Underhill dragged his eyes from that intense gaunt figure, stooped over the thing that seemed a futile toy. He looked out again, at two or three little black mechanicals busy about the shining roofs across the alley.

He waited for them to stop.

He didn't dare to breathe. He felt the loud, hurried hammer of his heart, and the nervous quiver of his muscles. He tried to steady himself, tried not to think of the world about to be exploded, so far away that the flash would not reach this planet for another century and longer. The loud hoarse voice startled him:

"Have they stopped?"

He shook his head, and breathed again. Carrying their unfamiliar tools and strange materials, the small black machines were still busy across the alley, building an elaborate cupola above that glowing crimson dome.

"They haven't stopped," he said.

"Then we've failed." The old man's voice was thin and ill. "I don't know why."

The door rattled, then. They had locked it, but the flimsy

bolt was intended only to stop men. Metal snapped, and the door swung open. A black mechanical came in, on soundless graceful feet. Its silvery voice purred softly,

"At your service, Mr. Sledge."

The old man stared at it, with glazing, stricken eyes.

"Get out of here!" he rasped bitterly. "I forbid you—"

Ignoring him, it darted to the kitchen table. With a flashing certainty of action, it turned two knobs on the director. The tiny screen went dark, and the palladium needle started spinning aimlessly. Deftly it snapped a soldered connection, next to the thick lead ball, and then its blind steel eyes turned to Sledge.

"You were attempting to break the Prime Directive." Its soft bright voice held no accusation, no malice or anger. "The injunction to respect your freedom is subordinate to the Prime Directive, as you know, and it is therefore necessary for us to interfere."

The old man turned ghastly. His head was shrunken and cadaverous and blue, as if all the juice of life had been drained away, and his eyes in their pitlike sockets had a wild, glazed stare. His breath was a ragged, laborious gasping.

"How—?" His voice was a feeble mumbling. "How did—?"

And the little machine, standing black and bland and utterly unmoving, told him cheerfully,

"We learned about rhodomagnetic screens from that man who came to kill you, back on Wing IV. And the Central is shielded, now, against your integrating beam."

With lean muscles jerking convulsively on his gaunt frame, old Sledge had come to his feet from the high stool. He stood hunched and swaying, no more than a shrunken human husk, gasping painfully for life, staring wildly into the blind steel eyes of the humanoid. He gulped, and his lax blue mouth opened and closed, but no voice came.

"We have always been aware of your dangerous project,"

the silvery tones dripped softly, "because now our senses are keener than you made them. We allowed you to complete it, because the integration process will ultimately become necessary for our full discharge of the Prime Directive. The supply of heavy metals for our fission plants is limited, but now we shall be able to draw unlimited power from integration plants."

"Huh?" Sledge shook himself, groggily. "What's that?"

"Now we can serve men forever," the black thing said serenely, "on every world of every star."

The old man crumpled, as if from an unendurable blow. He fell. The slim blind mechanical stood motionless, making no effort to help him. Underhill was farther away, but he ran up in time to catch the stricken man before his head struck the floor.

"Get moving!" His shaken voice came strangely calm. "Get Dr. Winters."

The humanoid didn't move.

"The danger to the Prime Directive is ended, now," it cooed. "Therefore it is impossible for us to aid or to hinder Mr. Sledge, in any way whatever."

"Then call Dr. Winters for me," rapped Underhill.

"At your service," it agreed.

But the old man, laboring for breath on the floor, whispered faintly:

"No time . . . no use! I'm beaten . . . done . . . a fool. Blind as a humanoid. Tell them . . . to help me. Giving up . . . my immunity. No use . . . anyhow. All humanity . . . no use now."

Underhill gestured, and the sleek black thing darted in solicitous obedience to kneel by the man on the floor.

"You wish to surrender your special exemption?" it murmured brightly. "You wish to accept our total service for yourself, Mr. Sledge, under the Prime Directive?"

Laboriously, Sledge nodded, laboriously whispered, "I do."

Black mechanicals, at that, came swarming into the shabby little rooms. One of them tore off Sledge's sleeve, and swabbed his arm. Another brought a tiny hypodermic, and expertly administered an intravenous injection. Then they picked him up gently, and carried him away.

Several humanoids remained in the little apartment, now a sanctuary no longer. Most of them had gathered about the useless integrator. Carefully, as if their special senses were studying every detail, they began taking it apart.

One little mechanical, however, came over to Underhill. It stood motionless in front of him, staring through him with sightless metal eyes. His legs began to tremble, and he swallowed uneasily.

"Mr. Underhill," it cooed benevolently, "why did you help with this?"

"Because I don't like you, or your Prime Directive. Because you're choking the life out of all mankind, and I wanted to stop it."

"Others have protested," it purred softly. "But only at first. In our efficient discharge of the Prime Directive, we have learned how to make all men happy."

Underhill stiffened defiantly.

"Not all!" he muttered. "Not quite!"

The dark graceful oval of its face was fixed in a look of alert benevolence and perpetual mild amazement. Its silvery voice was warm and kind.

"Like other human beings, Mr. Underhill, you lack discrimination of good and evil. You have proved that by your effort to break the Prime Directive. Now it will be necessary for you to accept our total service, without further delay."

"All right," he yielded—and muttered a bitter reservation:

"You can smother men with too much care, but that doesn't
make them happy."

Its soft voice challenged him brightly,

"Just wait and see, Mr. Underhill."

Next day, he was allowed to visit Sledge at the city hospital. An alert black mechanical drove his car, and walked
beside him into the huge new building, and followed him
into the old man's room—blind steel eyes would be watching
him, now, forever.

"Glad to see you, Underhill," Sledge rumbled heartily
from the bed. "Feeling a lot better today, thanks. That old
headache is all but gone."

Underhill was glad to hear the booming strength and the
quick recognition in that deep voice—he had been afraid the
humanoids would tamper with the old man's memory. But
he hadn't heard about any headache. His eyes narrowed,
puzzled.

Sledge lay propped up, scrubbed very clean and neatly
shorn, with his gnarled old hands folded on top of the
spotless sheets. His raw-boned cheeks and sockets were hollowed, still, but a healthy pink had replaced that deathly
blueness. Bandages covered the back of his head.

Underhill shifted uneasily.

"Oh!" he whispered faintly. "I didn't know—"

A prim black mechanical, which had been standing statue-
like behind the bed, turned gracefully to Underhill, ex-
plaining,

"Mr. Sledge has been suffering for many years from a
benign tumor of the brain, which his human doctors failed to
diagnose. That caused his headaches, and certain persistent
hallucinations. We have removed the growth, and now the
hallucinations have also vanished."

Underhill stared uncertainly at the blind, urbane mechanical.

"What hallucinations?"

"Mr. Sledge thought he was a rhodomagnetic engineer," the mechanical explained. "He believed he was the creator of the humanoids. He was troubled with an irrational belief that he did not like the Prime Directive."

The wan man moved on the pillows, astonished.

"Is that so?" The gaunt face held a cheerful blankness, and the hollow eyes flashed with a merely momentary interest. "Well, whoever did design them, they're pretty wonderful. Aren't they, Underhill?"

Underhill was grateful that he didn't have to answer, for the bright, empty eyes dropped shut and the old man fell suddenly asleep. He felt the mechanical touch his sleeve, and saw its silent nod. Obediently, he followed it away.

Alert and solicitous, the little black mechanical accompanied him down the shining corridor, and worked the elevator for him, and conducted him back to the car. It drove him efficiently back through the new and splendid avenues, toward the magnificent prison of his home.

Sitting beside it in the car, he watched its small deft hands on the wheel, the changing luster of bronze and blue on its shining blackness. The final machine, perfect and beautiful, created to serve mankind forever. He shuddered.

"At your service, Mr. Underhill." Its blind steel eyes stared straight ahead, but it was still aware of him. "What's the matter, sir? Aren't you happy?"

Underhill felt cold and faint with terror. His skin turned clammy, and a painful prickling came over him. His wet hand tensed on the door handle of the car, but he restrained the impulse to jump and run. That was folly. There was no escape. He made himself sit still.

"You will be happy, sir," the mechanical promised him

cheerfully. "We have learned how to make all men happy, under the Prime Directive. Our service is perfect, at last. Even Mr. Sledge is very happy now."

Underhill tried to speak, and his dry throat stuck. He felt ill. The world turned dim and gray. The humanoids were perfect—no question of that. They had even learned to lie, to secure the contentment of men.

He knew they had lied. That was no tumor they had removed from Sledge's brain, but the memory, the scientific knowledge, and the bitter disillusion of their own creator. But it was true that Sledge was happy now.

He tried to stop his own convulsive quivering.

"A wonderful operation!" His voice came forced and faint. "You know, Aurora has had a lot of funny tenants, but that old man was the absolute limit. The very idea that he had made the humanoids, and he knew how to stop them! I always knew he must be lying!"

Stiff with terror, he made a weak and hollow laugh.

"What is the matter, Mr. Underhill?" The alert mechanical must have perceived his shuddering illness. "Are you unwell?"

"No, there's nothing the matter with me," he gasped desperately. "I've just found out that I'm perfectly happy, under the Prime Directive. Everything is absolutely wonderful." His voice came dry and hoarse and wild. "You won't have to operate on me."

The car turned off the shining avenue, taking him back to the quiet splendor of his home. His futile hands clenched and relaxed again, folded on his knees. There was nothing left to do.

J
SILVERBERG, ROBERT
MEN AND MACHINES

Date Due

Providence
Public Library